In Praise of *and A*

Thundering White Crosses was absolutely wonderful!! I read it in one sitting and then cried when it was over, knowing it was the last we'd see of these colorful characters. I have read all three books of the trilogy and loved it. –B. Wood

Thundering White Crosses is an extraordinary conclusion to the extraordinary trilogy, *A Full Measure*!! J.M. Patton accurately describes the political and military lay of the land of this era. From the battlefield to the halls of Congress, this novel will keep you spellbound to the last word. – Steve Foust, MSgt USAF (Ret)

A Full Measure is a blockbuster trilogy. This third novel is an engrossing read! When is the movie?? – Mike Carrigan

Jake continues to track down the government mole who seeks to destroy our freedom and democracy. We hope that our country produces more people who possess the character of Jake!! Great, fast-moving book! – Steve Romberger

Drums of War continues the story from *West Point* with a mix of humor, romance, and drama of the onset of terrorism and the military missions to keep the United States safe. Another great read.. – A.S. Romberger, NMMI69

Once again, J. M. (Mike) Patton has knocked it out of the park! After just a few sentences into the novel, the reader moves from his own reality into the main character Jake's, Reading is experiencing *Drums of War!* — Tommy "T" Tatom

This story is the very fast-paced and exciting sequel to his first book West Point. I highly recommend it as not only an entertaining read but a look into the development of the bond between our military men and woman created by their unselfish service — Greg Graves, NMMI69

I recommend Patton's books to any reader of any genre. The characters are vibrant. The emotions enkindled are universal. He has captured not only the details of the West Point Military Academy experience but also the character traits that embody a graduate's service as an officer in the U.S. Army: Duty, Honor, Country. *Drums of War* reads like a thriller. — Wayne Springer

As a fan of military novels, I really liked reading Patton's second work, *Drums of War*. It ties in perfectly with his first book, *West Point*, of the trilogy. Its storyline and characters are both captivating and true to life. Patton's trilogy is an appealing story of military service during a very trying time in our national history, and I eagerly await the final book of this series. — Mike Herbert, CAPTAIN, USN (Ret)

I have read the first two books of the *Full Measure* trilogy, *West Point* and *Drums of War,* and found them connected and exceptional. As a cadet at USMA, 1963-67, I had similar experiences as those described for Jake Jacobs. — Dr. Daniel P Schrage, Professor Emeritus, Georgia Tech; COL USAR (Ret); Former SES Level 3, U.S. Army

ALSO BY J.M. PATTON
"A FULL MEASURE" TRILOGY

Book 1. West Point

A tale of honorable military commitment, love, and conflict. It gives the reader the experience of attending West Point—featuring the humor and heartbreak of daily life that slowly develops the panache of a West Point leader during the Vietnam Era.

Book 2. Drums of War

Following graduation from West Point, now 2nd Lieutenants Jake Jacobs and Patrick McSwain don the army blue. The Vietnam War is in its final throes of agony, and the seeds of international terrorism attack America on American soil. *Drums of War* is a rollercoaster ride of emotions. It is heartrending. It is humorous. It is thrilling.

THUNDERING WHITE CROSSES

A NOVEL

A FULL MEASURE
BOOK 3

J.M. PATTON

Publish Authority

This book is a work of fiction. Names, characters, places, and incidents are products of the author's imagination or are used fictitiously unless otherwise historically accurate.

Copyright © 2023 by J.M. Patton
Thundering White Crosses (*A Full Measure* series, Book 3)

All rights reserved. No part of this book may be reproduced or used in any manner without the prior written permission of the author, except for the use of brief quotations in a book review. For permission requests, solicit the publisher via the address below.

ISBN 978-1-954000-50-6 (Paperback)
ISBN 978-1-954000-51-3 (eBook)

Cover Design Lead: Raeghan Rebstock
Editor: Nancy Laning

Published 2023 by Publish Authority,
300 Colonial Center Parkway, Suite 100
Roswell, GA USA
PublishAuthority.com

Printed in the United States of America

Mark Anthony Runyan, RIP 2022
Friend. Cattleman. Amazing Teacher and Mentor to Our Youth
And
Chief Petty Officer Donald R. Patton, USN
Hospital Corpsman
3rd Marine Division (2) – RIP
For his service many Marines lived to go home
And
Midshipman First Class Steven O. Coats
United States Naval Academy
Class of 1973 -RIP
In our hearts and minds, he will remain forever young.
And
Jim Roth, Sr. – RIP
An Exemplary Individual

"**Duty, honor, country**: Those three hallowed words reverently dictate what you ought to be, what you can be, what you will be. They are your rallying point to build courage when courage seems to fail, to regain faith when there seems to be little cause for faith, to create hope when hope becomes forlorn. . .The unbelievers will say they are but words, but a slogan, but a flamboyant phrase. Every pedant, every demagogue, every cynic, every hypocrite, every troublemaker, and I am sorry to say, some others of an entirely different character, will try to downgrade them even to the extent of mockery and ridicule. . . But these are some of the things they do. They build your basic character. They mold you for your future roles as the custodians of the Nation's defense. They make you strong enough to know when you are weak, and brave enough to face yourself when you are afraid."

GENERAL DOUGLAS MACARTHUR

PROLOGUE

THUNDERING *WHITE CROSSES* is the third novel, following *West Point* and *Drums of War*, in the trilogy *A Full Measure*. The entire trilogy is a work of fiction. The setting for the three books is the last days of the Vietnam War through the next decade. It was a time of change: change in American society and change in the military. The Cold War continued, an all-volunteer military was established, and a progressive movement staked its claim, which is prevalent today.

John Paul Jacobs (Jake) and Patrick McSwain take the reader through their days at West Point to the challenges they encounter as officers in the United States Army. It is a dangerous world for a soldier. From their first day as cadets at West Point, they hold fast to the Academy's motto: Duty, Honor, Country. That commitment rises above self, though changes in society dictate that those words be diluted relative to an emerging political and military culture. The *A Full Measure* trilogy stimulates the reader's connection between cultural transition and contemporary times.

A continuing theme in *Thundering White Crosses* is that

military service is an honorable profession. History teaches many lessons, at least to the wise. Long term, no nation has endured the weakening of its military. Preservation of freedom is a responsibility of every citizen, and the foundation of that responsibility is military service or support of those that serve. Warfare is inevitable. If a nation desires to perpetuate the blessings of freedom, constant preparation for military victory is requisite. Every generation is faced with the prospect of severe trial by war, requiring those who serve to value liberty more than life: Duty, Honor, Country. If one generation fails, liberty fails.

What is in a book title? General Douglas MacArthur stated in his 1962 Farewell to the Corps speech — "The long gray line has never failed us. Were you to do so, a million ghosts in olive drab, in brown khaki, in blue and gray, would rise from their white crosses, thundering those magic words: Duty, Honor, Country." The specter of failure is haunting.

PART ONE

CHAPTER 1

2 June 1977
1600 Hours
Juan de Fuca Straight, Washington State

THE NINETY-FOUR FOOT, million dollars per linear foot Ditmar and Donaldson superyacht slowly cruised five hundred yards from the shoreline of the Washington Olympic Peninsula. The strait is often treacherous with its unpredictable tidal flows and thermally induced summer winds, but today a mild seven mile per hour breeze made for a moderately calm surface. Owned by Advent Pharmaceuticals, Inc., *Carpe Diem* boldly identified the vessel from the stern. Early June is within the preferred season to cruise the shoreline of the Olympic National Park. The air and water temperatures are crisp, but following superabundant winter rains, the rainforest is lush and vibrant with life, posing a spectacular view from the waters of the peninsula.

The yacht slept fifteen guests in luxury and was crewed by

nine, including a professional security detail and a master chef trained at the Culinary Institute of America at Hyde Park. The vessel, furnished in rich antiques and artisan woodwork, accommodates formal dining for twelve and an upper deck bar with a pool to top off an evening with a brandy and evening swim. Ninety million dollars bought an ostentatiously rich corporate amenity to impress, gain favor, and cut deals.

At the rail, the senior Senator from Delaware, Benjamin Townsend, and the chairman of Advent Pharmaceuticals, Jonathan Wisner, wore lightweight, down parkas while they smoked Cuban cigars and sipped Bowmore single malt scotch whiskey. In the discussion of financial matters, they generally disregarded the splendor of the lush shoreline. Senator Townsend had become a wealthy man from his financial relationship with Advent, and the privacy of the *Carpe Diem* was again the ideal place to discuss his newly submitted legislation that would further enrich Advent and himself. While their financial arrangements had always been technically illegal, certainly immoral, and definitely unethical, neither Townsend nor Wisner felt threatened by the facts of their corruption. The U.S. Department of Justice did not appear to care, and the members of the U.S. Congress cared even less.

From the shoreline of the Olympic National Park, final adjustments were made to the two M40A1 Sniper Rifles for distance, windage, target movement, and bullet drop covering the distance to the *Carpe Diem*. With the targets at five hundred yards, the shots were well within their effective range. Milliseconds apart, the two 7.62 x 51mm rounds, equivalent to the .308 Winchester, struck Townsend and Wisner center mass. They both flew backward from the impact and then lay sprawled on the deck, dead, before the fragments of goose down from the parkas they wore settled beside them.

Ex-Navy SEAL snipers Seaman First Class Simmons and Griffin extended a right-hand fist, "Enemies foreign and domestic," they said in unison. Ex-Chief Petty Officer Sizemore, working as their spotter, disassembled the rifles, placed them in two medium-sized duffel bags, and followed the two shooters for a short walk to their rented van. Within an hour, the contents of the duffel bags were scattered piecemeal in deep water at various points along Highway 101, never to be evidence in the assassinations. Chief Sizemore picked up his rental car in Olympia for his drive to the Seattle-Tacoma International Airport and a flight back to Little Creek, Virginia. Simmons and Griffin continued their drive to the Portland International Airport for separate flights to the vicinity of the Naval Special Warfare Group at Coronado, California.

"How are you feeling about all this?" Griffin asked Simmons on the drive to Portland.

"I'm ok with taking them out. No doubt we violated the law. But that Senator was grossly corrupt. The law allowed him to be corrupt. The country is better off with him gone."

"Patriots," Griffin said. "Only four hundred thirty-four to go."

Simmons laughed.

1600 Hours
2 June 1977
Office of the Dean
United States Military Academy
West Point, New York

JAKE WALKED to within three feet of the dean's desk and came to the position of attention. "Sir, Captain Jacobs reporting to the Dean of Academics as ordered."

Only seconds passed in silence, though it seemed longer. Jake continued to stand at attention in his green, Class A uniform awaiting Brigadier General Walton Pence to look up and acknowledge his presence. The thought occurred to Jake that he would have been intimidated five years earlier under these circumstances.

The General removed his reading glasses, set them on the desk, then leaned back in his overstuffed chair while eyeing Jake from top to bottom. Another half-minute passed as though he were lost in thought. To Jake's surmise, the ritual was theatrics. The General was establishing the fact that he was the alpha dog, which was unwarranted as a general is by default the alpha dog to a captain.

"At ease, Captain Jacobs. Have a seat."

General Pence smiled, indicating that his first impression of Jake was a good one.

"Welcome back to West Point, Captain. We are pleased to have you on the faculty. Four years out of the Academy, and you have made quite a name for yourself. Green Beret. Bronze Star, Silver Star, and a Purple Heart. Impressive. And a graduate degree in international politics from Georgetown. I'm sure you will be an asset to the Political Science Department and be a mentor to the cadets. Are you up for this environment again?"

"Yes, sir," Jake replied. "It is always heart-warming to return to West Point. I am looking forward to teaching classes, and working with cadets is always a pleasure."

"You are a bachelor, are you not?" the General asked. "Are your quarters adequate?"

"Yes, sir. I am still a bachelor, but that may change. Marriage is likely sometime during my assignment here."

The General smiled. "Excellent, Captain. I hope you will consider a wedding in the Cadet Chapel. I'm sure your colleagues would appreciate the opportunity to provide a crossed-swords ceremony for you and your bride. My family would be proud to attend. We would adjust your quarters, of course. I see that you are still wearing your insignia as an infantry officer. My understanding is that you are transferring or have already transferred to Military Intelligence."

"Yes, sir. I expect that the branch transfer will occur in the next few months. Security clearances are in the works, and I have some coursework to complete. Once done, I will be a Military Intelligence officer and a federal agent. The idea of not being an infantry officer will take some getting used to, but I'm adaptable. Military Intelligence has its own intrigue, and I am confident that it will be a rewarding path. Hopefully, my time with Special Operations will be useful."

"I'm sure it will be. Speaking of adaptable. You have come back to West Point at an interesting time. As you are aware, women were admitted to the Academy last year. That is a significant change in West Point's one-hundred-seventy-five-year history. Do you have any particular thoughts on that?"

Jake paused and forced himself to show no reaction to the

question. Among graduates, it was a highly debated subject. Some graduates liked the change, and some were vehemently against it. "I'm a soldier, sir, and a junior officer. I am not a policymaker."

General Pence laughed. "Well said, Captain, but surely you have an opinion."

Jake smiled, "Frankly, sir, I am undecided and waiting to see the results. On the one hand, I think it is fine. West Point-trained women can be a terrific asset to the Army and entirely appropriate for our new all-volunteer military. Equality in our society doesn't have anything to do with it. That is a different subject. What it does have to do with is what is good for the military and our mission to win wars. If women have come to West Point to be educated and trained in its proven traditional sense, then that's great. On the other hand, if this turns out to be politically driven social engineering that will fundamentally change West Point and its method of developing officers, then I think the country will suffer a terrible loss. Sir, perhaps it boils down to whether women have come to West Point or will West Point have to change what it is to accommodate them. Either way, sir, I am here to obey my orders, be impartial, and do my job to the best of my ability."

"Well said, Captain," the General said. "However, I think you will find that change is in the wind. The powers that be are out to close the cultural gap between civilian and soldier as a priority over mission. Time will tell. In the meantime, welcome back. Report to Colonel Rogers as soon as possible. He is the head of the Political Science Department, and he will get you settled and fill you in on his expectations.

As Jake walked down Thayer Road, his past days as a cadet flashed before him. He was home and satisfied with the prospects of the next three years.

1800 Hours
5 June 1977
Fredericksburg, Virginia

RETIRED MAJOR GENERAL Seth Osborne sat at the head of the large, hard maple conference table with four others in attendance. These five comprise the Benedict Arnold Tribunal. Like Osborne, the other four were also retired senior officers: one each from the U.S. Army, Navy, Marines, and Air Force. Retirement had come early for each, not in the normal sense of time in service, but because they had been forced out or fired by the executive branch for their refusal to toe the line of its political thinking concerning the Constitution and dilution of the military's mission. For these five officers of impeccable service records, it was traitorous for the government to seek cultural changes in the military that would weaken the Nation's defense, especially now with the Cold War threats of overrunning Europe by the Warsaw Pact. Thousands of lives were at stake. If the Soviet Union were to attack, the only option to stop the annihilation of Western Europe was to use nuclear weapons. That prospect was unthinkable for these officers. Their self-appointed patriotic stance was to uphold their oath of service by literally defending the country from enemies foreign and domestic. An equal threat to Soviet invasion of Europe would be the internal threat of men bent on destroying America. For these five officers, their obligation given upon entering military service had become one of action over words, and that obligation expired only upon death, not retirement.

The Benedict Arnold Tribunal, the existence of which was

necessarily held in strict secrecy, was composed of only the five retired officers. All five were deeply concerned about extensive corruption in the federal government, particularly with regard to corruption where foreign governments were concerned. Of specific concern was rapidly emerging relations with communist China, but there were other countries not considered a United States ally that were a breeding ground for political corruption as well. Trade agreements opened the floodgates for elected officials to peddle their influence to benefit foreign powers. While the executive branch was focused on how relations with Communist China would positively impact the long-standing Cold War with the Soviet Union, some members of the legislative branch opened their office door in the Capitol Building as though it were a candy store. The Benedict Arnold Tribunal's intention was to curb the onrush of corruption with the fear of death, believing that judicial means were an impossibility.

Legitimate authority? There was none, but the Benedict Arnold Tribunal considered its mission to be one of substance over form. That is, the mission was substantially superior and righteous over constitutional legality. The Tribunal's self-derived authority was the product of justification by argument from analogy. The applicable analogy being England's Star Chamber, effective from the late 15th century through the mid-17th century. Its purpose was to supplement the judicial system of the common-law courts in both civil and criminal proceedings. The Star Chamber was established to ensure the enforcement of the laws against prominent people who were powerful enough that the legal system might hesitate to convict them of their crimes. The Star Chamber had the flexibility to punish individuals for actions that were morally deplorable but not necessarily in violation of the letter of the law. It stood for equity for the common people when faced with crimes committed by the nobility.

"Mission accomplished, gentlemen," General Osborne said. "Senator Townsend and one of his corporate benefactors have been eliminated. We will have to see how that impacts Advent Pharmaceutical's business dealings with communist China. That makes four corrupt congressmen that have relayed, by their deaths, a warning message to their colleagues. Our operatives are safe, with no evidence for the FBI to connect them to the event. There remains no direct connection between the operative assignment and this committee. All documents concerning Townsend have been shredded, and all related communications destroyed. In short, another successful Tribunal mission has been completed."

"Have you any intel on FBI investigations?" Marine Corps Major General Lefevre asked as he tapped the eraser end of a pencil on the table. Lefevre was still attired from his afternoon of golf and looked more like a retired banker than a highly decorated Marine that had seen combat in two wars.

General Osborne took a sip of water before answering.

"Only that they haven't the slightest idea what they are looking for. They are culling through all the normal right-wing, militia-type suspects, but of course those are dead ends."

"Any scuttlebutt on reactions in Congress?" Army Colonel Joan Whitehead asked. "They all know that the four had major corruption in common. Surely those like them have raised a red flag."

"Yes," Osborn said. "They are all talking about it amongst themselves. Those that are guilty of selling their congressional influence are making the most noise. The deaths of four corrupt congressmen who considered themselves above the law are causing panic in the halls of Congress. *The*

Washington Register is already cracking Townsend's reputation. Scared straight is ok with us. If we are successful, then being scared will have a broad influence on the executive branch, flag officers that are political for their own self-interest, and even on the judicial branch. We will just have to stay the course and see what happens."

Colonel Whitehead smiled at the image of congressmen huddled up in a corner, expressing concern that their own indiscretions of selling out the American people had put them in the crosshairs of a sniper's rifle. Whitehead was a twenty-four-year Army veteran. Those that knew her well respected her as much as any dedicated male officer. Never heard to complain about the acts of discrimination against women in the military, she had overcome it all. The members of this Benedict Arnold Tribunal all recognized that Colonel Joan Whitehead was the toughest warrior at the table. At forty-five years of age and in civilian clothes, it was impossible to distinguish her from any attractive, middle-aged woman that had nothing to do with the military. Her bearing and presence were compatible with both the military and beau monde.

Admiral Stanley Monroe sat forward in his chair, nodding his head in agreement with all that Osborne had said. Wearing a light brown suit, blue shirt, and yellow foulard tie was in stark contrast to General Lefevre's casual golfing attire. The routine of wearing a dress uniform daily to wearing full-time casual clothing had been a difficult transition. Wearing a suit, even when it might be inappropriate, was, to him, a satisfactory compromise.

"I've surveyed our options for our next action. I'm saddened to say that it appears to me that House Representative Jim Gaylord is an appropriate candidate. He has been in Congress thirty-seven years, sits on the House

Permanent Select Committee on Intelligence. He has been in Congress thirty-seven years, and he is as crooked as they come."

"From Oregon, if I remember correctly," Osborne stated.

"Yes. Pure greed. He was wealthy the day he was born. Old Oregon timber money. Why he would sell his soul for more money is beyond me. According to sources, he is also chatty about information he gains on the Intelligence Committee. His behavior is beyond dangerous. To him, nothing is top secret. He leaks and shares classified information with everyone. Once again, it is an instance where the law does not apply to him. Not to his corruption, which is obvious, and not to his big mouth, which borders on treason. The chances that he has been compromised as a source of information by the Soviets is almost guaranteed."

Brigadier General Robert Perribone, United States Air Force, retired, had been silent up to this point. He was a man of few words, but when he spoke, people listened. He had thousands of hours in the cockpit of various fighters, and his record of aerial combat was astonishing. The dishonorable ending of the Vietnam War was his justification for being involved with the Tribunal. His loathing of the executive branch and corruption in Congress motivated him to uphold his obligation. It was his belief that the three branches of government operated above the law, and he, personally, was at war with them. His war was illegal but righteous, not unlike the actions of the Nation's Founding Fathers. To him, contemporary federal government was in the process of transubstantiating the Constitutional republic from a nation of law to a nation governed by an arrogant aristocracy, an oligarchy, bent on rule by a few for their own benefit. If the standards of Constitutional accountability did not change, if political corruption remained unchecked, the Republic of the United States of America would fail, and that failure would eventually result in a horrible civil war.

"I support action against Gaylord," Perribone stated without emotion.

"As do I," stated each of the other four members of the Benedict Arnold Tribunal .

CHAPTER 2

1600 Hours
1 July 1977
United States Military Academy
West Point, New York

JAKE MET Sara's flight at LaGuardia Airport at noon, followed by a late lunch at Antoinette's Bistro, a newly fashionable place to eat in the Bronx where chef Mary Prythurch served her popular Singaporean dishes. July is hot and humid in New York City. Jake looked like a tourist in his chinos and blue polo, and Sara was pleasing to the eye of those on the street in her flower-print summer dress. Jake and Sara both relished Mary's midday sandwich made from cumin-spiced beef, egg, and caramelized onion. They could have talked endlessly, but sensing that their table was needed, Jake asked for the check. Once outside, they continued their conversation as they walked the two blocks to Jake's Corvette for the drive to West Point.

Traveling north on the 9W, Sara was presented with the

awe-inspiring scenery along the Hudson River. It was the same drive that had overwhelmed Jake's sense of grandeur on that first day upon arriving at West Point eight years earlier. Dense forest covered the mountains of Bear Creek State Park on their left, and the mighty Hudson glistened on their right. She had become acclimated to the beauty of Colorado, but the beauty before her now was extraordinary. As they drove through the Highland Falls gate to the United States Military Academy, Sara could sense a change in the aura of her surroundings. Upperclass cadets walked along the granite wall toward the heart of the post in their pressed gray trousers with a black stripe down each leg, heavily starched short-sleeved white shirts with epaulets, and white service caps with a gold braid. It occurred to her that her impression of them was not so much about what they wore but how they wore the uniform. Their presence and bearing were astonishing, if not downright magnificent. They appeared to exude a quality of poise and confidence.

"I will drive on down Thayer Road to Trophy Point so you can get a quick view of the place," Jake said. "Things are a bit chaotic today. The new cadets arrived for the craziest day of their entire lives."

Sara was speechless. On the slab in front of Washington Hall, all thirteen hundred new cadets were in their company formations and in uniform. They were divided into seven companies of four platoons, with ten new cadets in each of the four squads of the platoons.

"We can't stop right now. The swearing-in ceremony will start shortly. The new cadets will march to Trophy Point in less than an hour to swear their obligation to serve in the Army and to defend the Nation against all enemies, foreign and domestic," Jake said.

Still staring at the sight before her eyes, Sara said, "They don't look like they just arrived today. How did they get them all in uniforms and look like they have been here a long time?"

Jake laughed. "Military efficiency and terror. Those new cadets are stunned. They have been yelled at, called every name in the book, measured and uniformed, run up flights of stairs multiple times, and had their skulls shaved to the bone. Every one of them is wondering what in the world they have gotten themselves into. They will remember the horror of this day for the rest of their lives."

2200 Hours
4 July 1977
Trophy Point
United States Military Academy
West Point, New York

ON THE PARADE GROUND, called The Plain, the West Point Band entertained those present in the reviewing stand with military medleys and familiar marches as a breathtaking display of fireworks flashed beyond the amphitheater over the Hudson toward Constitution Island. It was a traditional 4th of July festivity and impressive to all, both in sight and sound. The West Point Band members were all active-duty soldiers assigned to the Academy. They were professional musicians. West Point did not have a cadet band to speak of. There was no time for such an activity. The cadets were there to learn how to be combat officers, not musicians.

Jake and Sara sat on a bench adjacent to the post flagpole overlooking the Hudson River. The flagpole, the top part of which is one of three masts from the sinking of the Battleship USS *Maine*, a precipitating action of the Spanish-American War, holds the post-American flag. The other two masts sit atop the flagpoles at the Naval Academy and Arlington Cemetery. To the right of the bench, cannons of Revolutionary War vintage pointed toward the Hudson as they did when General Benedict Arnold aimed them at British ships of war. Massive links of chain were displayed, and Sara was amazed at their size as Jake explained that the chain was strung across the river from West Point to blockade British ships from sailing upriver. Jake continued to bring where they sat to life, "George Washington, on a surveying expedition, noted that this very location should become a military fort to control passage on the river. There were three forts. Fort West Point, Fort Clinton, and Fort Putnam, which is on the high ground behind us."

Military personnel at the event wore their Class A uniform, and the ladies added color to the midsummer celebration in bright summer dresses with perhaps an open, light sweater to curb the cool night air. The music, the military formality, and the presence of fashionable ladies proclaimed a moment of patriotic optimism and glittering romance.

As the band played and fireworks popped and crackled in the night sky, Jake came to one knee in front of Sara and opened the small box. Visitors within mere yards of the bench smiled as they knew what was about to happen.

"Sara. You have been in my heart before I even set foot on this ground. There has not been a single day since I was fourteen years old that I haven't loved you. All that we have been through has done nothing but make us stronger together. Will you marry me?"

Sara's face was aglow, her eyes welled with tears, and she

softly bit her lower lip to keep the almost uncontrollable smile from her face. With a single blink of her eyes, she enthusiastically said, "Yes. Jake. Yes. I love you so much," as she threw her arms around his neck.

"And Stephen Patrick," Jake whispered into her ear, "we will make adoption happen. He will be our son, in every way."

Sara was emotionally choked beyond reply. She merely squeezed Jake's neck a little tighter as a tear rolled down her cheek.

1030 Hours
6 September 1977
U.S. Capitol Building
Washington, D.C.

CONGRESSMAN JAMES GAYLORD, House Representative from the state of Oregon, leaned back in his large executive chair and paused mid-sentence. Lawrence Covington, the primary lobbyist for the Italian-based Sipaggio Aero Corporation, listened attentively. His objective for the day was to continue to entice Gaylord to support their F65S trainer and light strike aircraft. Though Gaylord was not the most critical vote to make the sale, his seat on the House Intelligence Committee made him an important piece of the puzzle that made a sale possible. And Gaylord knew it.

"As I was saying." Congressman Gaylord sat forward and reached for his cup of coffee. "The 8th Army brass in Germany has a lot to do with the decision. Right now, their war plans do not include small strike aircraft. But that could change. I would be willing to consider using my influence in that regard."

With eye contact, Gaylord's underlying meaning was conveyed to Covington as the office secretary knocked and entered the room.

"Congressman, your next appointment down the hall is in fifteen minutes," she announced.

Covington rose from his chair and extended his hand across the desk. He had learned what he needed to know. He now knew something about the 8th Army war plan, and he knew that Gaylord was a player. It was now a matter of determining what Gaylord's influence was worth in dollars.

1100 Hours
6 December 1977
U.S. Capitol Building
Washington, D.C.

EARNEST COBB STOOD along the wall of the hallway, casually reading a folded copy of *The Washington Register*. The hallway traffic was as it always is during the day, busy and crowded. Cobb was nondescript among the many congressmen, aides, secretaries, visitors, and lobbyists. His navy-blue-pinstripe suit, blue shirt, and red tie was like a uniform in this environment. Most everyone wore a power suit in their scramble to achieve some level of success in these halls of cutthroat politics.

Cobb had his assignment through CIA channels, to which he was well acquainted, though he knew of no specific person to be the source of the job he had to do. Since retirement from the Army, the CIA had used his special skills to take care of several inconveniences located in a number of countries, including the United States. The only rationale given for this assignment was that he was truly a patriot for taking it. After studying the dossier on Congressman James Gaylord and then destroying it, he agreed that it would be a patriotic act. Gaylord was a domestic enemy, but he could only guess why his work had to be accomplished inside the Capitol Building. It magnified his risk. Killing a congressman inside the Capitol Building would be off-the-chart risky.

Gaylord walked through the door of his office with a half-dozen file folders tucked under his arm to walk the thirty yards for his meeting. Cobb made another fold in his *Washington Register* and stepped forward to meet his target half the distance. With his head down, yet watching the distance to Gaylord close, Cobb palmed the handle of the #12, curved surgical blade—one more step before contact.

Cobb steered into Gaylord, slightly bumping him off balance, sending the file folders to the floor. Coinciding with the distracting bodily contact, Cobb slashed a two-inch-long, half-inch-deep, surgical cut through Gaylord's charcoal grey suit, upward from the groin through the center of the right femoral triangle. Gaylord felt the sting from the razor-sharp, surgical scalpel, but he was preoccupied with cursing the man walking away from him into the congested hallway and his files strewn on the floor.

There was hardly a bleed. That is until Gaylord kneeled to pick up the scattered file folders. That movement opened the near-severed femoral artery, and a copious amount of blood began to flow down his leg onto the floor. His feet were unstable in the slick pool of blood, and he was bewildered when he saw his hand covered in the thick, crimson liquid from massaging the stinging cut. Life is in the blood, and Gaylord's heart was pumping his life onto the floor of the Capitol Building.

The Capitol Police were on the scene in under five minutes, but Congressman James Gaylord bled out and died before they arrived. His last breath was coincident with Earnest Cobb casually walking down the steps of the U.S. Capitol Building.

0900 Hours
12 October 1977
Glayhoye Razvedyvatehoye Upcevlenie (Soviet Union GRU)
Moscow, Russia

COLONEL VLADIMIR YANOVSKI was ushered into the office of General Alexey Dmitrievich, the commanding officer of the main intelligence directorate of the GRU. The KGB dealt with internal matters. The GRU controlled foreign matters of espionage. Dmitrievich replaced the cap on his fountain pen and set it on his desk. If one can surmise one's personality by the organization of his desk, Yanovski could conclude that his superior was focused on detail, perhaps to a fault. It was not a working desk. It was a metaphor for superiority.

"What's your business, Yanovski?" the General asked.

"Sir, we have had contact with Wellspring."

Yanovski liked the codename given to the GRU's most secretive and prolific source of classified intelligence in the United States. The critical intelligence Wellspring had passed to the GRU in the past sixteen years would have made him a

Soviet hero if more than three senior officers had known that he existed. Even the KGB, internal security and intelligence, did not know of him. Outside of these three officers, no one aware of the codename knew who he was. Wellspring was an enigma. Rumors were plenty. It was whispered among GRU officers that Wellspring is a mole, American-born, and one cultivated through long-term GRU planning. He is a wealthy industrialist. Or perhaps in the highest levels of American politics. Or maybe he is in the military. Usually, the rumors were eventually written off as conjecture—he does not really exist.

General Alexey Dmitrievich raised his eyebrows and sat forward with his elbows on his desk, making a steeple with his hands.

"Wellspring. It has been a year since we heard from him. You, me, and only one other is privy to this source. What is the message?"

"Sir," Yanovski said as he handed the General an envelope containing Wellspring's message.

"It's disappointing in terms of gaining military intelligence. He is requesting assistance."

Dmitrievich read the message silently, then sipped his hot tea before looking up again at the Colonel.

"He is worried, and he is angry. Apparently, we have reason to be worried and angry as well. He has lost two of his primary sources of information. Gaylord and Townsend. Both assassinated."

"Yes, sir. There have been several assassinations in the past year, and all of them are associated with high-level individuals in the American legislative government. We were aware of those, but until now, we did not know that they had an impact on Wellspring. Frankly, sir, since it has taken so long to hear from him, I have been somewhat concerned that he somehow found out how his parents died and had turned on us."

"No," Dmitrievich said. "That's not a concern. As far as he knows, or ever will know, his parents had the misfortune of an automobile accident. Unfortunate, but we had to sever all ties to him. I don't question his loyalty to us. He is extremely cautious, as he should be. I am confident that when he has critical intelligence to pass on, he will do so. Suggestions to consider on his request?"

"I checked with our embassy in America, and the FBI has made no progress in solving the assassinations. None. They haven't so much as found any viable suspects. It seems to me that the only assistance we can give Wellspring is to track down the assassins ourselves. It is possible. We don't have the same restrictions the FBI does, though it would all have to be completely under the radar."

General Dmitrievich paused, took another sip of his tea, and reclined in his chair.

"Contact Colonel Vladimir Zhukov. Have him in my office within a week. He is in Czechoslovakia."

CHAPTER 3

1400 Hours
5 November 1977
United States Military Academy
West Point, New York

"YOU CAN BUY us dinner tonight at The Thayer Hotel," Patrick McSwain said to Jake. "You are still single. You can afford such swanky dining. I love that place."

Rebecca nudged Patrick's feet off Jake's coffee table, which was Jake's old cadet footlocker, and sat next to him on the sofa.

"Not hardly," she said. "It is our treat tonight. Thank you, Jake, for letting us stay the weekend with you."

"Now, don't spoil the man, Rebecca. He's just a lowlife. You know—Bronze Star, Silver Star, Green Beret Ranger stud, West Point instructor, and all-around American hero. There's no reason to treat him special. Make him earn a little respect."

Jake laughed. "Seems to me that just about describes you, except you don't have enough sense to keep your feet on the ground. Flying that Huey Cobra has given you brain damage.

Fumes from a gas leak, I reckon. West Point instructor? That's going to be you after your interview with Colonel Withers on Monday."

"Well," Patrick said. "That depends on whether or not the University of Virginia is actually dumb enough to grant me my master's degree next month."

"I see what you mean, Patrick," Jake said with a smile. "It is a bewildering question how such a great university can grant a master's degree in mathematics to someone that can only count as high as the number of his fingers and toes."

Rebecca laughed and leaned over to give Patrick a kiss on the cheek. "It's because he is brilliant in how he counts those fingers and toes."

"Yes. Had it not been for the Green Death, I would not be able to count that high. Besides, if I am selected to teach, it will be in plebe math. Calculus. If I make a mistake, they are too dumb to know it."

"Well," I just hope Colonel Withers is smart enough to bring you on board. Sara and I would love having you and Rebecca here.

"So, when is the wedding?" Rebecca asked.

"May. It will be a small wedding. Our parents, you and Patrick, and Wayne Barnes and his wife Emily. It will be in the Cadet Chapel, and I can hardly wait."

Patrick smiled. "Well, finally. We couldn't be happier. What about this new business you have going on with Military Intelligence? All I know is that they are spooks of some sort. You going to be a spy?"

"Not really a spook, though the branch can get pretty interesting," Jake said. "The transition from Special Forces is not one that I would have chosen had I not taken a bullet to my knee and got kicked out of the Green Berets. But I know that one's destiny is a guided tour. I have accepted that if God wants me in a certain place and a certain set of circumstances, He will do the doing. I'm just along for the ride, whether I understand it or not. I will have completed all my requirements to be a Federal Special Agent by the time I leave West Point. You get that, Patrick, not just an agent, but a Special Agent."

"Of course, you're special," Patrick said.

"I'm told I will be assigned to Army Counterintelligence or ACI. I will be dealing with national security crimes by Army personnel. You know, to investigate things like treason, spying, espionage, sabotage, and maybe assassinations. For the most part, it is like being an investigator, but it can involve other things. It will probably involve some time at the Berlin Wall. Who knows. With my time with the Green Berets, I might even find myself attached again to a Special Forces team somewhere, but in ACI, I think my biggest danger will be from sitting at a desk and getting fat."

Patrick laughed. "A federal agent, huh? So, you will have a badge, a gun, and wear a crumpled suit under a trench coat.

"Sure, but don't forget the fedora. No self-respecting spook can walk around without a cool hat."

1000 Hours
26 December 1977
Midland-Odessa Regional Airport
Midland, Texas

COLONEL VLADIMIR ZHUKOV stepped on Texas soil with counterfeit, but verifiable, credentials. For the duration of the mission, he was Daniel Levy. To any curious Americans, he was an Israeli businessman and petroleum engineer, not that he was likely to be questioned. The United States was the easiest country in the world to enter illegally. Midland was an easy place to enter. No one paid any attention to a petroleum engineer, foreign or otherwise, coming to the oil and gas-rich Permian Basin. Once in the country, he could move around at will.

General Dmitrievich knew Zhukov's skills well. If there was a man that could find out who was assassinating American politicians, it was him. Zhukov was Spetsnaz GRU. Where the FBI was restricted by law on U.S. soil, Zhukov was not. The Spetsnaz units were formed in 1949 and had developed into one of the best Special Forces in the world, extremely well trained, and by western standards, more than a little crazy. The units are expert at reconnaissance, conventional combat, assassinations, and sabotage. Like other Special Forces, the Spetsnaz are familiar with several makes and varieties of firearms, and they use a secretive form of martial arts named Systema that has its origin with the Cossacks of medieval times. Zhukov had the Spetsnaz technical skills and more. He spoke fluent English, was handsome, could fit in well with any social class, was brilliant at deduction, and was a stony-hearted killer if it favored his mission.

Colonel Zhukov boarded a flight to Dulles International Airport in Washington D.C. to meet his six-man team of Spetsnaz commandos that consisted of a captain and five enlisted men. They were all specialists at locating people in addition to their warrior skills. Zhukov sat in the privacy of his first-class seat and opened his briefcase in flight to memorize the address of the condominium safe house where they were to meet. Closing his eyes for the long flight, he visualized the steps it would take to identify the assassin or assassins. He needed to find one link in the chain and work from there. The problem was how many prospects would he have to process before he found that link. Those prospects were not well known, but the CIA and the KGB's Spetsbureau 13 (Department of Wet Affairs) had their lists of contracted and freelance assassins worldwide. In the case of the Russians, they had been in the assassination business since the 19th century. The hunt was on.

1400 Hours
16 January 1978
The Pentagon
Washington D.C.

MAJOR GENERAL SETH OSBORNE, retired, walked into Army General Matthew Brodrick's office, not in uniform but wearing a navy-blue suit, khaki-colored shirt, and a powder blue-tan and copper striped tie. General Brodrick smiled and came from behind his desk to meet his old friend and shake his hand.

"Good grief, Seth. You look like the chairman of General Motors rather than an Army Major General."

Osborne smiled. He and Matthew Brodrick had worked together on a number of occasions and had played more golf together over the years than they had a right to.

"Retirement. I can't find a thing wrong with it. Chairman of the Joint Chiefs. Top dog. You're looking well. It's good to see you."

"You as well," Brodrick said. "This job is keeping me off

the golf course, and that is not good. I'm so out of practice I would be afraid to play with you now."

Osborne laughed. "You know how it is. Major Generals, retired or not, never beat a four-star general at golf. That would indeed be in poor taste. I'm happy that you invited me for a visit, but as busy as you are, I'm thinking you want me to do something other than help improve your golf swing."

"Exactly right." Brodrick motioned for Osborne to sit on the office sofa as he sat in the adjacent leather side chair. "If I remember correctly, the last time you were assigned to the Pentagon, you did some poking around with Military Intelligence concerning Casper the Ghost."

Osborne smiled, crossed his legs, and thought for a moment. "Yes. That's a long-standing rumor. We didn't find anything to substantiate that. Zero. Nothing. Not a hint, but I suspect that Casper is real."

"That suspicion is why I wanted to talk to you. In the past year, we have had a pretty good idea that top secret information concerning our defense in Europe against a Soviet invasion has leaked in detail. Your thoughts?"

"Well, sir," Osborne said. "Those leaks could have come from a number of sources. We have ongoing investigations of military personnel in Germany. Military Intelligence knows about a couple of the traitors, but they are still gathering the proof the Department of Justice demands. They are not willing to prosecute unless they have better than an ironclad chance of conviction. It's ridiculous, I know, but the wait for a perfect case means the leaks continue. The leaks could be passing through East Berlin rather than Casper, and it is just as likely that they are coming from our own Congressional members that have access to intelligence information. Not that there are any outright traitors in Congress that I know of, but that outfit is about as loose-lipped as a barrel of monkeys sucking on ex-lax-laced bananas."

Brodrick laughed and reached for the pitcher on the coffee table to pour each of them a glass of water as he thought aloud. "So, you think one of those two scenarios is more likely than the existence of a Casper?"

"Not necessarily, General. Those scenarios are no more than possibilities. Personally, I'm confident that there really is a Casper the Ghost. Now he could be civilian or military, but there has been plenty of evidence over the past ten years to indicate that high-level intelligence has passed to the Soviet Union. And there are plenty of sources of that kind of information in Washington for a spy to gather. I think Casper is American born. A Soviet mole. He is off the radar, not that anyone is really vetting individuals for top-secret security. Sure, we examine people for security clearance, but we don't dig deep enough to uncover a mole. This guy was probably an Eagle Scout type of individual, a graduate of a prestigious university, and a family man. How many people like that are walking around D.C. rubbing shoulders with people who know top-secret information, the Soviets would love to get their hands on? What if the mole is a congressman or a high-ranking military officer? Or, what if he sits at the apex of government and is the president of the United States? Can you imagine the damage to the Constitution and freedom if we ever have a president that is bent on destroying America? Frankly, sir, with all the digging we did, we didn't have a clue about Casper, real or imagined."

The General frowned, then took a slow drink of water from his glass. He was visibly disturbed. "Well, Seth, that is all quite depressing. Which means it is probably worth the effort of poking around a bit. You have already spent some time looking for Casper. If he exists, you are the best person to look around some more. Want a job?"

Osborne laughed. "Not really, sir. I'm happy being retired. I would be hesitant to get myself tangled up with the same politicians that fired me because I disagreed with them. Corruption and sedition are creeping up on this country, and those sycophants don't like contrary opinions."

"Don't blame you for feeling that way, Seth. I can't put you back in a command position for obvious reasons, but I can put you on my staff for a special assignment. How long would the job last? Well, I don't know. The job would last until you find Casper, or you determine that he does not exist. And, of course, when I get replaced as chairman, the new one might want to shut the assignment down. I know that you don't really want the job, but I need you. Your country needs you."

Osborne leaned back a little further into the sofa and crossed his arms as he thought. "You are going to guilt me into this. I see how it is."

Both laughed at the uncomfortable truth.

"That's right," General Brodrick said. "Whatever it takes."

"I'll do it on two conditions. I have an office here, but I can work from home when I want. I'm not interested in fighting I-95 traffic every day. Secondly, I report to you and only you."

"Done," Brodrick said with a smile on his face. "I'm sure you remember Admiral Hollifield, retired Chief of Naval Operations. He is the one that put the bug in my ear about Casper. He believes Casper is real. I suggest you visit with him as you get your feet on the ground. He recommended that a Captain Jacobs might be of some use. Jacobs is currently an instructor at West Point, and he recently transferred to Military Intelligence from the Green Berets because of a combat wound. He hasn't had enough time with Military

Intelligence to have an opinion one way or the other. He is greener than green in the military intelligence world, but he's highly decorated for such a young officer."

"Of course, General. I will meet with Admiral Hollifield and consider Captain Jacobs."

"I wonder," Brodrick said, "what the Soviets call Casper."

CHAPTER 4

1530 Hours
15 March 1978
United States Military Academy
West Point, New York

WITH CLASSES FINISHED for the day, Jake leaned back in his chair, hands interlaced behind his head. His office was not much bigger than a closet, buried in the bowels of Thayer Hall, a multi-storied academic building. But besides being a workspace, it was adequate to conjure up a daily degree of cadet academic misery. He had to fight off the inclinations to make the work easier on the cadets when recalling the course load he carried as a cadet and how difficult it was to keep up in every class. But an easy class was not part of the West Point mission. His job was not only to have the cadets learn the course material, but he was to contribute to their learning to function under stress. It all folded into the current Bee Gees hit, *Staying Alive*. It was a popular song with the Corps of

Cadets since it reflected their daily mantra of staying alive in the Corps one day at a time.

With his eyes closed, listening to *The Closer I Get to You* by Roberta Flack and Donny Hathaway on the radio, Jake visualized his wedding to Sara in two short months. He could hardly wait.

His ecstatic state was shattered mid-song, with the door abruptly opening. "Whatcha doin', roomie?" Patrick asked in a loud voice. "Caught ya day-dreamin', didn't I? America will be much safer when this wedding business is a done deal."

Jake blushed, having been accurately accused. "And you would be much safer if you would have a little more compassion for a soon-to-be-fallen comrade."

"Nah," Patrick said. "You are going to be as miserable as I am— which is not at all. If you and Sara are as happy as Rebecca and me, you will get no sympathy here. You will be as happy as a pig in mud."

Jake laughed. "Only a Tennessee redneck would compare a happy marriage to a pig in mud."

"Lots of happy pigs in Tennessee. Say, what's with the meeting you had with Major General Osborne and Admiral Hollifield last week, if you can talk about it?" Patrick asked as he sat in the chair adjacent to the desk.

"Well, nothing classified about the meeting. General Osborne has an assignment from General Brodrick, and the Admiral suggested that I might be useful. It's an intelligence matter. I'm willing to help as time allows, but I have my boat loaded for now. We'll see. I will only be shuffling paper, looking for trends that will lead Osborne to one individual. Miracle mission. It makes looking for a needle in a haystack a piece of cake."

"Who are you looking for, if you don't mind me asking?" Patrick asked.

"I don't mind," Jake replied. "It's likely a dead end. Apparently, there has been a long-standing rumor that there is a Soviet mole. God only knows who and where. They call him—or her—Casper the Ghost, but it's only a rumor. That makes it dang near impossible to find someone that you don't even know for sure exists."

Patrick rose from his chair. "Good luck with that. Better you than me. Ok, grab your bag, and let's head for the gym. It's time for me to whip your butt in squash, then dinner at my place."

Jake grinned. "Even with my bad leg, I can handle you at squash. The last time you won was... Never!"

As Jake and Patrick walked toward East Gymnasium and the squash courts, cadets were scrambling to their intramural sport. Every weekday, except days scheduled for regimental parade on The Plain, at 1600 hours, the cadets participated in athletics. If a cadet was not on one of the twenty-five varsity teams, they played company intramurals in the fall, winter, and spring.

"Don't you miss all this intramural business?" Patrick asked. "Especially boxing. I miss seeing you coming back to our room with your cheeks all puffy and bruised, maybe even a little blood oozing out of your lip."

"You're sick, Patrick. It's a wonder I didn't have brain damage from the pounding I took every day."

Patrick laughed. "You seem to think you didn't have some brain damage. You went infantry. That proves there was some serious damage involved."

"Might be some truth to that, but here we are, back at West Point. Maybe it's a curse. So how is it having females in your classes? I won't have any until next year when they are Cows. My classes are only available to juniors and one class of seniors."

"I have no complaints," Patrick said. "It was a little shocking at first, but only because we didn't have any females here when we were cadets. They are as smart as the men, and as far as I'm concerned, they are as squared away as the men, too."

Jake shifted the strap on his gym bag to the other shoulder. "I'm sure that's right. You know, I'm not at all concerned about how the women will perform. All these cadets are simply persons, male or female, and they will step up to the task. They are as capable as men to be leaders. What does bother me is the social engineering of West Point and the entire military. Admitting women to West Point is not the problem. The problem is the federal government's determination to close the cultural gap, as they call it, between military and civilian life. In my opinion, there should be a cultural gap. The military, and specifically West Point, has a mission to be prepared to win wars. Its mission has never been to train social justice warriors. The military shouldn't mirror civilian life, and West Point shouldn't mirror a civilian university. Anyway. I think we are going to see significant changes in West Point. It usually takes twenty years for poor political decisions to manifest themselves into a disaster, and it only takes one president bent on fundamentally transforming America into a socialistic nation by turning our Constitution upside down."

Patrick thought a moment as they walked, then asked, "What kind of changes are you talking about?"

"Well, the value of West Point, or any service academy, is the underlying character and leadership skill of the officers it produces. If you wanted to make West Point look just like

Podunk University, what would you have to change? You would certainly have to get rid of a strict honor code. You can't kick someone out just because he was a thief or a liar, and you would have to tolerate cheating at some level. That would be a change that would have major ripples throughout the system. How about academics? You sure couldn't have cadets dismissed because they made a "D" or "F." That would be unfair to penalize a cadet for failure to uphold the standard. You would have to let cadets take the class over again, and when would they do that? In the summer? What would that do to summer training? That's not to say that the quality of academics would weaken because West Point academics will always be strong and up-to-date. But West Point has never taught that failure is acceptable. Failure at war is not acceptable. So, what are we teaching if academic failure is allowed? We all graduated with the equivalent of a BS in engineering. Well, that's not fair if you want West Point to look like Podunk U. So, let's have cadets select a major of any discipline. You know, graduate with a degree in sociology. Well—if you do that —what happens to the General Order of Merit? You can't have a General Order of Merit when the engineering student is ranked on the same system as the sociology student. There is a difference in difficulty. When one wants West Point to look like Podunk University, that becomes the mission, not that of making officer-leaders in the preparation for war, to lead citizen soldiers to military victory. And what about the plebe system? There's a purpose for that, you know. It builds leaders that can think and function under chaos and pressure. If that changes, how will that affect our national defense in times of war? You see, having women admitted to West Point is not the issue. The issue is making West Point fit the civilian culture. Make it politically correct. And it is not simply West Point. It is the entire military."

"Really?" Patrick asked incredulously. "If that is true, I'm depressed. Surely not."

"Hang on, buddy. It's coming. There are powerful people that want to destroy this country. Political blunderings have made sure that America has not won a war since World War II. Korea and Vietnam had disastrous results. If the top of the political food chain means doing harm to defense and American freedom, then there are military officers that will carry it out for their own self-interest. It will only take a couple of three-star superintendents to turn West Point upside down and make it appear to be a good idea. Don't get me wrong, some of the world's most powerful politicians at home and abroad are the ones that want a new world order. Apparently, their agenda includes morphing our military into an institution composed of social warriors. In time, they will determine what politically correct is and force the military into conformity."

"Sounds like prophecy," Patrick said. "I know you are a lot of things, Jake, but I didn't know you were a prophet."

Jake laughed. "I'm not a prophet, but I am a person that thinks we have an obligation to interpret contemporary events in terms of reality."

"What reality? Everyone has a different sense of reality."

"Well, I think my sense of reality is biblical and historical. For someone else, reality might be only world history. What caused other nations to ultimately fail? If you want to know the future, look at the past. Degeneracy slowly crushed every higher civilization in history. The military? Look at what happened to the military in the Roman Empire. It degenerated right along with the degeneration of society corporately."

"I see. So, back to our Highland Home on the Hudson, do

you think any of those changes are good for West Point?" Patrick asked with a tone of doubt in his voice."

"You know, Patrick. I don't know if the changes are good or bad. Right, or wrong. But I'm confident that whatever the changes are in the military, for the sake of a homogeneous culture, will impact the long-term history of the United States. On a positive note, West Point and its graduates will always be bright, shining stars amongst a galaxy of stars. Duty-Honor-Country will not diminish."

CHAPTER 5

0900 Hours
1 April 1978
GRU Headquarters
Moscow, USSR

COLONEL VLADIMIR YANOVSKI properly marched into General Alexey Dmitrievich's office, came to attention three paces from the General's desk, and saluted.

"Yes, Colonel, what is it?" the General asked without looking up from the report he was reading nor returning the Colonel's salute.

"Sir, a sealed message has come from our consulate in Washington," Yanovski said as he stepped forward and handed the envelope stamped "Of Special Importance" to the General. He immediately stepped back and returned to the position of attention. Unless dismissed, he would stand fast should the General have instructions for him.

Dmitriievich broke the envelope's seal, leaned back in his chair, and began reading the coded communication with the assistance of his code key, giving the Colonel no indication, by facial expression, of his reaction. Having read it once, the General sat forward with elbows on the desk and read the message a second time. The General then leaned back in his chair once again as he gathered his thoughts. "Wellspring."

Overcoming his intense curiosity, Yanovski calmly asked if the General had any instructions for him concerning the matter.

After a long pause, the General said, "Apparently, Wellspring has uncovered an investigation underway to determine if he truly exists and, if so, to find him. Note these names, Colonel Major General Seth Osborne, U.S. Army-retired, and Captain John Paul Jacobs, who is a Military Intelligence officer and instructor at their army military academy. Wellspring is not concerned but wants this investigation on our radar, so to speak. He is convinced that the findings will be that he does not exist. The U.S. must not be seeing this as a priority. Otherwise, they would have personnel involved other than a retired general and a junior officer. I don't think there is too much to this investigation, but I want everything you can gather on these two officers. Contact Colonel Zhukov and have him return to Moscow for a meeting. You are dismissed, Colonel."

Yanovski saluted, executed an about-face, and marched to the door.

1900 Hours
20 April 1978
Washington, D.C.

RETIRED CHIEF PETTY Officer Sizemore was pleased with another assignment following the assassination of Senator Townsend. Retirement was enjoyable in some respects, but he missed the camaraderie of being in a SEAL unit and the adrenaline rush he got on a mission. The action was addictive and could not be matched or replaced in civilian life. Missions like that of Senator Townsend, and this one, were exceptions, and he hoped for more opportunities to energize his slow-paced retirement. He backed the plush, stolen conversion van between the parking stripes until he felt the gentle tap of the van's bumper against the four-foot concrete wall on the third floor of the parking garage. The Chief then moved to the back of the van and removed the tinted window on the right panel door and reaffirmed that he had a clear shot to the front door of the congresswoman's condominium. It would be a relatively easy shot. A three-hundred-yard shot for a SEAL sniper is an uninspired challenge. However, the rush of adrenaline from executing the details of the kill and exiting the scene undetected would still be satisfying.

The Chief had been provided a dossier on the congresswoman, and he had confirmed it with his own research. Pulling the trigger on Congresswoman Margo Whiteside would not cause him to lose a twinkling of sleep. She was from the State of California and had been in Congress for twenty-seven years. It was a mystery why her constituents continued to vote for her, given that it was rare for her to do anything that was in the best interest of her California constituents. By all appearances, her very existence in Congress was to gain power over others and to amass personal wealth.

Retired Chief Sizemore found numerous news snippets suggesting that she had passed information to her husband, who had turned that information into several hundred million dollars. One instance was an awarded government contract to a publicly traded corporation where her husband took a large position in their stock. As soon as the announcement of the contract was made public, the stock price significantly increased, and her husband immediately sold the stock for a gain in the millions. Conversely, there were instances where a stock was due to suffer a major decrease in value because of the loss of a government contract. A short sale of stock, which was a tactic of selling a stock at the current value and then buying it at the decreased value, also made Margo Whiteside and her husband millions. Insider trading on the stock market was not their only means of cashing in on her congressional position. Real estate speculation was equally productive, though it could hardly be classified as speculation. When the federal government sells property at ten cents on the dollar to her husband, it has all the appearance of a gift. On one such occasion, a military base closing by congressional edict had all non-military assets sold to the Whitesides while a corporate buyer stood by to pay them ten times what they paid for it. The military base was not an isolated incident. Her twenty-seven years in Congress had put hundreds of millions of federally owned buildings into their hands at a mere fraction of their value.

Congresswoman Margo Whiteside was also universally known for her influence peddling. If one were to line her coffers with coins, just about anything could get done in Washington, D.C. Even the most liberal-minded in her political party were embarrassed by her flagrant actions, but never had she been publicly reprimanded, prosecuted, or otherwise punished for blatantly breaking the law. That was about to change in a draconian manner.

Congresswoman Margo Whiteside's last moments were at hand. The black Lincoln Town Car pulled to the curb in front of her condominium. With his weapon easily effective to a thousand yards, Sizemore ran the bolt of the Remington 270 to chamber a 130-grain Berger VLD (Very Low Drag) round. The untraceable rifle and ammunition were purposely chosen. They were common. They were used by thousands of deer hunters, which eliminated any ironclad presumption that the assassination was executed by a military-trained individual, and the Weaver Micro-Trac scope was appropriate for the same reason. To a military professional like Sizemore, the gear was adequate for this mid-range shot.

Whiteside's security guard stepped out of the car from the front seat and took a full minute to scan the area for any threats. Security details were now common for any members of Congress that could afford the luxury. The assassination of Gaylord in the Capitol Building created a new avenue of employment for security guards. Chief Sizemore smiled. Had Whiteside's guard been a real professional, he would have required she move or hire additional men to be stationed in the buildings within range of the condo. A sniper positioned in a building or parking garage was an easily identified risk.

Finally, the security guard opened the curbside rear door of the Town Car. The moment the congresswoman exited the car to enter her condo, the back of her head became the target. Sizemore squeezed the trigger. The bullet penetrated the back of her head and explosively exited below her nose, taking all of her lower jaw with it. To ensure there would be no immediate pursuit of him, Sizemore cycled the bolt to chamber another round, fired, and saw the security guard drop lifelessly beside Margo Whiteside.

Without a moment's hesitation, Sizemore donned a

charcoal newsboy cap, put on oversized, horn-rimmed sunglasses, slipped on a bulky blue blazer, picked up a bouquet of spring flowers, and exited the van. Should someone see him descending the stairs or casually walking to his pickup truck two blocks from the garage, their recollection would likely be that of a middle-aged man in a blue blazer, a fashionable Ivy League cap, and a bouquet of flowers.

1700 Hours
22 May 1978
United States Military Academy
West Point, New York

LIEUTENANT COLONEL (LTC) Diego de la Cruz, a Spanish language instructor at West Point and an officer in the Philippine Army Special Warfare Brigade, had a three-year assignment coinciding with Jake's return to the Academy. Like any true warrior, de la Cruz would prefer to be on-task with a unit rather than teaching cadets. That was especially true since the Special Warfare Brigade had only been formed since January. He was missing out on the initial organizational matters, but though absent from the Brigade, he was thankful for his selection to be a special operations officer. There was no doubt in his mind that his assignment to West Point would somehow lead him to opportunities unimagined.

The Colonel worked diligently to stay physically fit and to keep his military skills honed to a razor-sharp edge. That honing became a more productive activity when Captain John Paul Jacobs approached him about Escrima. A few months ago, Jake had heard that the Colonel was skilled at the art and was working out alone in the gymnasium several times a week, so Jake asked the Colonel if he would be willing to teach him the Filipino martial art.

While Jake's motive was primarily to stay in shape, de la Cruz saw it as an opportunity to develop a worthy sparring partner. It did not take long for Jake to recognize that Escrima was a skill that he intensely desired. He was already skilled in hand-to-hand combat, but Escrima offered specific skills not so familiar with other special forces operatives. There would be no awarding of colored belts involved with training with the Colonel, though the Colonel was a black belt, master three. Jake already had credentials of a different quality. He had a Ranger Tab and a Green Beret flash. Both were a death-dealing set of skills if called upon. His boxing experience gave him the capacity to think under pressure and to apply knowledge calmly rather than simply reacting emotionally. Combined, Jake's hand-to-hand combat skills and his boxing experience made him a fast learner and a worthy opponent.

Today was like every session with de la Cruz. After six months of training, they still followed the same training routine. They stretched and completed a series of exercises to warm up, then individually practiced a series of basic movements and footwork. It was all about repetition. Muscle memory, offensive and defensive. De la Cruz wiped sweat from his face and neck, then moved to the side of the mat to pick up two twenty-four-inch rattan sticks. Jake eyed the sticks, as they were somewhat shorter than the ones they had used before.

"Let's talk about weapons," de la Cruz said. "First, let's be clear that Escrima, for a military man, like yourself, is not about sporting martial arts. For the soldier, Escrima is about delivering the maximum amount of damage and death as quickly as possible. It is not a sport. It's about life and death combat. Escrima combat doesn't last long. How would you categorize what you already know, Jake?"

Jake thought for a moment, then stated, "Boxing. I'm no professional, but I know a little bit about it. Most of my hand-to-hand combat training was lethal techniques that combine various martial arts. I was an Army Special Forces representative for a new system being developed at Quantico. It only lasted a month, but it was some intensive training. The Marine Corps is forming what they call LINE, or Linear Infighting Neural-override Engagement. Good stuff, but it will be a few years before it is fully integrated for troop training."

"I've heard of LINE," de la Cruz said. "You have a solid foundation."

Jake asked, "How does Escrima compare to other martial arts used by foreign military or foreign governments? If I were to find myself in combat with some Special Forces killer, would Escrima help me get out of a jam, or would my best move be to run?"

De la Cruz laughed. "Jake, I'd say that what you already know about combat at close quarters would serve you well. Escrima is one of the top ten deadliest martial arts in the world. Knowing the basics of Escrima well will give you favor against any Special Forces operator. One more year of our training together will make you good. Another year after that will make you one of the most dangerous men I know."

"And then I will grow old and no longer be dangerous to anyone except myself," Jake said with a smile. "I doubt I will find myself in a situation again where I need to be dangerous. As a Green Beret, yes, but as a desk jockey in Military Intelligence, no way. Unless I need to fight my ex-roommate over who is going to pick up the tab for lunch."

De la Cruz shook his head without smiling and said, "So, when is the wedding?"

Jake smiled, "This Saturday, the 27th. Cadet Chapel. I hope you can make it. Sara and Stephen Patrick will get here on Wednesday. I can hardly wait. We'll be off to Colorado on Sunday for a full month's leave and a honeymoon week at Lake Tahoe. Think I'll grow a beard."

De la Cruz raised one eyebrow. "You may have to rethink that beard. The wife will be in charge of grooming from now on. You may think you are in charge, but you won't be."

CHAPTER 6

0930 Hours
27 May 1978
United States Military Academy
West Point, New York

JAKE, Patrick, and six other officers, in dress blues with sabers, congregated at the main entrance to the Cadet Chapel, awaiting guests to arrive for the wedding of Captain John Paul Jacobs and Sara Mosher. To the officers and all West Point graduates, the chapel was a structure with which they were intimately familiar. They had sat in the pews for Christian services on almost two-hundred Sundays during their four years at the Academy.

Chapel was no longer mandatory at the service academies. The Supreme Court ruled in 1972 that the mandatory aspect of attendance was a violation of a cadet's civil rights. Government policy became that the academies must diversify to gain a more egalitarian character, or perhaps better stated, that the academies conform to the cultural trend in America to remove God from its institutions, contrary to the precepts set forth by the Founding Fathers. To many, including Jake, the decision was a crushing blow to the warp and woof of that which made West Point officers honorable, spiritually courageous, and effective leaders in the chaos of warfare.

Jake meandered toward the alter, a two-hundred-foot walk that was seventy-two feet wide. The majesty of the military gothic chapel never failed to overwhelm him with emotion. Its fifty-six-foot ceiling dwarfed an individual's sense of self-sufficiency. Colorful flags adorned the walls, and stained-glass windows extolled the praise of God and the memory of departed graduates of the United States Military Academy. Jake paused and stared at the twenty-one-panel window above the chapel's main door and its tribute:

> "To our graduates who died in the World War, proudly their Alma Mater claims her own: may she have sons like these from age to age."

Over the altar hung the painting "Peace and War," and on the walls were black marble shields with the names, ranks, and dates of birth and death of the generals of the American Revolution. Around the tower, figures representing the Odyssey for the Holy Grail came to life. Above the door is a carved two-handed sword that represents King Arthur's Excalibur, and there are twenty-seven panels, each depicting military individuals in biblical history. The chapel organ is esteemed, being the largest church organ in the western hemisphere with its twenty-three thousand five hundred pipes. As Jake absorbed the majesty of the chapel, Patrick came to Jake's side and said, "What better place to consecrate your marriage to the woman you love? None, I think."

Jake smiled, "This is the most important day of my life. I can't think of a better place to seal my love for Sara. I am truly blessed, and thank you, Patrick, for standing by my side. Sara, this place, and you make this day one of incomparable joy."

"Well—I don't want to get all hokey, especially in my dress blues and saber, but you and Sara deserve all the happiness in the world. I am so happy to be your best man."

"And Stephen Patrick, too," Jake said. "Brent Mosher signed the legal documents yesterday. When we say our 'I do's,' Stephen Patrick will legally be my son. I was a bit surprised that Mosher gave very little resistance to the adoption. Go figure."

Patrick smiled. "No doubt God worked all that out."

"Exactly," Jake replied.

1000 Hours
27 May 1978
United States Military Academy
West Point, New York

MAJOR TOM HARDER, one of the post chaplains, performed the wedding ceremony. Harder had been a lacrosse all-American at West Point, graduating five years before Jake and Patrick. He loved his assignment back at the Academy, weddings being his favorite. Harder and Jake had spent time together playing racquetball, and Harder was aware of the circumstances that made this wedding extraordinarily special. His exuberance was obvious as he performed the ceremony.

With Stephen Patrick standing between them, Jake and Sara gave their vows to love and cherish until death do us part.

Those attending who knew the couple's journey to the altar wept. It was a joyous moment framed in a setting that announced the splendor of their commitment to each other.

1100 Hours
2 June 1978
GRU Headquarters
Moscow, USSR

COLONEL ZHUKOV and General Alexey Dmitrievich sat in leather armchairs facing each other around a large, round coffee table, engaged in idle conversation as they waited for the General's secretary to bring coffee. Zhukov had taken advantage of his return to Moscow to visit family in the city and was filling time with pleasantries about his visit with family that held little interest for either. Such conversation was protocol, but it was considered a waste of time by the General and the Colonel.

A small consolation to his visit with Dmitrievich was that he would have a few hours in uniform after months in the United States wearing only civilian clothes. He missed the military environment. After twenty-plus years in the Soviet Army, he felt out of place when not emersed in formality and uniforms. Washington, D.C., had initially been a pleasant change of environment. However, as the weeks passed with little results in finding those responsible for assassinating American politicians, his days had become frustrating and boring. With little positive expectation, he hoped that General Dmitrievich had called him back to Moscow to reassign him to a military unit.

At last, the secretary delivered the coffee and poured the steaming beverage into two Herend Queen Victoria green teacups and saucers from a silverplate coffee pot. When finished, she bowed slightly and then departed.

General Dmitrievich wasted no time crushing Zhukov's faint hope of returning to a military unit.

"So, Colonel. I'll not keep you long in Moscow. I am sure you are anxious to get back to Washington. Bring me up to date on your progress."

Zhukov set his cup on its saucer and leaned back in his chair. "Unfortunately, I do not have a great deal to report of a positive nature. We have made inroads as far as intelligence sources. That is, we have established a social contact with an agent of the FBI that is attached to a task force to investigate the assassinations. He is an unrestrained individual. As a result of that contact, we know what the FBI knows. At this point, sir, the FBI is running around without a clue. They are under a lot of pressure from Congress to put a stop to it. Fear and paranoia are abundant in American politics these days. We are investigating about a dozen individuals that have military skills, but they are no more than prospects. We haven't found any of them that indicate they are involved. It seems, General, that we are only waiting for the FBI to present us with a suspect or a lead. We will continue to look at individuals that could possibly be involved. Other than that, General, there is not a lot to report."

"Disappointing but not surprising, Colonel. Apparently, it is going to take some time to clear this up. Good job, though, on developing the FBI contact. What about that other matter? Have you any opinions about those two officers looking into Wellspring?"

"As you are aware, the Americans call him Casper,"

Zhukov said. "That situation seems irrelevant to me, sir. A retired two-star and a junior officer? That is not really a serious inquiry into whether Wellspring, or Casper, exists, much less identifying him. Frankly, sir, dealing with this situation is nothing more than a distraction from our primary assignment of finding those who are assassinating politicians."

General Dmitrievich paused and sipped his coffee. "I don't disagree with your assessment, Colonel. It does seem to be a waste of time. The likelihood of them stumbling into anything significant with respect to Wellspring does seem remote. Very remote."

Colonel Zhukov nodded but did not reply to the General's statement. He sat silently. In his experience with senior officers, he could sense that there was a "but" hanging in the air.

"Wellspring is expecting some kind of response from us," the General said. "We don't hear from him often, but when we do, it is either to deliver worthwhile intelligence or to express a genuine concern. From what you are telling me, we have nothing to deliver that will satisfy his request for assistance. I'm not so sure that the simple continuation of our present course is enough to set his mind at ease."

"What do you have in mind, General?" Colonel Zhukov asked. While he would not argue with the General, he remained hopeful that he was not about to be ordered to exercise an aggressive action of some kind. He and six Spetsnaz soldiers being on American soil was risky enough without highlighting their presence.

General Dmitrievich continued to sip his coffee as he thought in Zhukov's silence. "Well—I think we cannot afford to insult the most important foreign agent we have. We must respond. We must demonstrate that his requests have our full attention and that we will respond."

Disappointed but expressionless, Zhukov said, "Yes, sir. Your orders?"

"Take Major General Osborne and that Captain out of play. No one will make much of it."

1030 Hours
4 June 1978
Durango, Colorado

SARA HAD DRIVEN the sixteen miles from the cabin to Durango, leaving Jake with a leisurely morning while she bought groceries. Their six-day honeymoon to Lake Tahoe was as anticipated. It was perfect. On the one hand, they hated to see it end, but on the other hand, they were anxious to get to Colorado, retrieve Stephen Patrick from Sara's parents, and settle into their family life. Jake had thirty days of leave, most of which would be used to prepare for the move to West Point. They would keep the cabin. When Jake did have extended leave, they needed someplace to go, and the Durango cabin would suit that need well.

Jake sat on the porch in sweatpants and a T-shirt sipping a hot cup of tea with his bare feet extended to the railing. The only thing out of sync with perfection was that Sara was not there with him. He mused that it would take a lifetime not to feel her absence when they were not together, even if it were only for a few hours at the grocery store.

Sipping his tea, Jake noticed the dark sedan turn off the paved highway onto the dirt road winding toward the cabin. At a half mile, he could not make out the color. Dark blue? Or maybe black? The cabin was the only destination for the road, so Jake sat upright, waiting for the visitor to arrive.

The blue sedan pulled up to the front of the cabin. The sticker on the windshield indicated that the car was a rental. A man that looked to be about the size and age of Jake emerged from the car and walked toward the porch, and Jake stood to greet him. He wore jeans and a green polo shirt, but it struck Jake odd that he was wearing plain-toed, black dress shoes, identical to those that he himself wore when in uniform.

"Good morning, sir," the man said with a smile on his face.

Jake returned the smile, an unconscious response to the man's friendliness. "Good morning."

"I'm sorry to bother you. I sink I am lost. I am on the road to Wallecito Lake. Is this the right road?"

"Yes," Jake replied. "That is the right road to Vallecito Lake," Jake said, correcting the man's pronunciation of the lake's name. Jake's senses were heightened. The man's substitution of the "W" sound for the "V" sound was slightly disturbing. Perhaps it was a speech impediment.

"All you need to do is go back to the highway and turn right. It will take you to the lake."

It struck Jake as another oddity that the man would drive half a mile off the highway to get directions when there was a gas station and restaurant within sight of the turnoff. He could not have seen Jake sitting on the porch from that distance.

"Are you on holiday?" the man asked with a friendly, disarming smile.

Jake paused, collecting his thoughts about the man's question. It was probing. It was somewhat out of context for a simple conversation concerning directions to Vallecito Lake, and Jake was bothered by the man's use of the word "holiday."

Americans used the word "vacation." Europeans said "holiday."

"Every day is a holiday, sir," Jake said as he turned toward the screen door. "You have a nice day."

"I will be on my way. Zank you for giving me direction," the man said as Jake stepped through the door. The man then walked to his car and drove down the road to the highway. Jake watched through a window until the car turned toward Vallecito Lake.

Jake was a bit disturbed by the encounter. He could not quite put a finger on what bothered him, but he did not like the interaction. He told himself not to be paranoid. Still, he could not overcome thoughts of how the man had misapplied his "th" sounds with an "s" or "z." And what about the "v" sound? It came out as a "w." From his Russian studies, he knew that those errors were common for a native Russian who is speaking English. But, although he couldn't place where he was from, this man had an American accent. What was it about this guy? Finally, in his internal argument, Jake convinced himself, "Well—everyone in the States comes from somewhere."

CHAPTER 7

1100 Hours
10 June 1978
Durango, Colorado

"THANKS FOR INTERRUPTING our honeymoon to help us make the move to West Point," Jake said to Patrick.

Patrick laughed as he unlatched the loading door of the trailer rental. "The interruption is my pleasure, Jake. Payback for all the times you have destroyed my social life over the years. If I could figure out how to get that euphoric look off your face, I'd consider the trip a total success."

"I doubt that is going to happen anytime soon," Jake replied. "Life is just about perfect, except for having to deal with the hired help."

"Me and Rebecca? I'm glad you are going to be paying for our expertise with room and board. We have moved three times already."

Jake grinned. "Sure, you will be paid what you are worth. A plate of beans and a slice of bread twice a day."

Well, I'm thankful for that. I thought you were going to feed us C-Rations. How much of this stuff are you and Sara carting back to West Point?"

"Not so much. The furniture stays since we are keeping the cabin, but clothes, personal things, and toys make the trip."

"Are you sure you want to get rid of your Corvette," Patrick said with a raised eyebrow. "That is an extreme move, buddy."

"Absolutely," Jake said with conviction. "We are going to town this afternoon to finalize the trade. The Vette for a new Ford Bronco. As much as I love my Corvette, it's time for a family automobile."

"Huuumph. I suppose. When Rebecca and I have our first, I will likely be doing the same thing. Sounds too painful to think about right now, but when the time comes, I reckon I'll kiss her goodbye."

Without looking at Patrick, Jake smiled and said, "Rebecca or the Vette?"

"Very funny, Jake. Rebecca is far more sexy than a Corvette. One thing is for sure. We will never sell her 1967 Oldsmobile 442. Colonel Daddy would have a fit if we did. He loves that car. Rebecca would be disowned if we sold it, and I'd be dead."

"Well, I guess your Vette's days are numbered then."

"Talking cars again," Rebecca said as she and Sara came off the porch. "According to my dad, old men are still eighteen when it comes to cars."

Sara chimed into the conversation, "We are keeping my VW Bug for me to run around in. It is a stick shift, just like the Corvette. Jake will have to wind up his imagination to feel like he's driving the Vette again."

"Ha," Patrick said. "That would take some imagination."

"Alright," Jake announced as he clapped his hands as if to get everyone's attention. "The women are ready. Stephen Patrick is excited about us getting a truck, and Patrick and I are ready to kick this Vette to the curb. Lunch, then the dealership."

1430 Hours
10 June 1978
Durango, Colorado

STEPHEN PATRICK COULD NOT SIT STILL. He was excited about the Ford Bronco, and he had a new question at a rate of about one per minute. At six years old, trucks are cool. Sports car cool and motorcycle cool does not materialize into an obsession until the mid-teens, and for many, that obsession is stable until their grown children take the keys away.

Jake and Sara stopped, before leaving Durango, to pick up some choice steaks to grill. Having Patrick and Rebecca stay with them for a few days merely added to the near-perfect June. As far as Jake was concerned, his leave from West Point could not get any better.

"Are you having any buyer's remorse?" Sara asked as they wound their way down the highway from Durango to the cabin. "I wish we could have kept the Corvette. I know how much that car meant to you."

Jake smiled and glanced at Sara. "I'm good. Me, you, Stephen Patrick. It doesn't get any better than this. The Vette is just a car. You look great in this Bronco, and I couldn't be happier."

1430 Hours (MST)/1630 Hours (EST)
10 June 1978
Fredericksburg, Virginia

RETIRED MAJOR GENERAL Seth Osborne stepped through his front door to retrieve his briefcase from his car parked on the circle drive. It was Saturday, and he was wearing a worn pair of baggy khaki pants and a powder blue polo. It had been a typical Saturday. A decent breakfast set the day in motion. It was followed by returning phone calls, some of which related to the activities of the Benedict Arnold Tribunal. These were veiled in such a way as to prevent any curiosity about their meaning. Tasks completed or not, from mid-morning through early afternoon, his hours were dominated by eighteen holes of golf with his usual foursome.

He and his wife, Lorraine, had made their way to West Point in late May for Jake and Sara's wedding. As always, he was awed by the majesty of the post. Having not been a graduate of West Point himself, he experienced brief yearnings that he had been, but ROTC at Michigan State had served him well. He was satisfied with the path it had provided him. Still, West Point was magical. While his attendance at the wedding was merely a courtesy extended to his only subordinate in the pursuit of the reality of Casper, once he stepped foot on the post, he was glad that he had come. The essence of West Point was an aide-memoire to the years he had dedicated himself to the U.S. Army and to defending the freedom of the American people.

Returning from the golf course, Osborne got out of his car and casually walked toward the front door of his residence. As he reached for the door handle, he eyed the folded *Washington Register* under the handcrafted, wicker rocker on the porch and reached down for it. The moment he did, the report of a rifle shot replaced the serenity of his suburban neighborhood, and sharp fragments of the brick porch column peppered his face deep enough to draw blood. Had he not reached down for the newspaper, the sniper's planned headshot would have been perfect, as his shots always had been before. Being no stranger to combat, Osborne was not surprised at how fast he found himself in the prone position, scrambling for cover. Instinct and training took him out of the sniper's sights. His first thought on running his hand over his stinging and bleeding face was that he had been hit, then he realized the small gashes were superficial. Osborne heard the roar of a vehicle. A moment passed before he peeked around the brick column in time to see the non-descript, white van pull from the curb on the other side of the street and hurriedly drive out of the neighborhood. Osborne was intuitively aware that his reaching for the newspaper had foiled the Winchester 308 full metal jacket from finding its target.

Within two minutes, Osborne had jerked a towel from the downstairs bathroom to mop his bleeding face and was on the phone to General Brodrick's Pentagon office. Flushed by adrenaline, he advised Brodrick's aide of the incident, not expecting the General to be in his office on a Saturday. But he was, and he quickly came on the line. "This has to be connected to my efforts to verify the mole. Casper," Osborne said. "There is no other reason for an assassination attempt on my life. The sniper was parked at my neighbor's house across and down the street. I can hardly believe he missed at that distance. Luck was with me today."

General Brodrick was as amazed as Osborne. "We will

send a Military Police unit immediately and notify local law enforcement as well. For Pete's sake, Seth, stay inside until they get there."

"General, I'm concerned about Captain Jacobs," Osborne said. "He is on leave a few miles outside Durango, Colorado. Since they came after me, he may be in danger as well. I tried to call, but no answer."

"Ok, Seth. I'll take care of it. We will get a unit in play out of Fort Carson and coordinate with the Sheriff in Durango. I'm boiling mad about this. If this is Casper, he just made the biggest mistake of his traitorous life."

1445 Hours (MST)
10 June 1978
Durango, Colorado

JAKE TURNED the Bronco onto the dirt road from the highway toward the cabin. Patrick and Rebecca were close behind. Patrick had been talking about the Bronco since they had left Durango. "I could do a Ford Bronco. Really. I could. All we need is a little Patrick on the way and I would run out and get us one."

"Sure, Patrick," Rebecca said. "You would cry for days if you had to sell your Corvette."

"Of course I would," Patrick replied. "But they would be tears of joy. After watching Jake and Sara with Stephen Patrick, I know how happy we are going to be someday with a pack of McSwains running around the house. I love you, Rebecca."

Rebecca smiled and squeezed Patrick's hand. "And I love

you. Every day is a holiday with you. Little McSwains or not. Whenever that happens, I'm happy with it."

Jake pulled up close to the split-rail fence in front of the cabin, and they all got out of the new Bronco. Stephen Patrick was on the run the moment his feet touched the ground. Jake and Sara had no idea why he was in such a hurry to get into the house, but they knew that in his mind there was some urgency in his mission. Everything he did during waking hours was with urgency.

For no particular reason, Jake and Sara stood to admire their new family automobile, and without a word said, they gave each other a loving hug. Shared contentedness marked the moment. They had taken a small step forward as a family. Neither could imagine greater blessings in life than what they now had.

From the line of trees adjacent the broad valley of tall grass and wildflowers three hundred meters distant from where they stood, the report of a Russian made Dragunov sniper rifle with a PSO-1 4x24 telescopic sight was immediately heard and the 7.62x54mm round arrived at twenty-seven hundred feet per second at the exact moment Jake opened the door of the Bronco. Targeted for Jake, center mass, the full metal jacket projectile scarcely nicked the metal frame around the door, but that was enough to change its trajectory. Without conscious thought, Jake grabbed Sara's hand and pulled her to the ground, then covered her with his body. It was the reaction of combat training. Get down to reduce the availability of yourself as a target and find cover. Patrick had the same response to training with Rebecca as he pulled her down, using their car as a shield.

Patrick opened the driver-side car door, reached under the seat, and pulled out his Colt 1911 45 caliber pistol and two extra magazines. He rose above the hood of the car and fired seven quick rounds in the general direction of where he thought the attack had come from, ejected the magazine, inserted another, and dashed toward the assumed attack origin. While Ranger School training had not been enough to convince him to have preference for the infantry over his Cobra gunship, it did make him the kind of soldier that runs toward the sound of gunfire rather than one that runs from it. Changing direction every few steps, he quickly covered the distance to the trees, pistol ready to engage the enemy. Once there, Patrick carefully searched for the assassin. After ten minutes he had not found him, but he did find the sniper's weapon. Patrick took off his T-shirt, tied it to a tree to mark the spot, and headed back toward the cabin with the Dragunov.

As Patrick came around the hood of the Bronco—he was horror-stricken. Sitting on the ground was Jake holding Sara in his arms, her blood covering the front of his shirt. Jake rocked forward and back as he held her, his face tilted skyward, incapable of making any sound between gasps of breath and the horror he felt inside. Jake's all-consuming agony and tear-drenched face sealed the essence of the tragedy. Sara was dead.

PART TWO

CHAPTER 8

1300 Hours
14 June 1979
United States Military Academy
West Point, New York

JAKE HAD BURIED SARA, his wife of only two weeks, exactly one year ago to the day. It was a simple funeral reserved for close friends and family. The hillside location of her grave was only a tenth of a mile from the cabin. Her white stone marker was beneath a massive pine tree overlooking the picturesque valley of tall grass, wildflowers, and grazing horses that she had admired so often from the front porch of the cabin. It was a beautiful piece of ground for Sara. Jake had purchased the land in the valley and put it in a family trust to be held in perpetuity. Sara's valley would remain pristine, perhaps for a hundred years or longer.

Jake passed another year as an instructor at West Point. There was to be one more year of this assignment then he and

Stephen Patrick would have major changes in their environment and routine. West Point was a near-perfect place to mourn the loss of Sara, for himself, and for Stephen Patrick. The on-post school was a good one, and Stephen Patrick adjusted well to new friends. Jake carried the roles of mom and dad without hesitation and appreciated every moment he spent with his son, though in a broad sense, his life was fractured. He was a soldier one moment, a soccer or baseball parent the next, then a homemaker until he tucked Stephen Patrick in for the night. It was a common routine for families everywhere, but for Jake, the motivation came from his loss of Sara and his love for their son.

With Stephen Patrick at his Cub Scout meeting for the afternoon, Jake walked into the Thayer Hotel in civilian clothes for lunch with Admiral Hollifield. The Admiral stood from his table in the dining room to greet him and shake hands.

"It is great to see you, sir," Jake said with a broad smile on his face. "Where is your beautiful wife?"

"You are looking well, Jake," the Admiral responded as they sat. "She is at home. She is involved in just about everything. She gets more done than any person I know."

Following a few minutes of idle chit-chat, Jake asked, "What brings you to West Point, Admiral? Business or pleasure?"

Any casual observer would obviously think that Jake and Hollifield were father and son rather than two unrelated officers. And that observation was true but for the absence of blood relation.

Hollifield smiled. "Well,—I came to visit you. So, this is a trip for pleasure. I thought lunch together was long overdue. That's what I like about retirement. I like the luxury of doing things simply because I want to."

"I'm glad you came, sir. It's been way too long. We need to do this more often. I suspect I may have an assignment closer to your neighborhood in another year. I've enjoyed being an instructor, but I'll be ready to get back to a unit."

Following their meal and light conversation, Admiral Hollifield leaned back in his chair and lit a cigar.

"So, how is it really going, Jake? The truth will do."

Pausing while looking down at his empty plate, Jake gathered his thoughts before speaking.

"It has been a year, Admiral. Truthfully, every day is the same. One minute I'm fine. The next, I'm shattered. I am calm and relaxed one minute in God's will and purpose, and then I'm angry at God for taking Sara from me. Oh, I may have the outward appearance of handling the loss of Sara and how I lost her, but that's a lie. Frankly, sir, I have been thinking about resigning my commission. I have a son to raise alone. I don't see how I can do that in the Army. It wouldn't be fair to him when I get deployed to God knows where at a moment's notice and for how long. And what if I did get killed? I can't leave him an orphan."

Jake stopped talking. He knew he had said more than intended and more than the Admiral probably wanted to hear.

Admiral Hollifield sipped his after-meal coffee before responding. "Are you asking me for advice, Jake?"

Jake smiled, "Yes, sir, I suppose I am. I apologize for going off the deep end."

"No apology needed. I can't imagine what I would be going through if I lost Suzanne. That would suck the wind out of my sails, just like it has yours."

Both laughed at the sailor's metaphor.

"Well, Jake," the Admiral said in a fatherly tone. "Others might tell you that you will get over your loss in time, but those people are nincompoops. Fact is, Jake, you will never get over mourning your loss. You will carry this sorrow for the rest of your days. So quit expecting it to go away. It won't. "

Jake nodded, a layer of tears clouding his vision from what he recognized as truth. The Admiral's words were direct, unemotional, and a cold statement of fact. He needed objectivity, and the Admiral was giving it to him. Both he and the Admiral knew that decision guided by emotion is the gateway to a bad decision and self-induced misery. But knowing that and applying the precept under tremendous emotional stress are two different things.

"What time will do for you is clarify what you have to do," the Admiral continued. "I've learned a few things from you, Jake, even if you are Army. You've taught me that our circumstances are the reality of God's will and purpose for our lives, not our will. Yes, that will and purpose are well beyond our understanding, but the fact stands, like it or not. Suffering, like prosperity, moves us forward in God's plan. God is sovereign. Embrace it. You can start by understanding that Sara is fine. She is in perfect happiness."

Jake sat motionless, the Admiral's words rolling through his mind like the impetus of a rapidly moving locomotive.

Admiral Hollifield took another sip of coffee, then continued. "You're a soldier, Jake. Resigning your commission is tantamount to trying to overthrow God's will for your life. Ridiculous. If your destiny is to be out of the military, circumstances will take care of that. Meanwhile, you follow the colors. And, when Stephen Patrick is a twenty-year-old, are you willing to have him carry the burden of knowing that because of him you gave up your calling in life? That's not you. You are not the first one in the military that raises a child as a single parent. The military is a family. You will be surprised at how much help comes out of the woodwork when you need it."

The Admiral paused.

"Now, on the subject of you getting killed in combat and leaving Stephen Patrick an orphan. Could happen. Might not. Either way, we are back to God's sovereign will and purpose. You move forward with confidence and courage that the manner and timing of your death is God's business, and his business is perfect in every aspect. If you were to fall, Patrick and Rebecca would snatch Stephen Patrick up in the blink of an eye. I just pray that when Stephen Patrick is of age, he will have the good sense to attend the Naval Academy."

1600 Hours
14 June 1979
40th Army Headquarters
Afghanistan

COLONEL VLADIMIR YANAVSKI entered his dirt-riddled tent, aggressively removed his battledress shirt, and sat on his cot. It was an uncomfortable place to sit, but it was the only place to sit. He had been angry for months about being made General Dmitrievich's scapegoat, and the anger intensified daily. The flap of the tent parted, and his new tentmate, Major Valentine Popov strolled into the tent. A gust of dirt followed him that glistened in the ray of sunlight. Popov sat on his cot facing Yanavski.

After several minutes of silence, Colonel Yanavski asked, "So what did you do to deserve this horrible assignment, Major?"

Popov frowned. "I think I'm here because I hate the Army, I have tried to resign numerous times, but command will have none of that. I hate it, and they know it."

"Well, your superiors have put you in a bad situation. It doesn't get much worse than this."

"And you, Colonel? If you don't mind me asking, why are you here?"

Colonel Yanavski swung his feet up to lay back on his cot. "I don't mind the question. I was the aide to General Alexey Dmitrievich. I'm here because I followed his orders."

The Major's eyes grew wide. "Dmitrievich? They don't get much higher in rank than him. Following orders doesn't sound like a bad thing."

"It's a bad thing when everything goes wrong, and the General needs someone to take the blame," the Colonel said. "Apparently, the higher one goes in rank, the less he takes responsibility for his own decisions. In my case, I got all the blame, and my army career is over. Just like yours."

"What was the bad decision?" the Major asked.

Colonel Yanavski paused. "It doesn't matter. Let's just say that the person that was to benefit from the order is angry because things did not go according to plan. Very angry. Dmitrievich sacrificed me to save his own skin."

"So. Do you have any idea how we can get out of this mess?"

"Not a clue," Yanavski said with a laugh. "We will be at war with the Afghans before the year is out. I think you can plan on being dead not long after that. Just like the Army intends for you to be."

1000 Hours
2 July 1979
United States Military Academy
West Point, New York

PATRICK WALKED into the gymnasium as Jake and Lieutenant Colonel Diego de la Cruz stepped to the mat for their final round of sparring for the day's training. His eyes widened as he took note of the eight-inch wooden knives the combatants carried in each hand. While he was aware that Jake had been learning the art of Escrima from the Colonel for the past two years, he had not paid much attention to Jake's exercise activity because Jake rarely said anything about it. The knives changed his curiosity. Stephen Patrick was at the far corner of the large mat practicing the basic footwork of Escrima. Though only seven years old, de la Cruz had convinced Jake that Stephen Patrick was not too young for the exercise and the basic skills of Escrima. Stephen Patrick loved it.

"Are you ready, Colonel?" Jake asked.

De la Cruz laughed. "Are you ready? That's the real question."

Jake smiled, then initiated the attack, giving de la Cruz no quarter. His left-hand knife slashed downward toward the Colonel's right shoulder, aiming to cut the target diagonally, from right shoulder to left hip. It failed. De la Cruz's masterful footwork pulled him a fraction of an inch out of range and positioned him for a counterstrike to the left side of Jake's neck. It would have been a deadly move had Jake not kept his feet moving. The Colonel's knife missed Jake's neck, and that miss was to Jake's advantage. Without pause, Jake's left-hand knife initiated a horizontal figure eight beginning at the Colonel's right shoulder, a downward diagonal slash across the chest, shoulder to hip, then completion of the figure eight slashing diagonally, left shoulder to right hip. It would have been a crippling and fatal execution had the knives been real, though it would not cause instant death. Without hesitation, Jake flawlessly used his footwork to move his body to the Colonel's left side and immediately made, to the point of contact, a slash across the right side of the neck. In less than five seconds, the battle was over.

"Outstanding, Jake," de la Cruz said. "I liked it better last year when you didn't know jack about Escrima. I liked winning every time."

"You are still the master. I just get lucky sometimes," Jake said with a smile on his face.

"See you next week. I'll get you next time." De la Cruz walked off the mat as Patrick came to Jake on the mat.

"I had no idea, Jake," Patrick said. "Escrima is some deadly stuff."

Jake wiped his face with a towel. "Yeah, a fight doesn't last very long with four knives flailing in every direction. It is all about training and muscle memory."

"Well, it's a good thing I won't see any of that in the cockpit of a Cobra. As for Stephen Patrick, he is looking pretty dangerous."

"He is doing great, and he has a healthy respect for not abusing the skill," Jake said. "But should it occur, a schoolyard bully is in for a surprise and is likely to learn a thing or two if Stephen Patrick can't talk his way out of a fight, even without a deadly weapon. What are you doing slumming with us real soldiers?"

"Real soldiers. That's funny, Jake. I walked over here from my department head's office. Crazy, I know, but I had a conversation with him that shocked me. I had a plebe that violated the Honor Code three months ago, and they didn't have the Honor Board meeting until last night. Can you imagine? Three months. It used to be that the Honor Board would convene within twenty-four hours. They found him guilty, a true bill, but guess what?"

"They didn't kick him out," Jake said disgustedly. "They gave him a bunch of tours to walk and asked him, politely, not to violate the Honor Code again."

"Exactly! My department head, Colonel Matthews, told me that this is how it is going to be now. West Point is now going to rehabilitate rather than separate cadets from the Corps for an honor violation. That's crap, Jake."

"That's one of the changes. And there are other changes that are more subtle. A lot of instructors are seeing insubordination. It is not unusual now to hear of cadets arguing with officers about anything. I wonder how that is going to play out when they graduate and are serving in a unit. You reckon that will have an impact on combat readiness?"

"I've seen some of that, too," Patrick said. "I had a cadet go off on me because he failed a calculus exam. He said it was my fault because the exam was too hard, and like always, every cadet taking the course gets the same exam. I reported the incident, but nothing came of it."

"You are giving me heartburn, Patrick."

"And what about all this sexual assault and sexual harassment business? Unbelievable! Where are they getting these cadets? Reform school?"

"I never thought that sort of thing would be a problem at

the service academies, but it is. Apparently, the occurrence of sexual assault is common these days. I don't know what to tell you, Patrick," Jake said solemnly. "All the service academies are under attack. Slow deterioration in the name of cultural engineering. God save America."

CHAPTER 9

0830 Hours
6 August 1979
The Pentagon
Washington, DC.

GENERAL BRODRICK ENTERED his office with Major General Osborne already seated, nursing a hot cup of coffee. Osborne rose when the General entered. "Sorry I am late. Everyone seems to have the crucial news of the day for me. I need my aide to run interference every time I step out of my office."

"Get you a couple of those West Point linebackers on your staff. That might work."

"Too small," the General said. "Maybe a couple from Notre Dame or USC." Brodrick moved to his desk as his secretary set a cup of coffee in front of him. "Ok, Seth. Bring me up to date on Casper."

"There is not a lot to give you, General, other than to say that it's a gut cinch we have a mole. Casper is the real deal.

Otherwise, there would not have been an attempt to assassinate me and Captain Jacobs. We hit a nerve somehow during our inquiries. I am still grieving over the fact that Captain Jacob's wife was killed."

"How is he doing?" the General asked.

"About as well as one might expect under the circumstances. I offered to relieve him from the assignment, but he would have none of that. I wouldn't go so far as to call his attitude inordinate revenge motivation, but his commitment to finding Casper is extraordinary. He is not going to rest until he does. He thinks, and rightfully so, that Casper is the cause of his wife's death. His attitude is an asset. In fact, Captain Jacobs may be the best thing we have going for us. You could assign him to Iceland, and he would still be obsessed with finding Casper."

"He still has another year at West Point, correct?"

"Yes, sir. It is a good environment for a couple of reasons. He needs time to mourn, and he has the time and resources to do the grunt work to find Casper. He is processing a ton of paperwork to compare what security breaches may have been made, what personnel may have had access to that information, and where that information may have been passed to the Soviets. It's a very complicated process of trying to find a needle in a stack of needles. Unfortunately, the process is a nightmare. Security is pitiful. The White House. Congress. Government employees and contractors, and military personnel. There are potential leaks everywhere."

General Brodrick leaned back in his chair and sipped his coffee. "Other than his motivation, I take it you think he is the right man for the job. There are others of higher rank and more experienced."

"Yes, sir," Osborne said without hesitation. "Jacobs is

young and inexperienced. However, he has completed all the requirements to be a Military Counterintelligence Officer. He could be more productive in the mission if he were a field grade officer, simply as a matter of perception, but promotion to major is at least three years out. Once he is promoted, he could be inserted with greater presence into any counterintelligence unit, even time in Moscow. And he is a decorated Green Beret. That alone gives him some credibility. He is the right man for the job, General. Time will take care of the details."

"I agree. It sounds to me like Jacobs will do a satisfactory job. I know this business may take years. I am concerned about the assassinations as well. Three months ago, Senator Cohen was assassinated while fly-fishing on the Provo River in Utah, and two weeks ago a federal judge was found dead in his swimming pool under questionable circumstances. The FBI appears to be running in circles. I'll leave you to complete your mission. I know the assassinations are not your concern. The FBI will get a handle on that."

"Yes, sir. I understand."

Brodrick cleared his throat and said, "I'll take care of the matter with Captain Jacobs. Early promotion to major will raise a few eyebrows, but it's not all that unusual."

Osborne smiled. "How about Lieutenant Colonel, Sir? That sounds even better."

"Don't press your luck, Seth."

1300 Hours
1 September 1979
United States Military Academy
West Point, New York

"MAJOR! HOW DID THAT HAPPEN?" Patrick said to Jake with a grin on his face. "Ok. Who did you bribe to get that done."

Jake laughed. "No bribe. Looks. Good looks. The Pentagon simply put my picture next to yours for comparison. Major, and no major. If you need some extra captain brass, I have some I don't need anymore."

"Hmmm. Apparently, you do have what it takes to become a general officer. Congratulations, Jake. You deserve it."

"Seriously," Jake said. "I have no idea what this is about. As far as my career goes, Military Counterintelligence is a road to nowhere. The rank of major is likely the last promotion I'll get."

"Good," Patrick said jokingly. "I'm looking forward to ordering you around. Get my coffee. Make my bed. Tell me funny jokes. You know, strategically important military stuff."

"Speaking of military stuff," Jake said. "I will be off to the 766th Military Intelligence Detachment in West Germany in a few days. It looks like I will be there for a couple of weeks."

"Doing what, exactly?"

"Snooping around, mostly," Jake said, being as baffled as Patrick about the assignment. The 766th, as you might imagine, is deeply involved in the spy-catching game and the shenanigans out of East Germany. The Soviets are always working to gather intelligence out of the 8th Army Headquarters. If open warfare were to flare up with the Soviets, their knowing our strategy could do immeasurable harm. Anyway, my being there for a couple of weeks is a fishing expedition to see if there is a lead to the mole responsible for Sara's death."

"Sic 'em, Jake. We will take care of Stephen Patrick while you are gone."

0900 Hours
15 September 1979
766th Detachment of the Berlin Brigade
Berlin, Germany

THE MISSION and purpose of the 766th was one of cooperation with other allied counterintelligence operations and tasked to identify traitors selling top secret plans for the military defense of Europe against the Soviet Union. As the Cold War intensified, Berlin was a hotbed of spy versus counterspy activity. Consequential? The 766th mission shouldered the burden that if the Soviet Union were to attack NATO in Central Europe, the United States and allies would have to make a choice between surrender or the near unthinkable use of nuclear weapons in Germany. The dedicated intelligence operatives that fought this silent war were known as Huminters, highly skilled in espionage and counterespionage. Spycraft, often referred to as the second oldest profession, has it historical roots in betrayal. That is, the craft of turning an enemy's citizenry into traitors and preventing the enemy from doing the same. With respect to the Cold War, Berlin was a silent battlefield, and Casper represented a worst-case scenario for America in this life-threatening game of treachery.

"Have a seat, Major," Colonel Nickolas Carver, commander of the 766th Detachment of the Berlin Brigade, said in a gruff, authoritative tone. Once seated behind his massive oak desk, he gave Jake a long, disapproving stare. "I'd be less than truthful if I said that I welcome you to my command. We are doing important work here, and we don't have time to nursemaid some hotshot West Pointer nosing around our top-secret operations. Just because you have security clearance doesn't mean you should have access. I've read the file on you. You have never actually had a Military Intelligence assignment, much less one for foreign counterintelligence. You have no experience, and how you made major in six years is beyond me, even if your mother was the Queen of Sheba. Granted, I do respect what you did in the Green Berets, but most of that is redacted. In short, Major, I'm not happy."

Jake paused, stone-faced, revealing not one iota of expression to indicate his thoughts. He was not a plebe at West Point, but he had been one. Outflanking an abusive superior was not new to him. He was not about to let the arrogance of rank blockade vindication of Sara's murder.

"Hotshot, or not, is irrelevant, Colonel. I am not interested in the specifics of your operations here. I am interested only in information from your operations that may indicate a traitor, or traitors, on American soil. I am not a threat to your territory. However, Colonel, I am visiting your command with purpose and authority from the Chairman of the Joint Chiefs of staff, and I believe you have your orders as well."

Colonel Carver passed through a look of surprise on his face to laughing aloud. "I do believe, Major, your response borders on insubordination to a senior officer. But, apparently, you have the authorization to do with me as you will. Well played, Major. How can we help this mission of yours?"

"I am looking for a pathway to someone at the highest levels of counterintelligence within the Soviet Union, her allies, or surrogates that may provide information on their moles on American soil. Berlin and your unit are as good a place to start as any."

"You are talking about Casper, aren't you?"

"Might be, Colonel. Might not. You have your limits for disclosure, and I have mine."

"Hmmm," Carver said, giving him time to think. "Very well. And what if this pathway of yours threatens to compromise one of our operations?"

Jake smiled, "Take it upstairs, Colonel. You and the higher brass get paid to make those kinds of decisions. I'm just a major."

1300 Hours
22 September 1979
American Embassy, Moscow
Moscow, USSR

CAPTAIN PAUL COLE, a seasoned naval officer, was the Military Attaché to the United States Embassy in Moscow. He had been on station for over a year and was experienced in the intricacies of spycraft on an enemy's home soil. Infiltration of the embassy and its day-to-day operations by the GRU was a constant threat. Jake's meeting with Captain Cole would be brief, and he was scheduled to return to West Germany later in the day.

"GRU General Alexey Dmitrievich is the man that knows exactly who and where Casper is in the United States, if Casper actually exists," Cole stated. "He would be Casper's primary control officer. However, you will not get any information from him directly. He is the highest-ranking officer in the GRU, and he is a powerful player in the Communist Party. Untouchable, in my estimation. I have visited with him on several occasions at diplomatic social events. My impression is that he is a cold-hearted man that hates America."

"How about subordinates?" Jake asked.

Cole motioned toward the sitting area in his office and carried a glass of water as he sauntered toward it to sit. Jake followed and remained silent, recognizing that the captain was thinking about his question.

"Ordinarily, I would say that his staff is as untouchable as Dmitrievich himself. However, something happened about a year ago. We don't know what it was, but his aide-de-camp, Colonel Vladimir Yanovski was suddenly out of favor and fired from his position. It must have been something bad. We have kept tabs on Yanovski since then, not as a priority matter at all, but it's clear that his career in the Soviet Army is in the toilet. We have pretty much written him off as no longer being a significant player. My recollection, which we can verify, is that he was exiled to some barren outpost in Afghanistan. There is a war brewing there. If Dmitrievich wanted Yanavski silenced, or dead without having to give a direct order himself, Afghanistan would be the place to send him."

This information from Cole hit Jake like a thunderclap. His instinct told him that he should grab this thin thread to see what might unravel. Yanovski's banishment might offer a sliver of hope to gathering specific information about Casper. If so, it would be the first actionable material they had received in the hunt for this elusive master spy.

"What do you reckon would be the chances of interviewing Colonel Yanovski?"

Captain Cole threw his head back in laughter.

"Pretty slim, I would say, Major. I can't imagine how you might be able to sit down and visit with a Soviet Colonel located at an isolated outpost in hostile Afghanistan. Not to mention that the Colonel is a hundred times more likely to be motivated to shoot you rather than talk to you."

CHAPTER 10

1030 Hours
12 October 1979
United States Military Academy
West Point, New York

JAKE SAT in his small office in Thayer Hall, mindlessly drumming the eraser end of a pencil against his desk pad with competing thoughts battling for attention. The moment one train of thought would begin, another would push it aside and demand attention. Then another. Then another. The only thing he was consciously aware of as a fact was that he would accomplish nothing unless he recaptured his concentration on one issue at a time. Thoughts of Sara were always with him, regardless of whatever else he was doing. It was as though she sat in his office with him, sat in the passenger seat as he drove, or lay next to him as he fought to go to sleep. Even in her death she was his moment-by-moment companion, present to comfort him or encourage him. It was not only the loss of her that kept her foremost in his mind, but he was also haunted that she had caught a bullet that was meant for him. These thoughts fueled his obsession to find her killer. Casper. Embarrassing as it was, he was often caught making what appeared to others as some off-the-wall comment to himself. Jake did not mind if he was criticized for it. He would trade sanity for Sara's presence, real or imagined, anytime.

West Point had depth of personnel in each academic department, so his two-week absence to Berlin did not have an impact on the instruction of his classes. Jake interpreted the lack of conversation about his absence as a confirmation of his self-determined priorities. He was committed to belief in his maker first, his fatherhood to Stephen Patrick second, his obligations as a soldier third, and temporarily, as an instructor at West Point fourth. Though unspoken, the Army appeared to support that stand, so long as it got its pound of flesh.

When Jake returned from Berlin, he shared every detail about his findings with Major General Osborne and Admiral Hollifield. Together, they decided to hold the information to themselves. The prospect of turning Yanovski was too remote to involve higher chain of command, and the task of locating the Soviet Colonel in Afghanistan was complex, if not impossible. Much of the conversation between the three officers concerned the international complexity of capitalizing on the information Jake had brought them. Colonel Vladimir Yanovski was a disenchanted aide-de-camp of General Alexey Dmitrievich, the highest-ranking GRU officer and Casper's direct handler. Though a defection was unlikely, Yanovski would be an ideal prospect to betray Dmitrievich and Casper. Yanovski might take them immediately to Casper's doorstep. Yet, Afghanistan was a problem. The Soviet Union was escalating its presence, and an overt military action against the government of Afghanistan was imminent. How could they tap any information that Colonel Yanovski held about Casper when a United States military action could be politically disastrous, and how exactly could they locate and interrogate a Soviet army officer in the chaos that was Afghanistan?

Looking back in history, a nine-year war was on the horizon. For the Soviet Union, it would prove to be a foundering that would ultimately give the United States and her allies victory of the Cold War. The cost of that victory being complex alliances and enemies that, in twenty years, would not only bring horrendous terrorist attacks to American soil but a twenty-year war where American soldiers would walk and die in the footprints of the Soviets. For all, the Soviet-Afghan war was costly, including the loss of two million of the Afghan population that perished. Forty years later, the American government learned what every farmer and rancher know based on common sense. That is, there are shortcomings attached to a saddled donkey. They are often unpredictable. Though presumably domesticated, a donkey may well throw his rider and beat him within an inch of his life. And woe to the mountain lion that sets his sights on livestock for an appealing meal with a donkey around. Regrettably, the academic intelligentsia that swaggers through the halls of Congress do not possess the same level of common sense as the farmer.

The foundations of the Soviet-Afghan War were laid by the Saur Revolution, a 1978 coup d'état. Afghanistan's Communist party—the People's Democratic Party of Afghanistan—took power and immediately began implementing land reforms, creating policies to modernize the country, and implementing other dictated reforms that contradicted the Afghan people's cultural traditions and political structure. Within a few short months of gaining political control of the country, the policies of the new Marxist–Leninist political party—"the Democratic Republic"—and its Soviet ally aggressively extinguished political opposition and executed thousands of political prisoners. By the time Colonel Yanovski was assigned to Afghanistan, there was widespread, open rebellion. The Communist party itself experienced deep internal rivalries between the Khalqists and the Parchamites. As Jake returned to West Point from Berlin, the People's Democratic Party General Secretary, Nur Mohammad Taraki, was assassinated by the second-in command, Hafizullah Amin. That event distressed the Soviet Union. Amin was pro-American.

The Soviet government, under the leadership of Leonid Brezhnev, breached the Afghan border with the 40th Army, orchestrated another coup (Operation Storm-333), assassinated General Secretary Amin, and consecrated their puppet, Babrak Karmal. The Soviet invasion was based on the Brezhnev Doctrine, which called for Soviet intervention where socialist rule was under threat. The Organization of Islamic Cooperation demanded the withdrawal of Soviet troops, and the United Nations General Assembly essentially did likewise. Afghan insurgents, called the Mujahideen, were aided financially and militarily by the United States, the United Kingdom, and others. While the Mujahideen, which was essentially communist in its political doctrine itself, waged guerrilla war over most of the countryside. By installing Karmal as the new leader of the Democratic Republic, the Soviets were confident that they could withdraw their troops in less than a year. However, the USSR was in a bear trap of its own making that lasted until General Secretary Mikhail Gorbachev withdrew Soviet troops nine years later. While the specifics of his future were unknown to Colonel Vladimir Yanovski as he sat in his dirt-riddled tent, he was aware that he had to find a way to escape from Afghanistan and his exile. Unconsciously perhaps, he understood the characteristics of the donkey. The United States government did not.

0300 Hours
29 October 1979
Afghanistan

THE US AIRFORCE C-130 Hercules banked sharply in a right turn and climbed for altitude above the twelve thousand feet it had dropped its two passengers. It was a HALO (High Altitude Low Opening) jump. But, by HALO standards, it was from low altitude as twelve thousand feet was considerably lower than the thirty thousand feet it might have been. Jake had made a half-dozen of these jumps when he was a Green Beret, but that was not enough experience to eliminate his anxiety. Jumping out of an airplane into a dark void came nowhere close to being fun for him and jumping into the rugged mountains of Afghanistan made it less so. Imagining himself landing in the middle of a Soviet outpost made the hair on the back of his neck stand up. And what about getting lost in the dark as he drifted downward? He could guide his parafoil, but that was only useful if he knew where to guide it. Had it not been for Green Beret Master

Sergeant Timothy McDade leading him to their destination, Jake would have had to dig deep to find any semblance of a calm performance of duty. The flashing light strapped to McDade's leg was like a lighthouse in a stormy sea, guiding Jake to the designated landing zone to meet up with a Green Beret team on the ground.

The controlled landing of McDade, then Jake, was textbook-perfect, that is, until they touched down on the jagged rocks on the slope of the mountain. Undesired excitement began with their loss of balance and ended with both jumpers lying in a heap on the ground, wrapped a couple of times in the shroud lines, and dragged fifteen yards across the rocks. Jake's shoulder slammed against a boulder, his left shinbone was painfully scraped, drawing blood, and his helmet made several head-numbing contacts with the rocks. Jake thought at first that his shinbone had been shattered. The pain was excruciating. When he finally came to a stop, his first reaction was to reach down to check the damage to his leg. It was not broken, but his hand was covered in blood from the brutal scraping the rocks had given him. Quickly cutting the shroud lines that entangled him was imperative, but each time Jake cut a line to free himself, the chute would catch the wind and roll him, tightening its grip. At the moment, all Jake could think about was the prospect of the wind pushing the chute down the mountain rocks with him in tow. And that mental picture made disentanglement requisite.

"Woo-hoo," exclaimed McDade. "It doesn't get any better than that, Major! Don't you just love this stuff? What a rush, and we get paid to do it."

Jake could not see his trembling hand in the dark, but he could feel it. Never—that is until now—in a hundred years would he have imagined that a head down, free fall at one hundred eighty miles per hour into a big black hole from twelve thousand feet would ever be as terrifying as it was. Anticipation of landing in rough terrain in the middle of a hostile army compounded his collywobbles.

As McDade finally untangled himself, rolled up his parachute, and stuffed it under some rocks, he said, "Aren't you glad you're not an Air Force officer, sir? You would have missed all of this."

Jake laughed. "Well, Sergeant—I was considering a transfer mid-air. Wearing the blue made a lot of sense at the time. I have to hand it to those Zoomies. They are apparently a lot smarter than I am."

CIA AGENTS ASSIGNED to the US Embassy in Kabul were plentiful and fed intelligence to Langley, Virginia, daily. Afghanistan was in chaos, and so was the embassy since the assassination of the United States Ambassador to Afghanistan, Adolph "Spike" Dubs, nine months earlier. Irrespective of numerous "who dunnit" speculations surrounding the murder, it was clear that the Soviets had ordered it. They were the only player that had anything to gain from it. The covered CIA agents operating out of the embassy were busy gathering information on Soviet troop movements, Afghanistan politics, and anything that would enlighten the US of the impending Soviet invasion of Afghanistan. With a fair amount of grumbling, the agents followed orders to locate Colonel Vladimir Yanovski and coordinate with the Green Beret team wanting to get their hands on him.

The six-man Green Beret team was tactically scattered

amongst the mountainside boulders to maintain fields of fire in all directions. It was a cold camp. No fires were allowed, so the protocol was cold chow and chilly nights. Upon Jake's arrival at the team's camp, three miles from Yanovski's outpost, tactical planning began in earnest as to how they would put the two opposing officers together for an undisturbed chit-chat. Snatching the Colonel from a Soviet outpost undetected had its complications. Unless it all went perfectly, the team might have to fight their way out and then be on the run across the country with the Soviets in hot pursuit.

On top of that, their action would likely be diplomatically considered a US attack on the Soviet Union. That scenario was *non est gratum*, not acceptable. While the politicians back home have no qualms about putting soldiers' lives at risk, getting caught ordering such a mission or taking responsibility for it is preposterous.

"You're not going to like this, Major," First Lieutenant Allen Polanski said.

Jake put the spoon full of cold, canned beanie weenies in his mouth, set the can down on the rock next to him, and chewed as he looked up at Polanski with expecting eyes.

"We will guide you in, but you will be on your own once we put you with Yanovski. He speaks English, so talking to him won't be a problem. How you strike up a conversation with him is up to you. We'll put you in a Soviet uniform. Yea, I know. Don't get caught. Getting shot as a spy would ruin your day."

Jake swallowed the beanie-weenies and then took a long swig of warm water from his canteen.

"When?" Jake asked.

"Near sundown, sir. We will put you on him as he leaves

the mess tent. Have your conversation. You will have the cover of darkness on your way out, and we will pick you up."

"And extraction from this lovely country?" Jake asked.

"CIA, Major," Polanski said. "We will hike six klicks east of our position to the meetup, and they will get you to the embassy in Kabul. From there, they will arrange to fly you out as a member of embassy personnel."

Jake nodded his head to indicate that the plan for extraction was acceptable. "How will you get your team out, Lieutenant?"

"No problem, sir. A little hike and a helo extraction. You don't need to worry about us."

Jake picked up his can of beans and leaned back against a boulder. "So, the plan is to drop me off in the middle of a Soviet outpost, alone, in a Soviet officer uniform, to strike up a conversation with a Soviet colonel who may immediately blow the whistle to get me killed, and if I survive that situation, I am to casually stroll out to catch a plane home. Is that about it?"

"You're a Green Beret, Major. Piece of cake."

Jake paused before putting another spoonful of beans in his mouth.

"Roger that. And Providence, Lieutenant."

"You might be the bravest man I know," Staff Sergeant Jimmy Macadangdang said as he spread K-Ration peanut butter on what was labeled "Cake" on the can.

Jake smiled, "No. I'm thinking you are the bravest. It takes a brave man to put forty-year-old peanut butter from a can on a brick of questionable substance and eat it. You deserve a medal."

Macadangdang laughed. "Sir, if I wore a medal for every one of these I've et, I couldn't stand up."

"He likes it because it tastes like roadkill," Sergeant Lopez inserted. "I passed through West Virginia once. I was lucky I didn't have to stop to eat. Luckier still, I made it through without some local mistaking me for a bear and violating me."

"Very funny, Lopez. At least we don't try to make tacos out of everything. Fish tacos. How disgusting is that? And the bears? They are pretty sweet once you get to know them. They have feelings, too, ya know."

CHAPTER 11

1800 Hours
30 October 1979
Afghanistan

JAKE AND SERGEANT First Class Jerome Swisher casually walked through the main entrance to the Soviet outpost thirty-five miles from Kabul. Security was pitifully lacking for an army that would be invading a foreign country in fifty-six days. Jake, in starched Soviet battlefield dress wearing the rank of major, carried a holstered 9mm Pistolet Makarova. With his natural tan and unkept beard Sergeant Swisher passed as a native-born Afghan. He wore the familiar pErAn -e tumbAns, a long top that covers the knee and loose-fitting trousers, and his turban was solid black tied above his forehead and matched his untrimmed beard. His clothing was authentic down to the sandals, as they had taken it all from a captured Afghan soldier four days ago. Swisher slung an old, fully operational Enfield British 303 diagonally across his back to complete the charade. Though a 19th-century rifle, Swisher had total confidence in the weapon. It was the preferred weapon for many Afghans over the more modern AK-47. The age of the rifle did not bother Swisher in the least. He had fired over a thousand rounds from the 303. It was as reliable as the American M1 Garand. Whatever it hit had a hole in it and went down.

JAKE AND SWISHER meandered through several twists and turns in the camp before arriving at the large mess tent near the center of the outpost. The Soviet battalion was smaller than those of the US Army, but still, it was a full battalion by Soviet standards. The outpost held three hundred seventy-eight officers and men consisting of three rifle companies with attached machine gun, artillery, mortar, and service units. Swisher was exhilarated by the risk of their parody. Jake, not so much. While Swisher's Russian was acceptable, Jake's language skills were at the Dick and Jane reader level. En route to the mess tent, Jake tried to keep his eyes forward but occasionally had to make do with friendly nods in Russian.

Standing idle outside the mess tent for five minutes waiting for Yanovski was agonizing. Jake and Swisher imitated a genuine conversation, which appeared normal enough, but the hair on the back of Jake's neck would stand up every time he had to return a soldier's salute. Was a proper West Point salute the same as a Soviet Union Army salute? That might have been a good question to ask before he walked into the lion's den and saluted a lion.

"That's him," Swisher whispered as Yanovski exited the mess tent.

A dozen steps later, Jake approached the Colonel, came

to the position of attention, and snapped a salute which caused Yanovski to come to a stop and return the salute instinctively.

Spoken in low-toned English, Jake said, "Colonel Yanovski. I am Major Jacobs, Military Counterintelligence, United States Army. For your sake, sir, please hear me out for one minute."

Without thought, the Colonel's right hand moved to his sidearm. Jake remained motionless to diminish any perceived threat the Colonel might have. Yanovski's facial expression revealed his astonishment. Astonished, as in beyond imagination, that an American intelligence officer would be openly speaking to him in the middle of an enemy outpost.

"May we talk, Colonel?" Jake said in a calm voice.

Yanovski was speechless, but he nodded in the affirmative.

"Obviously, it is not in my best interest to spend a lot of time with you today, so I will be direct if I have your permission to do so. Is that acceptable to you?"

Still speechless, Yanovski nodded in the affirmative.

"Thank you, sir," Jake said. "You are a highly respected, professional officer, Colonel. Otherwise, I would not be here. How would you like to get out of this hellhole?"

Colonel Yanovski was stunned. He had run countless scenarios through his mind about how he might be able to do that very thing, but each was a dead end, impossible based on General Dmitrievich's banishment of him to misery and probable death. In the span of time that it takes for a deep breath, the Colonel responded.

"I want to defect to the United States."

With no sign of emotion, Jake said, "That would please us as well, but you must understand that we will expect full and honest cooperation from you."

"Agreed," Colonel Yanovski said and extended his hand to seal his word.

"Walk out of the west gate at 1800 hours tomorrow," Jake said, shaking the Colonel's hand and nodding toward Sergeant Swisher. "He will pick you up, and you will be out of Afghanistan within forty-eight hours."

"Will I be hunted?"

"No. Colonel Yanovski will be dead."

0930 Hours
12 November 1979
GRU Headquarters
Moscow, USSR

COLONEL VLADIMIR ZHUKOV marched smartly into General Alexey Dmitrievich's office, the heels of his twelve-inch, black boots loudly announcing his military presence and bearing. Coming to the position of attention three feet, precisely, from the General's desk, Zhukov executed and held a perfect salute until it was returned.

"Good morning, Colonel. How was your travel from Virginia?

"Excellent, General," Zhukov said, knowing full well that his response ended the conversational pleasantries. General Dmitrievich did not waste time on such, especially on subordinates. Had the conversation been with a superior, the conversation would likely be an extended one, well-researched as to what that superior would most enjoy talking about.

"Any progress on the assassinations in America?" Dmitrievich asked.

"None, sir. There have been no more assassinations that we are aware of for months. Our source in the FBI has no enlightening information either. There is nothing new to report since your order to stand down."

"Just as well," the General said. "It appears that Wellspring is satisfied. For the moment."

Zhukov was cautious. The attacks on Osborne and Jacobs were ordered, but General Dmitrievich was not going to take personal responsibility. Colonel Yanovski's transfer to Afghanistan was proof of that.

"Are there any adjustments to our orders, Sir?"

Dmitrievich leaned back in his chair and paused.

"Yes. I want you and one of your men to stay in Virginia and continue the investigation. Send the remainder of your team back to Moscow. We will keep them on standby should the circumstances change. It could be that there will be no more assassinations, which would please Wellspring greatly. Colonel Yanovski may have been correct in thinking the assassinations had nothing to do with them being sources of information for Wellspring. It could be it was simply bad luck for him."

"Could be, sir. Colonel Yanovski is a perceptive officer."

"Was a preceptive officer."

"Sir?" Zhukov asked with a look of puzzlement.

"He is dead, Colonel," the General said with an absence of emotion. "He was killed less than two weeks ago in Afghanistan. A mortar attack by the Mujahideen."

CHAPTER 12

1000 Hours
15 November 1979
The Pentagon

THE J2, Joint Staff Directorate of Intelligence, supports the Chairman of the Joint Chiefs of Staff, General Brodrick, as well as the Secretary of Defense. Two-star Rear Admiral Mark Brownfield, United States Navy, held the J2 position. His job is to coordinate joint intelligence doctrine and architecture to support joint warfighting intelligence capabilities. As a privileged son of Massachusetts, Brownfield was a well-connected officer of twenty-three years in naval service. The timeline of his promotions to a two-star flag officer was meteoric compared to other officers, spectacular performers or not, and his Harvard education provided the requisite paperwork to socialize with the Washington elite. To complement that door-opener, Brownfield was a master of charming interaction with people, a perk to any social gathering. He topped off his naval qualifications as the paragon of good looks in his dress blues. Brownfield was a skilled commander in the East Room of the President's residence in the White House, a successful social climber among the social and military hierarchies but was otherwise regarded with contempt by most Navy combat veterans.

General Brodrick was smart. He knew the background and character of the officers on his staff. But, contrary to prevailing belief, he had little input as to who held positions on his staff. The appointments were politically weighted. It bothered him that selection of the directorates and chiefs was determined more by politics than by qualifications of the officer. As for himself, he assessed his appointment as Chairman of the Joint Chiefs of Staff to be a bit of a congressional compromise. He would have preferred a position a few notches down in the military hierarchy. Too much acclaim is often a liability.

As far as General Brodrick was concerned, the purpose of this meeting with Brownfield and Senator Samuel Zendt was to appease the Senator's incessant demands to be kept abreast of all matters military. Brodrick did not like these beltway games, but they came with the job.

"Admiral Brownfield, give Senator Zendt a short version of our intelligence on the situation in Afghanistan," General Brodrick said.

"Yes, Sir," Brownfield responded. "Senator, we have every indication that the 40th Division of the Soviet Army will initiate an invasion of Afghanistan within the next ninety days. Probably sooner than later. The Soviets are not pleased with the political chaos on hand. They have their man in charge, but there is widespread rebellion against the puppet government in the rural areas. And when I say widespread, I mean a large majority of the people of Afghanistan. The likelihood, Senator, is that a Soviet takeover in Afghanistan will not be as quick and easy as the Soviets might think. Given some support to the rebels, we might think of this situation as the Soviet Union's Vietnam. We all know how painful Vietnam was for us."

Senator Samuel Zendt, in his early thirties, held a junior position on the powerful and prestigious Senate Armed Services Committee. It was customary that those on the committee have prior military service, considering their duties. Zendt had none. His selection was purely political. The left-leaning members of Congress favored Zendt to be the President of the United States in a couple of decades, and the thought that he would not be President seldom crossed his mind. He was sure of it.

"So," Zendt said. "You're implying that the United States supports the rebels in Afghanistan in the hope that an extended war will drain the Soviet Union of resources as Vietnam did for us? We have been hearing this type of scenario for months. Granted, the idea beats an all-out war with the Soviet Union in Afghanistan, but I tend to think that our best option is not to get involved at all. The rebels are basically as communist as the Soviets. You are suggesting that we support communists to fight communists."

General Brodrick coughed to break the conversation between Zendt and Brownfield. "Senator, any recommendations will come from the Joint Chiefs. I'm sure that General Brownfield did not intend to interject his opinion on what action, if any, should be taken. I agree, sir, that our intelligence has not changed much in the last couple of weeks. If an invasion does occur, the executive and legislative branches will request our thoughts on the matter, but until then, we will keep developing alternative plans for consideration."

Zendt remained expressionless. His contempt for the military was not well known, but his key supporters were aware of his feelings and agreed with him. This meeting with General Brodrick and Major General Brownfield did nothing to indicate outright contempt, but it did leave both officers with the sense that something was amiss. Senator Zendt did not evoke confidence that he was playing on the same team, or for that matter, that he supported a strong military presence anywhere.

"Is there any intelligence of a specific nature, that is, intelligence that would impact national security?" Zendt asked.

"None that comes to my office, Senator. As you know, Military Intelligence and the CIA manage their operations with tight security. Details of an operation don't necessarily become known at my level, or yours, until they are pertinent to us. Otherwise, Senator, we would be flooded with information that has no value to you or us at all."

Expressing his assertiveness, Zendt slightly raised his voice and stated, "As a member of the Armed Services Committee, General, I expect detailed briefings from you. I'm sure I don't need to remind you that the military is controlled by duly elected government officials and not the other way around."

Thinking specifically of the twenty-year-long Vietnam fiasco, General Brodrick sarcastically said, "Of course, Senator. I am aware that the military merely executes the decisions of our civilian government on strategy and, ultimately, tactics of all military actions. You can count on our full cooperation."

1530 Hours
16 November 1979
West Point, New York

AS THE WALL clock clicked to the half-hour, Jake announced that his class of fourteen third-year cadets should place their examination blue books on his desk and that they were dismissed. After an hour and a half of answering essay questions, the cadets were numb between the ears, and they wasted no time leaving the classroom to hustle back to the barracks to change clothes for athletics. Though a Friday, they could not yet celebrate that the week was done. They still had long hours ahead of them preparing their rooms for Saturday Morning Inspection, studying for another half-day of classes, and a brigade pass in review. Only then could they claim the weekend.

Patrick came through the door as the last cadet came out. Jake was made suspicious by the smile on Patrick's face.

"So," Jake said. "What have you done this time to put that grin on your face? I'm guessing you did something that will embarrass me."

"Such disrespect. I did something alright. Rebecca is pregnant!"

Jake tossed his head back and laughed. "Well, congratulations. I didn't figure you knew how to make that happen."

"Very funny, Jake. We couldn't be happier. By the way, where did you disappear to a couple of weeks ago? We were up for steaks on the grill, and you were nowhere to be found."

Jake laughed. "Wish I could have made it. I can't give you a lot of detail, but I was vacationing in Afghanistan wearing a Soviet Union uniform in the middle of their army. It was an operation with a high-level pucker factor. I was glad to get home in one piece. West Point was a welcome sight."

The look on Patrick's face was one of shock. "Afghanistan! Is that a country or something? I swear, Jake. This spook stuff is going to get you in trouble. It's worse than that gung-ho, Green Beret business."

"Speaking of gung-ho, they tossed me out of a C-130—in the dark—at twelve thousand feet! The jump wasn't too bad, but the landing was brutal."

"Ok. I won't pester you for the details right now, but you can fill me in over those steaks. You and Steven Patrick should come over Saturday afternoon, and we will slide them onto the grill."

"Will Sunday work? Steven Patrick and I are going camping tomorrow. His Webelo Cub Scout troop is having a campout. He has to learn how to cook a piece of bacon on a leaf or something like that. Funny. If he were in the infantry, he wouldn't need the leaf. He'd eat it raw."

"I'd bet money on the terrified mothers of his Cub Scout troop. I can just hear all those Army officer dads. 'Be a man. Go ahead and climb that cliff. Don't worry about that broken arm. Shake it off. We'll have it looked at when we get home. That bone sticking out is no big deal. Don't be a sissy—kill that rattlesnake and eat it.' Being a scout at West Point is a dangerous business."

Jake laughed out loud, knowing there was some truth to the jest.

"Afghanistan, huh," Patrick said. "Did you find what you were looking for?"

"I think so." Jake rubbed the back of his head as his mind returned to a more serious subject. "I think we may have a credible source that may help us find the biggest traitor this country has ever had."

"Casper. How are you going to manage all this? I mean, how are you going to take care of the demands of your career path and search for Casper at the same time?"

"I probably won't," Jake said in a saddened tone of voice. "Finding this traitor is more important than my career. I will find him. He is responsible for Sara's death. He gave the orders to assassinate me and Major General Osborne. I wish that bullet had taken me rather than her."

CHAPTER 13

1000 Hours
5 January 1980
The Pentagon
Washington, DC.

JAKE AND MAJOR General Osborne poured cups of steaming coffee from the silver coffee service provided by his secretary and sat comfortably at the informal area arranged for discussions. Once the pleasantries were completed, Jake took the initiative to get down to business.

"General, I have completed two weeks of interviews with Colonel Yanovski. The FBI and the CIA interrogated him extensively before that. They almost brought him to the brink of insanity to clear him for my interview with him. He has been given the code name The Otter, a strange name, but that is what it is. From now on, that is how we should refer to him."

"Were the interviews productive?" Osborne asked.

"Yes, and no," Jake replied. "Yes, to the extent that he could identify Casper as a high-ranking military officer or a congressman that has access to military intelligence. In either case, it is possible that Casper does not have direct access but has indirect access through relationships with those that do. By the way, he confirmed that Casper's Soviet code name is Wellspring. He indicated that Casper's intelligence has become more specific and valuable over the past ten or fifteen years, which may indicate Casper's advancement either in the military or in the political arena. He is their most productive agent, which makes him our greatest threat. We suspected all that to be true, but now we have some degree of verification. So, yes, The Otter's information is valuable with respect to our field of investigation."

Osborne sipped his coffee as he considered what Jake had told him. "And the "not so productive?' "

Jake smiled, "That information covers a broad field of suspects, sir. The number of high-ranking military officers and politicians that have access to top-secret information is staggering. As for military officers, it could be any well-connected officer at the battalion level or above, from lieutenant colonel to four-star general. A battalion commander would have access to limited strategic information, but if he were socially connected, he would know more than he probably should. The same goes for a congressional suspect. Even a staff member would be a possible suspect. So, the 'no' is that we have a confirmation, but not necessarily information that will narrow our search in a meaningful way."

"Do you need to interview The Otter again?" the General asked.

"Perhaps, sir. But not right now. He is housed at Fort Belvoir, Virginia, and in custody with USA INSCOM, the United States Army Intelligence & Security Command. They will interview him regularly concerning other matters for a time, then set him up with a life in the United States. His interview with me is confidential, even to the commander of INSCOM, and I must say, the commanding general is not happy with me. Lieutenant General Nathan Hawk, the Director of Defense Intelligence, has let it be known that a lowly major does not have the authority to keep intelligence from his command."

"I've known Hawk for years. He is a good man, but his position is appointed by the President. He has been the director for nearly six years. That's too long for someone to wield that much power. So, what's next, Major?"

Jake paused and sipped his lukewarm coffee.

"Well, sir. I do have a suggestion that you may not find favorable."

Osborne smiled. "Let's have it."

Jake squirmed a bit, knowing that his suggestion would be a sensitive one directed toward senior officers.

"Well, sir, I would like to form an air-tight group for the investigation going forward. Since all ranking officers and congressmen are suspect, we can't afford the normal chain of command protocols. I suggest that all investigative information be held by this group only. That would exclude you, sir."

Osborne's eyes widened in surprise.

"Such an arrangement would put you in a position of deniability with other flag officers. It would not be good for you to report the progress of this investigation to Casper inadvertently. That is not likely, but it is possible. I would suggest that we use Admiral Hollifield as a liaison. He would know everything that I discover, and if something were to happen to me, you would have a solid connection to the facts. This way, General, you would have limited knowledge of our progress, and you could legitimately report to your superiors without jeopardizing the mission. I realize that this is a highly unusual request, but I think it best for you and the mission."

Osborne crossed his legs, sipped his cold coffee, and considered Jake's proposal for a full two minutes. Jake silently sat, expecting a rejection of the idea.

"Under circumstances of lesser importance, Jake, I would say that you are absolutely out of your mind. But I think you might have a good idea. I'm not crazy about not knowing what's going on in my command, but I do understand the necessity of it. It would keep the facts covered. Admiral Hollifield? I trust him to tell me anything that is critical for me to know. He would be an excellent choice as a liaison—a solid patriot. Good judgment. I would sign off on that if he is willing to do it. The last time I talked to him, he and Suzanne were quite happy with retirement."

Jake nodded. "If it is alright with you, sir, I will approach him on the matter?"

"Certainly. If he agrees, then the three of us will have to meet."

1800 Hours
9 January 1980
Major General Osborne's Residence
Fredericksburg, Virginia

"SO. WE ARE ALL IN AGREEMENT," Osborne said to the Benedict Arnold Tribunal. "We currently have two congressional targets. Both are anti-Constitution and corrupt. However, it is the decision of this committee to postpone any action until we know the results of the presidential election in

November. The election may eliminate the need for our work altogether. If it has a favorable result, we may have a strong executive that will return some sanity to the Nation."

Major General Joan Whitehead leaned forward to indicate that she had a comment or question. "Seth, does your 'off-the-books' assignment from General Brodrick conflict in any way with your obligations to this committee? Not knowing the extent of your assignment causes me some concern, considering the risks we are taking here."

Osborne sat forward, placed his elbows on the conference table, and smiled. "Normally, I would be duty-bound not to share information about the assignment, but under the circumstances, I will. There is a Soviet mole in the high echelons of our government. His code name," he hesitated, then said, "or her code name, is Casper. Wellspring is the Soviet's code name. We'll just presume that Casper is male. He may well be the most dangerous and traitorous spy in American history. All we know at this point is that the information he is passing to the Soviets is copious, highly classified, and ravaging the security interests of the United States. Potentially, the information Casper is passing to the Soviets could determine the ultimate survival of our Nation. Because of the nature of the information he is passing, it is likely that he is a high-ranking military officer or a highly influential member of Congress. My assignment from General Brodrick is to determine the validity that Casper truly exists, which we now know that he does, and to identify him. Our work on this Tribunal is important. I assure you that my assignment to find Casper is equally important and related."

Air Force Brigadier General (Ret) Robert Perribone asked, "What happens if you do identify Casper?"

Osborne paused. "I've given that question a lot of thought.

As we are all aware, most federal prosecutors hold their careers as their highest priority. It is likely that the justice system will demand overwhelming, unrealistic proof to move forward with a trial. Prosecutors will demand an ironclad case as a prerequisite to move forward, which means that Casper would never be prosecuted. Secondly, suppose he was brought to trial. In that case, there are many at high levels of government that would be embarrassed, or worse, entangled in their complicity of providing the Soviets with top secret information. Those people would jump through hoops to keep a trial from happening. Again, personal careers would trump the best interest of the Nation. I feel that the members of this committee may ultimately be tasked with reasonably weighing the evidence and taking action to obtain justice for the American people. So, this committee is deeply involved in this assignment I have from General Brodrick."

CHAPTER 14

0900 Hours
3 March 1980
Admiral Hollifield's Office
Camp Lejeune, North Carolina

ADMIRAL HOLLIFIELD STROLLED into his office, and Jake and John Hanraty came to the position of attention.

"Good morning, Sir," they said simultaneously.

"Good morning, gentlemen."

The Admiral set his briefcase next to his desk, surveyed the room, then sat in his desk chair. "Thanks to the Marine Corps, we have a place to work. Thank God we are not in Washington. A man could easily get snake bit in that place."

Jake and Hanraty both smiled. They had missed the Admiral's refreshing candor.

"Jake. Thanks for getting me out of the house for a couple of days a week. I needed a break from all my lollygagging. Retirement is a curse."

Jake laughed. "The pleasure is mine, sir. I appreciate your willingness to jump into a difficult situation."

"And you, Hanraty," the admiral said with a smile. "I see that you still haven't found any clothes that fit, or an iron, for that matter."

Hanraty smiled, thrilled to be working for Admiral Hollifield again. He had missed the old sailor.

"Thank you, Admiral. I'm glad to be working with you again."

"Well, let's get to it," the Admiral said. "We need to find this Casper fellow as quickly as possible. Otherwise, Jake, your career is going to be in the toilet. Lieutenant General Hawk, the Director of Defense Intelligence, is not happy with you."

"And me, Admiral?" Hanraty asked teasingly. "Is my career going down the toilet, too?"

Admiral Hollifield leaned back in his chair and laughed.

"John, your career has always been down the toilet, but you are the most indispensable person on this team. No other person in the world can find a needle in the haystack like you do."

All laughed as Jake nodded his head in the affirmative.

"Ok. Here are the parameters. Based on what The Otter said, we start with Washington, DC, and commutable areas. Casper is high-ranking military or civilian government and well connected to the executive or legislative branches. By well-connected, I mean that he is positioned to tap into high-level intelligence in his job or through social contacts that have access to that kind of intelligence. It appears obvious that some of those social contacts are with individuals in Congress. That place leaks like a sieve. We know that war plans for the 8th Army in Europe have consistently been passed to the Soviets by Casper, but we will not start our search with NATO command. The Otter says Casper operates out of Washington. We will expand our search if we come up empty-handed here. Jake, to whom do you think we should start looking?"

"Sir. I think John can start making a preliminary list of suspects. If he's military, he is high ranking, probably colonel and above. The Otter says that Casper has been active for at least ten years, with the quality of intelligence drastically improving over that period. That may indicate advancement in his position. So, an eliminating factor may be an inconsistency of a prospect's exposure to intelligence. For example, a prospect may have access now, but he may have had zero access five years ago. That being the case, his name might be shuffled down the list a few notches. We are looking for someone that has a consistency of access. Now, a congressman might be a little different because his access may be purely through social contacts, committee assignments, or positions on the periphery of top-secret information. If access is an eliminating factor, the filter is some different. We probably can't look at a congressman through the same lens that we would a military officer.

"How long do you think this list of suspects may be, Jake?" the Admiral asked.

"Well, Sir, until we can eliminate suspects by logical impossibility, the list is every military officer above the rank of colonel, every representative and senator in Congress, high-level congressional staff, and even some lobbyists. Until we make those eliminations, the only people exempt from speculation are the three of us in this room and Major General Seth Osborne. Initially, everyone else could be Casper. Determining who has access to intelligence and for how long they have had access will bring that list to a workable size."

Hanraty sat up straight in his chair, ran his fingers through his hair, and raised his hand to speak.

"This is not high school, John," Hollifield said. "Feel free to butt in whenever."

"Yes, Sir. I can whittle that list down considerably, but it will take time. A first pass may take several months. Most files will take minutes to eliminate while others will require some deep digging."

"Excellent," Hollifield said as he lit his first cigar of the day. "Jake, what is your schedule?"

"I will finish up my assignment at West Point the first week of June, but I can meet with you and John as often as needed. I have been selected for the Army Command and General Staff School at Ft. Leavenworth, Kansas. As you know, Admiral, that selection is a critical career requirement. The course doesn't start until next January. Patrick has been selected as well. I can arrange to work here until then, or I can request postponement of CGSS. Either way, I can be available."

The admiral smiled. "You and Patrick on the same post again? You would think the Army would figure out that they need to keep you two separated. Lord, help us. For now, Jake, keep the assignment at Leavenworth. There is no need to completely blow up your career. Take your thirty-day leave in June as planned. You will be here full-time for five months, but you will obviously need to make a few trips while at Leavenworth. As far as I'm concerned, they don't come any more trustworthy than Patrick. If you want to use him as a sounding board, feel free to do so."

"Yes, Sir."

"John. Get to work. I will be in the office a couple of days a week. Jake. Wrap it up at West Point, take leave, then get back here. Any reservations?"

"Only one, Sir," Jake said. "I'm a little concerned about Stephen Patrick being around all these Marines. Sara would be greatly disappointed if he decided he wanted to be one."

All laughed.

1800 Hours
5 April 1980
United States Military Academy
West Point, New York

"LITTLE LEAGUE BASEBALL," Jake said to Patrick as they leaned against the bleacher seat behind them. "I can remember those days back in Comanche. Steve Ross and I were on the same team, and even then, Sara was there watching us. Great days. Stephen Patrick seems to be a natural."

Patrick grinned. "Well, you playing catch with him for an hour every day makes a huge difference. You two seem to be doing well, Jake."

There was still a spring chill in the air, but the returning foliage was displaying the beauty that was West Point. Jake and Patrick were nearly unidentifiable as soldiers, wearing faded jeans, sneakers, and disreputable t-shirts. As usual, Jake wore the faded Dodgers baseball cap Sara gave him in junior high. Patrick's statement had shifted Jake's thoughts from baseball to life without Sara.

"It's all one day at a time, Patrick," Jake said, almost in a whisper."

Patrick paused and then laid a hand on Jake's shoulder

without saying a word.

"Some days, I am so angry I want to lash out at everyone. On those days, I question why God would take Sara away from me and Stephen Patrick. It's like happiness went sliding down the drain. Forever. I've never felt such heartache. Before that day, I thought my faith was as solid as a rock. I found that it wasn't. That alone feels like a crushing defeat."

Jake paused, and Patrick remained silent. Not only did Patrick not know what he could say that would be comforting, but he also thought that perhaps it best to let Jake get these things off his chest. Knowing Jake's sorrow to its depths was impossible.

"It is all incomprehensible, beyond human understanding, exactly why there is such suffering. All I know, most days, is that God has a plan and purpose for each of us. It is hard to imagine that Sara's death is a positive thing in any shape or form, but I do have faith that God ultimately works all things for good in the life of the believer. We all have an appointment to die. That faith is all that I have. All I really know is that I must give God credit for perfect wisdom and focus on legitimate thoughts and actions regarding that wisdom. Hardest thing I have ever had to do."

Patrick nodded that he agreed with Jake, as he was silently thankful that he was not fighting that kind of a personal battle. The thought of such a thing was frightening.

"So," Jake said. "Are you and Rebecca happy about coming to Colorado for a few weeks in June?"

"Of course we are," Patrick replied, relieved to have Jake change the subject. "You are going to do all the cooking, aren't you? Rebecca and I will be on vacation."

"So long as you like peanut butter and jelly sandwiches, I am."

CHAPTER 15

1000 Hours
6 May 1980
Lieutenant General Nathan Hawk's Office
Director of Defense Intelligence
Washington, DC

"GENERAL BRODRICK, thank you for the meeting on such short notice," Lt. General Hawk said as he cordially shook General Brodrick's hand. I hope it wasn't an inconvenience."

Brodrick smiled and shook his hand as though they were the best of friends. They were not best of friends as in bonded brothers, but they had done a considerable amount of mutual backscratching over the years. Both could claim that they had been a positive influence on the other's career.

"Not at all, Nathan. Your request was a good reason to get away from the office. This is a Tuesday that feels like a Monday. Chaos every time the phone rings."

"Have a seat. This won't take up much of your time. Coffee? Tea?"

"Water would be fine," Brodrick replied. "What can I do for you?"

"A foursome of golf on Saturday. If you can. But the main thing I wanted to visit with you about is this mysterious assignment you have given to Major General Seth Osborne. He is retired. He is basically a civilian. I don't know what you have him doing, but I'm getting all kinds of flak from INSCOM, the Intelligence and Security Command, and from some of their unit commanders."

Brodrick smiled, then took a slow gulp from his water glass. "What kind of flak are you talking about, Nathan? Seth is not involved in anything that would warrant a problem for you or INSCOM."

"Well, Military Intelligence is annoyed. Seth has this Major Jacobs carved out of the normal path of their operations. It is rumored that Jacobs is doing some undercover investigating that leaves Military Intelligence in the dark. It would be a shame to ruin the Major's career by alienating the commanders that he works for. In short, sir, there is some resentment about this mysterious sideline operation you have going on with Seth Osborne. Even Senator Samuel Zendt has called me. He is a turd and aggravates me to no end. I have no idea why he thinks your operation is such a concern to him."

Brodrick leaned forward with a smile on his face. "Well, Nathan, as you are aware, I don't have to explain any of my operations to you, sideline and mysterious or not. But, out of courtesy, I will this time. It has been rumored for years that there is a high-level Soviet mole in our ranks. That is pure conspiracy theory. The speculation is not good for us. Seth's assignment is to prove that the mole either exists or doesn't, and Seth is the perfect person for that assignment. He is a fanatic about chain of command, and I will know everything he knows. Of that, I am confident. Major Jacobs? Unfortunately, his career is sacrificial to a greater cause. I assure you, Nathan, that there is no mole. There is no doubt in my mind that the intelligence leaks attributed to Casper, the theoretical mole, come from the US Army Europe and US European Command. The 66th have ongoing operations that will ultimately prove that to be true, and that will put an end to all these Casper rumors."

"What if they do prove there is a Casper?" Hawk asked.

"They won't. Even if they came up with a viable suspect, they would never be able to get sufficient proof to make it into more than pure speculation. Our judicial system would crush any attempt to pursue the matter. No. Given some time, Seth Osborne's investigation will come up empty, and the assignment will be closed."

General Hawk leaned back and sipped his glass of water as he considered what Brodrick had told him.

"Alright, Sir. That doesn't solve my problem of being pestered by INSCOM and Senator Zendt, but I can manage all that. I'm satisfied that your operation is no threat to my command. We will all ride this out. Too bad about Jacobs, but like you said, it is for the greater good of the service."

1800 Hours
20 May 1980
Senator Lloyd Prather Residence
Arlington, Virginia

LLOYD PRATHER WAS a farmer from Pennsylvania, at least, he was a farmer thirty-seven years ago, but he had been a politician for so many years he had forgotten what farm dirt looked like. He was one of those in the Senate that was not visibly corrupt. No one could directly tie him to payoffs and backroom shenanigans. Still, his multimillion-dollar wealth left many curious as to how he had managed to accumulate such on a congressional salary. Wealthy for sure. Powerful in the Senate without question. He was the vice chairman of the Senate's Select Committee on Intelligence. While all Senators have access to classified intelligence, the Select Committee's knowledge of security matters is expanded to include intelligence sources, methods, and covert operations. The President can, and occasionally does, restrict from the committee knowledge of certain covert operations, but not from the chairman and vice chairman. Senator Prather, as vice chairman, had full access to the smallest details of intelligence, including the who, what, and where of all covert operations. At the age of seventy-two, he boasted of being in the prime of his life, his political career nowhere near its apex.

Senator Prather's Cadillac Deville pulled into the circle drive of his lavish residence. He was glad to be home and anxious to see his wife of almost fifty years. Because of the hour, he would have to hustle to change clothes for dinner with friends. Coming to a stop, he simultaneously turned off the motor and pulled the door handle. No sooner had he turned to shut the door than he felt a strong arm across his chest from behind, and only momentarily, the sting of a thin five-inch blade puncture the base of his skull. The lights went out as the blade fully penetrated to its hilt prior to the attacker moving the tip back and forth, slicing through the brain stem. With Senator Prather's brain severed from his spinal cord, death occurred immediately.

1330 Hours
22 May 1980
Major General Osborne's Residence
Fredericksburg, Virginia

"IT WASN'T US," General Osborne said emphatically. "The Tribunal did not even have him under consideration."

Brigadier General Robert Perribone, USAF (Ret), spoke louder than usual. "Well, from what I'm hearing, it is presumed a gut cinch that it was a Tribunal assassination. It looks like the others. I don't like it. It smells like someone knows about the Tribunal and is setting us up. That would be a heck of a note if we got fried for the one assassination we didn't arrange."

Admiral Stanley Monroe sat forward and joined the conversation. "I feel the same way, Robert. Makes the hair stand up on the back of my neck, but we need to remain calm and see what happens. If Senator Prather's assassination is a set-up, we will know soon enough."

"Gentlemen," Osborne said. "Stanley is right. It is a time to remain calm. We don't know much about Prather. It is likely that someone wanted him dead, and it has nothing to do with us. It has been two days. If this were a set-up, we will know that soon enough."

1400 Hours
22 May 1980
The Pentagon
Washington, DC.

VICE ADMIRAL BROWNFIELD, Director of Intelligence on General Brodrick's staff, stepped into the General's office, thinking he would sit at first. But Brodrick's body language indicated that this was not to be a pleasant meeting.

"Yes, sir. You wanted to see me."

Brodrick gave no indication that the Admiral was invited to sit. "Yes. Senator Prather was assassinated. That is insane. We have to get to the bottom of this and stop all this nonsense. What do you know about it?"

"Not much, General," Brownfield said. "It's like the other political assassinations. Someone is taking out some of the most powerful people in Congress. The FBI is clueless. Finding who is responsible is their responsibility."

"Well, make it your responsibility as well," Brodrick said in a tone that indicated a direct order, though meaningless at best. "What else are you hearing on this?"

"Nothing directed toward the assassination itself, but it has caused a few rumors that impact the Senate. Senator Prather's death will shuffle the composition on the Select Committee on Intelligence. There are fourteen remaining on the committee, and one of which will move to vice chairman. That will leave one seat open."

"And?" Brodrick asked.

Admiral Brownfield stiffened, fully expecting Brodrick's mood to worsen. "Senator Samuel Zendt."

"Good Lord. What does he have to do with this? He is on the Armed Services Committee."

"Probably not for long, Sir," Brownfield said. "Rumor has it that he is making a play to fill the opening on the Intelligence Committee, and he apparently has the support of his political allies to make that happen. By the time the Senate gets through exchanging favors, Zendt will likely get the appointment. It would be a huge step up for him and his long-term ambitions. It's a power position, and eventually, he might rise to chairman or vice chairman."

General Brodrick was stunned. "I'll have to think about that. Very bad news, Admiral Brownfield."

2330 Hours
24 May 1980
Parking Garage, 30th Street Station
Philadelphia, Pennsylvania

SENATOR SAMUEL ZENDT pulled his car into the 30th Street Station parking garage on Market Street and slowly drove to the third floor. Few autos were parked at this hour, and he parked as far as possible from the stairwell leading to the next floor up. Nervously, he walked to the stairwell carrying a briefcase with twenty thousand dollars in one-hundred-dollar bills neatly stacked in it. One car passed as it descended toward the street. Zendt turned his back to the car as it approached.

Upon reaching the fourth floor, Zendt scanned the few parked cars until he spotted the dark blue Mercedes sedan with deep tinted windows. As he approached the car, he could plainly see that a back seat window was halfway down, as he had been told it would be. Without hesitation, Zendt slid the briefcase through the open window and then immediately turned back toward the stairwell. As he opened the door, he heard the Mercedes engine start and the distinctive sound of it driving to the lower floors toward the street.

With payment made, Senator Zendt relaxed, knowing that his seat on the Senate Select Committee on Intelligence was secure.

CHAPTER 16

0800 Hours
2 June 1980
United States Military Academy
West Point, New York

JAKE SAT ALONE in the conference room adjacent to the office of the head of the political science division, Colonel Matthews. The conference table, made of cherry and massive, was a hold-over piece of furniture and beautifully worn from decades of use. Like most things West Point, it projected grandeur and charm. He was nervous about the meeting but aware that it was best not to appear so. It was his exit interview at the end of his three-year teaching assignment. While he was confident that he had done a good job teaching, he was somewhat anxious about criticisms he might receive about his absences while chasing Casper. The evaluation was to go into his permanent file, which could either aid his future career or bring advancement to a dead stop.

Colonel Matthews stepped into the room, file folders

under his arm, and Brigadier General Walton Pence, Dean of Academics, came in behind him. Jake had expected Colonel Matthews but not the dean. Anxiousness turned to the sense of butterflies in his stomach as he rose from his chair to the position of attention.

"Good morning, Major Jacobs," Matthews said. "General Pence will be joining us for the interview this morning. Be seated. This won't take long."

"Major Jacobs," General Pence said as he took a seat at the end of the conference table. "I trust my joining the interview is not a bother. I was in the Colonel's office and thought it would be interesting to sit in."

"Not a bother at all, sir," Jake said with a smile.

Colonel Matthews opened the file, glanced at it, then leaned back in his chair. "I understand you will be on special assignment in the Pentagon for a few months, then off to Command and General Staff College at Ft. Leavenworth."

"Yes, sir," Jake said, knowing full well that a standard response would indicate that he was anxious to get back to a combat unit and command rather than an academic environment. Leaders want to lead, and that is what superiors want to hear.

"You're an early major," the Colonel said. "Outstanding combat record. Your performance as an instructor here is also outstanding. Your record will reflect that. I am hopeful that you would like to return to West Point again in some capacity."

"Thank you, sir. I'm sure at the right time that would be an excellent opportunity for me."

General Pence leaned back in his chair and crossed his legs as though he were sitting in someone's living room. "Tell me, Major, you have now been here for three years and are about to see the first class of women graduate at West Point. What is your take on this? Informally, of course."

Jake was not surprised at the question. He had been prodded with the same question by more people than he could count since his arrival.

"The women? They are sharp, motivated individuals. I could say the same thing about the male cadets."

Pence laughed. "That was an excellent, diplomatic answer, Major. There have been significant changes since women were admitted. Surely you have more to say about those changes."

"Yes, sir," Jake said without hesitancy. "Changes at West Point. I do have personal opinions that I'm willing to share, but it really doesn't have much to do with women being admitted. It appears to me that women being admitted is simply a catalyst for an ongoing overhaul of military standards in general and at West Point specifically. It is politically and culturally engineered. Women have nothing to do with that. They will make fine soldiers."

"Do you have specifics? Exactly what changes have you seen since you were a cadet, excluding the obvious fact that there are female cadets?" Colonel Matthews asked.

Jake smiled, not knowing exactly how either of these two senior officers felt.

"Alright, sir. All three of us being graduates of West Point in earlier times, I presume that we share, to some degree, like experiences. Our Founding Fathers were smart men. They understood that culture in a nation would sway in the wind, to and fro, in terms of its principles, thereby making it necessary, or at least desirable, that there be a fixed standard of leadership in the military. One based on character and integrity. They set West Point apart from other institutions of higher learning for a specific purpose. In 1802 the Founding Fathers established the United States Military Academy to set a high standard for military officers and ensure military readiness for war. That standard has served the United States extremely well for one hundred and seventy-eight years. During the Civil War, the first test of the theory, there were sixty critical battles. In fifty-five of those battles, a West Point graduate commanded both sides. In the other five battles, a West Point graduate commanded one of the opposing sides. The Class of 1915 was the class that the stars fell upon. Fifty-nine of one hundred sixty-four graduates became general officers in World War Two. Through the years, names such as Grant and Lee and Sherman and Eisenhower and Pershing and Patton and Bradley and MacArthur come to mind. Hundreds of other graduates fall on the list of those named who have held the West Point standard without wavering, as designed by the Founding Fathers. Our Alma Mater says it right. 'Let Duty be well performed, Honor be e'er untarned, Country be ever armed, West Point, by thee.' "

"What about modernization of the military based on changing times?" the Colonel asked. "Don't you think it a bit short-sighted to leave West Point and the military as a whole antiquated and obsolete?"

Jake chuckled, and all three laughed when Jake said, "I certainly don't intend to be flippant, sir, but West Point has had indoor plumbing for quite a long time. I'm confident that West Point will continue to provide an excellent curriculum that reflects changing times and technology. Relatively speaking, West Point will always be a high-quality learning institution."

"As the dean, I certainly agree that West Point performs well in its academic curriculum. We are constantly looking for ways to not only keep up but to look ahead at future needs. West Point is a forward-looking education."

"Specifically, Major, what makes you think West Point will not accomplish all that it always has in the past?" Matthews asked.

"Well, Sir," Jake said without hesitation, "after my three years as an instructor, I see a trend to make West Point like other colleges. To make West Point fit in with contemporary culture. A major break from West Point's history is the deterioration of the Honor Code, where cadets now get a pass in many instances. I see the character-building travail of daily cadet life diminished. I see cadet attitudes formed that mirror those of their peers at other universities, some of which are socialistic and disrespectful. I see numerous sexual assaults, which are common on many university campuses. That has become a plague at all the service academies. Sexual assault at West Point defies logic to me as to how cadets of that character were admitted in the first place or why the academies do not have an ironclad, no-tolerance policy against it. The changes are subtle, I'll grant you that, but I can't help but wonder how they will impact the defense of the Nation a few decades in the future if the trend of re-culturalization the military continues. In just the short time since I graduated, the number of graduates that stay in the military after their five-year commitment has dropped drastically. Why is that? Hopefully, that negative trend will reverse itself, but I doubt it will. Many of the cadets today have the attitude that they are here for the free education and the benefits of a West Point education in civilian life. Fewer today than in years past have a genuine desire to be career combat officers. I think it prudent to ask ourselves the hard question. If, in forty years, America finds herself in a long, bitter conventional war—will we persevere?

Our mission has not been to make captains of industry but to make warrior leaders. If the training changes, will the results change as well?"

General Pence smiled. "So, you think West Point is going to hell in a handbasket."

"Not at all, General," Jake was quick to say. "You asked me specifically about the changes I have seen, but they don't encapsulate my opinion of West Point or its future. Relative to fluctuations in American culture and politics over time, West Point will always be an exceptional institution. While there may be more cadets unmotivated to be career officers, there are many who are dedicated to military service. There will always be extraordinary combat commanders that emerge from West Point. I am confident of that. And of the overall curriculum? Outstanding. As technology changes, the curriculum will change to meet those challenges. I do hope to return to West Point someday to be a part of the future preservation of our Nation."

"Interesting perspective, Major," Brigadier General Pence said sincerely. "I hope you do return. I tend to agree with most of what you have said. Unfortunately, and I'm sure you would agree, the military, the service academies, are subject to that sway of the wind with respect to the culture and politics. The Founding Fathers set that in play as well. We are soldiers. Not politicians. We have these exit interviews often. Similar concerns and conclusions have been expressed by most. We wish you well on your next assignment. And certainly not a secondary matter, I want to express the Academy's deep condolences for the loss of your wife."

Jake nodded, pushing back on the emotions that threatened to bring tears to his eyes.

"Major Jacobs," Colonel Matthews said as he handed Jake

a black, rectangular box with a beautiful Monte Blanc ballpoint pen with the Academy crest on the clip. "It is not as good as a bonus check, but it is a token of the Academy's appreciation for the job you have done here. Thank you, Major. You are a fine officer."

CHAPTER 17

1800 Hours
6 June 1980
Durango, Colorado

"UNCLE PATRICK WILL BE HERE TOMORROW," Jake said to Stephen Patrick. Jake sat in the rocking chair on the front porch of the cabin as the early evening cooled. It was the same chair Sara had sat in, rocking slowly while admiring the valley with its tall grass gently blowing in the breeze and its array of colorful wildflowers. The view was unhindered by other cabins or structures for a mile or more, and other than the sway of the grass and flowers, the only movement was the slow grazing of a half-dozen horses.

"And your grandma and grandpa Lowell will be picking you up the day after to go stay with them for two weeks. You will have a great time."

"What will we do?" Stephen Patrick asked as he continued to roll a toy truck up and down the steps.

Jake grinned. "Well, they live in California now, so I know

you will be going to Disneyland and the beach to swim in the ocean. What fun. I remember when I was your age, the undertow kind of scared me until I got used to it."

Stephen Patrick looked up at Jake with deep concern. "Under toad? Will he hurt me?"

Jake was at first puzzled by the question, then laughed. "No. It's not a toad, like a big frog. It's an undercurrent of the water caused by the waves. It just feels funny on your feet."

Satisfied that some huge toad would not attack him, Stephen Patrick went back to running his truck up and down the step.

"I wish that Mom were here to go with me," Stephen Patrick said without looking up.

"I do, too, Son," Jake replied. "I wish that more than anything."

Stephen Patrick rolled the toy truck to the top of the step and roared like a truck engine under stress.

"But I'm glad she is with Jesus and happy. We'll be ok, Dad," he said nonchalantly.

"How old are you? Are you twenty years old?"

Stephen Patrick laughed. "No, Dad. I'm only nine. You know that."

0930 Hours
9 June 1980
Camp Lejeune, North Carolina

JOHN HANRATY silently sat in a heavily worn chair in front of Admiral Hollifield's desk while the Admiral read the report prepared for him. These moments were always unsettling. No matter how satisfied the Admiral might be with the work, there was always a display of pursed lips, grumbling, and heavy thumping of his cigar on the ashtray. If the report was disturbing, the Admiral's tone always projected his displeasure at the messenger, but Hanraty had learned from the experience of working with the Admiral that there was no personal criticism involved. It was simply the Admiral's reaction to the substance.

When finished reading, the Admiral leaned back in his chair and puffed on his cigar. "I suppose we should be happy to have eliminated most of the military, but seventy-three officers are still a considerable list. As far as Congress goes, there is not much reduction from the four hundred thirty-five."

"Yes, sir," Hanraty said. "The military is easier. Since an officer would have to have assignments that put him in contact with the right kind of top-secret information over a long period of time, it is a matter of investigating his assignments. If the officer did not consistently have access to pass to the Soviets, then he would drop down the list of suspects. Of course, most officers might have some information of value throughout their career, but it would not be information consistent with what Casper is passing. Congress is a different story, sir. Most everyone that has been in Congress for five years or more is at least a plausible candidate. Even if one is not directly connected with intelligence, they rub shoulders and make concessions with impunity. The vetting of Congress will take time."

"Enlisted personnel?"

"Not likely, Admiral. Enlisted personnel do have access to high-level information and intelligence, but it is almost always restricted to one specific situation. For instance, Military Counterintelligence is currently working on building legal cases on enlisted personnel in Berlin, whom they've verified, that have passed war plans for the 8th Army in Europe. That is a serious situation, and they will get them. But Casper appears to have a much broader range of information for the Soviets that includes war plans, weapons development, and strategy at the highest level. If Casper is military, he is high-ranking and has consistently had assignments over the years that gave him a broad view of intelligence."

Hollifield walked to the sofa table and poured coffee into Marine Corps coffee mugs for himself and Hanraty, then sat again behind his desk. He thumped his cigar against the edge of the crystal ashtray, stuck it in his mouth, and created a cloud of smoke around his head.

"Sir," Hanraty said, indicating an additional note for the Admiral's consideration. "I've been asked by several people here at Lejeune exactly what we are doing. They are curious as to our assignment."

Hollifield smiled. "That's natural. Just stick to the cover story. Tell them that I am writing a book on the Korean War, and you are assisting me with research. No one, and I mean no one, knows what we are doing except Major General Osborne and Major Jacobs. As strange as it is, in terms of normal chain of command, even Osborne doesn't know any details. He only knows that I am involved. The less he knows, the more legitimate his answers will be to higher command. I admire the man for the position he has taken. It's not easy for a general officer to subordinate himself out the line of communication."

"Got it, sir," Hanraty said. "How is the book coming along?"

"Splendid. Simply splendid."

1300 Hours
14 June 1980
Durango, Colorado

"SO, tell me again why we are digging this godawful trench halfway up the mountain," Patrick said.

"You mean, why am I digging this twenty-five-yard trench while you lean on that shovel yakking," Jake replied.

"Yeah. That's what I mean. Don't you think three feet deep and three feet wide is a bit extreme for a two-inch pipe? My rate for labor will break you."

Jake stopped to catch his breath. Digging the dirt with a shovel was not so bad, but all the rock in the ground was making it a more significant project than he had imagined. "To explain it one more time, we are digging a crawl space for a water pipe from the well to the house. The pump will be connected to a propane generator so I can fire it up if the electricity goes out. If a pipe does burst, I can crawl in there to fix it. The generator in the crawl space will be accessible through the closet in the master bedroom. That way, I can take care of the generator and the pipes no matter how much snow is on the ground."

"You are going to blow yourself up with that generator."

Jake smirked. "It will be vented, genius."

Patrick continued to lean on the shovel and stared down the valley as though he were in deep thought. "Well, if you lived in Tennessee, you wouldn't need all this."

Jake roared with a laugh. "If we were in Tennessee, all we would need is a shack and an outhouse."

"That's just downright silly, Jake. We've had indoor bathrooms for a couple of years now. Not to change the subject, but what prompted you to buy up this entire valley?"

Jake took another breather on the shovel. "I see your game. You're changing the subject to keep from digging. To answer your diversionary question, it's because I want most of this land to stay the same. Forever. Sara is buried up on the hillside, and I don't want people building cabins up this valley. At least not a big part of it. I'm buying other real estate in the area as well. One of these days, I am going to retire. I'll be right here with Sara."

"I understand, Jake," Patrick sadly said. "I would feel the same if it were Rebecca. "I wish Sara could have been with us for our West Point assignment. She would have loved it."

"That very thought ate on me the whole time I was there."

CHAPTER 18

2100 Hours
6 September 1980
White House, East Room
Washington, D.C.

A COUPLE HUNDRED "WHO'S WHO" guests gathered in the East Room of the White House. As part of the president's executive residence, the room is used for dances, receptions, and press conferences. It was a mixed crowd of attendees, but all were of importance to the president's administration. Formal dinner wear was worn by most men, evoking the thought of a waddle of penguins, but star-studded military officers from every branch added a diversity of splendor and piquancy to the event. As for the ladies present, it was multi-colored formal gowns with presentations of cleavage of a competitive nature and displays of gemstones that would make a cat burglar's mouth water. All in all, the Royal Court of France's Louis XIV at the Palace of Versailles three hundred years earlier had nothing to lord over the pomp and circumstance of an American White House event in 1980.

Vice Admiral Brownfield sidled close to Senator Samuel Zendt with his glass of 1970 Taittinger Comtes de Champagne Blanc de Blancs Brut, which to him was simply white wine. "Good evening, Senator."

"The same to you, Admiral," Zendt replied. "I intended to seek you out. I'm glad you found me instead."

"I wanted to congratulate you on your appointment to the Select Committee on Intelligence. That is quite a plum. Well deserved."

Zendt raised his glass as a salute of sorts. "As the Directorate of Intelligence on staff of the Chairman of the Joint Chiefs, I think we have much in common. I'm looking forward to working with you in ways that are mutually beneficial. I've heard rumors that you are interested in running for Congress when you retire from the Navy."

"I'm considering it," Brownfield replied openly. "Perhaps in the '84 election cycle."

"Democrat or Republican?"

"Whichever will get me elected." They both laughed.

Senator Zendt sipped his Chardonnay. "I could be helpful in that. I would be glad to help you get elected. You and your wife should come out to my farm in Virginia some weekend. It would give us a chance to get to know each other better."

"I'd like that," Brownfield replied without hesitancy.

"Having someone I trust on General Brodrick's staff could be helpful to me as well. After all, we are on the same team."

0555 Hours
12 October 1980
Afghanistan (6 miles NE of Pakistan border)

OPERATION AFGHAN-063, originating with the Pentagon and coordinated with the CIA, was not the kind of large-scale operation that engenders a name to be remembered for years to come. It had a file reference, and that was it. It did not involve the movement of full divisions toward victory over an opposing army. It only involved ten Green Berets. Their mission was simple but one of importance in the Russo-Afghan War, which was now in its eleventh month. The Green Beret team was to train and supply the Afghan rebels with FLM-43 Redeye, man-portable, surface-to-air missiles to use against Soviet aircraft. The Redeye had a range of forty-five hundred meters, an M222 Blast Fragmentation warhead, and traveled at five hundred and eighty meters per second. Armed with the Redeye, the Afghan rebels, the Mujahideen, could make the Soviet's air war an expensive one.

The team had trained a dozen Mujahideen soldiers on the border of Pakistan with the intention that they could train others on the use of the weapon. They had slipped across the border with a half dozen horse-drawn carts loaded with Redeyes and were now six miles into rough terrain. The immediate area rarely had any Soviet presence other than a flyby of a fixed-wing aircraft or helicopter, and relatively speaking, as a covert operation, it was low risk.

Master Sergeant Glen Zeplinski and Staff Sergeant Raul Velasco trudged along behind the first cart filled with Redeyes, occasionally sidestepping a fresh pile of "road apples" dropped by the horse pulling the lead cart. At each half hour, Zeplinski made radio contact with the E-3 airborne warning and control system (AWACS) that circled in Pakistan air space close to the Pakistan-Afghanistan border northwest of Quetta. The other eight Green Berets were spaced in pairs throughout the column. Progress was slow in the couloir, a mountain trail barely passable for the loaded carts. The route was chosen because the trail was narrow at the bottom of a steep gorge, providing cover from any prying eyes of routine surveillance aircraft. To be spotted would be purely accidental.

The moment sunrise broke, calamitous gunfire erupted from the boulders on both sides of the couloir. A Soviet-sized company of two hundred infantrymen had opened fire from well-concealed positions and reigned destruction upon the small column. The daybreak tranquility was shattered with deafening explosions and the loud rattle of small arms fire. The narrow trail was in mayhem. Shrapnel, rocks, dirt, and body parts from horses and men impregnated every square inch of air along the column. Velasco immediately went down, dead, and Zeplinski took cover as well as he could behind a boulder and shouted into the microphone of his radio, "Jayhawk1 to Jayhawk2! Ambush! Ambush! RPG's. Automatic weapons fire! I say again. Ambush."

No sooner had Zeplinski made the call to Jayhawk2 than two Soviet Mi-24 attack helicopters, known as the Hind to most, but known as the Shaitan-Arba, or Satan's Chariot, to the Mujahideen, fell in line a hundred meters apart to attack the column. The Hinds were armed with the 12.7mm Yak-B Gatlin guns, with a fire rate of four thousand to five thousand rounds per minute, and two pods of UB-16 S-5 rocket launchers of sixteen rockets each.

Master Sergeant Zeplinski keyed his mic as the Hinds made their approach.

"Jayhawk2. They knew we were coming. They knew where we were."

As life ebbed away from his wounds, speech became impossible. Zeplinski stopped trying to use the radio and looked into the sky for a moment of peace in the knowing that eternity was next.

The AWACS responded, but there was no callback.

CHAPTER 19

0930 Hours
5 June 1981
The Pentagon
Washington, D.C.

THE WASHINGTON REGISTER and the *New York Globe* had simultaneously released headline articles, with information scrumptiously intriguing, on the ambush in Afghanistan that had taken the lives of ten Green Beret soldiers. Neither newspaper focused on the loss of lives. They were only soldiers. They had signed up for that kind of work, knowing it was dangerous, so the repercussions were merely a matter of volitional responsibility in the reporter's mindset. The articles made it clear that the only important detail was that a covert operation was attempting to put Redeye missiles into the hands of the Mujahideen. 'It is exactly how the Vietnam War started,' they stated. 'The executive branch is overriding the power of Congress', they said, and for the most part, Congress was enjoying its opportunity to throw punches at the president's administration. Covert operations always had a way of exploiting political opportunities. What the articles lacked in veracity was that the Soviets had been tipped off with the details of the operation by a traitor. That fact was the bigger story, had they known it, but the media was more than happy in the immediate response of kicking the dog.

"I think it was bad luck," Lieutenant General Nathan Hawk said. "I'm not believing that the team was ambushed because of a leak at the intelligence level. If there was a leak to the Soviets, it came from the CIA. I have absolute confidence in the personnel in Military Intelligence."

Major General Seth Osborne (Ret) set his cup of coffee in his saucer lest he spilled it as a result of a rush of moderately controlled anger.

"You're wrong, Nathan. We have a spy, a Soviet mole, in our ranks. He is the most dangerous traitor in the history of the United States, and this ambush shows us how dangerous he is. We must come to grips with the fact that he is plugged in at the highest levels of intelligence."

Hawk sat back in his chair, offended by Osborne's demeanor and what he interpreted as an assault on his domain, the military intelligence community.

"Well, I've heard you say before that if there is a mole, he could be a congressman. I don't think there is a mole, but if there is, he is not military. I'm sure of that."

Osborne smirked but held his tongue. Hawk was possibly wrong, but the three stars on Hawk's shoulders called for Osborne to withdraw from pressing the point.

"Seth, I in no way intended to insult you, but you are retired. General Brodrick asked you to look into this matter, but you are taking it too seriously. It's my opinion that your inquiries should be shut down."

"That's a misplaced priority, General," Osborne said, trying not to be accusatory but still laying the facts on the table. "A traitor in our midst trumps the protection of personal territories."

Lieutenant General Hawk's body language clearly indicated that he was insulted.

"Alright, gentlemen," General Brodrick said. "That's enough of that."

Brodrick had remained silent throughout the discussion and had let the two officers play out their positions on the matter. It was time to step in before things were said that would escalate to a bad relationship between the two.

Hawk and Osborne turned their attention to General Brodrick.

"Nathan. To an extent, I agree with both of you. I tend to believe that there is not a mole at all, but if I am wrong about that, would you have me stand in front of the President and apologize for ignoring the possibility? Don't you think it prudent of me to at least have Seth check it out?"

"So, this is a cover-your-ass operation," Hawk stated.

Brodrick laughed aloud. "Of course it is. If you were in my shoes, you would do the same. Not only that, but I would wager that half the decisions you make are motivated by covering your ass. We didn't get these stars on our shoulders because we failed to do exactly that."

"Ok, General," Hawk said. "I see your point. I just don't like it."

"Good. General Osborne and Major Jacobs will run this down, mole or no mole, and then we will be done with it. I suspect it will take a year, or two, to vet this out. In the meantime, General Osborne's assignment is proactive. No one can criticize the assignment if this thing slips sideways."

"What about this Major Jacobs? He has been made a field grade officer without time in grade, and he is not under the control of Military Intelligence. This assignment makes him a renegade. His peers and his superiors have a strong resentment against that sort of thing."

"I'd say promote him to Lieutenant Colonel," Osborne said, meaning the suggestion in jest. "Eisenhower was promoted to temporary Lieutenant Colonel only three years out of West Point. Jacobs has been out of the Academy for eight years. He's dragging his feet as far as I'm concerned."

"Ridiculous," Hawk said, stunned that Osborne would make such a suggestion.

Seeing the opportunity to twist the knife, Osborne continued. "Not so ridiculous. We have given Jacobs a great deal of responsibility in this business with Casper, and it may have caused the loss of his wife. Personally, I know there is a Casper because it almost cost me my life as well. If he is expected to hob-nob with flag officers and members of Congress, then the rank would give him a lot more credibility. Promote him temporarily. You can always revert him back to his rank based on time in grade when the mission is completed. Give him the tools he needs to do the job."

"Surely you wouldn't do that, General Brodrick. Jacobs is no Eisenhower. Not even close," Hawk said.

Brodrick was in thought as the two officers looked at him in silence. Finally, he spoke.

"Well, as you so aptly put it, General Hawk, as a cover-your-ass kind of operation, that's not a bad idea for my command as Joint Chief, or your command as the Director of Defense Intelligence. Whether General Osborne and Jacobs deliver Casper, or they don't, you look a whole lot better having gone the extra mile to support the mission. It's a matter of perception. With either result, we win."

General Osborne was stunned that Brodrick was considering the promotion, and General Hawk's mind was circling around the consequences of appearing not to fully support the vetting out of the country's most deplorable traitor if, indeed, he existed at all. On the off chance that there was a Casper, he would look pretty good for having thrown his weight into the mission.

General Hawk leaned back in his chair and took a sip of his coffee, thinking of how to reverse his position without appearing to be self-serving on the matter.

"I'll defer my support to your decision, General Brodrick. If this is something you want to do, then I'll back that one hundred percent."

General Brodrick smiled, and General Osborne smirked, both recognizing the skill by which General Hawk played the game.

CHAPTER 20

0800 Hours
15 November 1981
Camp Lejeune, North Carolina

ADMIRAL HOLLIFIELD ROSE from his chair behind the desk as Jake entered the room, and John Hanraty did the same. Jake's trips to Lejeune were always pleasant. While their meetings were informal, by military standards, they still held the aura of Hollifield's presence. He was still considered by those that had served with or under him to be the best Chief of Naval Operations that had ever held the post. Jake had a special love and respect for the man that extended back to his days as a cadet at West Point. He would never forget their first meeting in a Philadelphia restaurant after the Army-Navy game.

"Well, there he is," Hollifield said enthusiastically while extending his hand. "Lieutenant Colonel John Paul Jacobs. The youngest lieutenant colonel in decades. Congratulations."

Jake smiled, and he blushed. "Temporary lieutenant

colonel. When we get this assignment wrapped up, I will be pushed back down to major, maybe even captain. Pushed completely out of the Army if some have their way."

"Maybe. Maybe not," the Admiral said. "I suspect you are none too popular at the officer's club, but, hey, who cares. You can always order those wallowing in envy to drop and give you fifty."

Admiral Hollifield moved back behind his desk, picked up his cigar, and created a cloud of smoke around his head.

"Now that you have completed the Army Command and General Staff College, you are still considered to be on a viable career path, and you are probably ahead of the game with your promotion. A lot of officers don't like it, but there is a lot to be said for being ahead of the game, even if it is temporary. Don't let criticism throw you off. People like you who are committed to a noble goal always bring out both envy and resentment in others. Like Aristotle said, 'Criticism is something we can avoid easily by saying nothing, doing nothing, and being nothing'. Jake, I know you have the character to ignore slander and not be bitter about it."

"I'll take your word for it, Admiral. Your advice has always been right on target."

"Stephen Patrick? What's his take on living on a Marine Corps base?"

Jake laughed. "He is being ruined. I think he is impressed. He saw a Harrier land yesterday, and his eyes were as big as saucers. Wouldn't that be something? A Marine in the family."

"Wonderful," the Admiral said. "I'll see what I can do to encourage that. A ride in a Harrier might be just the ticket."

"No fair, Admiral."

The Admiral created another cloud of smoke, then said, "Let's get down to it. Your office is down the hall, Jake, next to

Hanraty's. The word I have from Major General Osborne is that General Brodrick has put a cap on how long we can pursue this project. Jake, you have a one year at a time assignment here, but that is it. If we cannot wrap it up in a reasonable time frame, then it is over. No Casper. I know that sounds like an indeterminate time, especially since counterintelligence operations can last a lot longer than three years, and they usually do.

As you know, Jake, you are the front man of the operation. Remember, as far as most know, you and Major General Osborne are the only people involved, and his knowledge of what we find is limited. He has a lot of pressure from military and political snoops. This gives him plausible deniability. The worst thing that could happen is that Osborne report the details of our work directly to Casper."

Jake and Hanraty nodded their heads.

"John, what do you have for us?" Hollifield asked.

Hanraty handed Jake and the Admiral a list of names. "This list can be reduced, or expanded, based on future findings. However, at this point, these twenty-five individuals have been identified as having access to intelligence that we are confident has fallen into Soviet hands. Each has held positions over a long period of time, with intelligence access that match the intelligence believed to have been passed.

"What kind of intelligence are we talking about here, John?" Jake asked.

"It could cover a lot of things," Hanraty replied, "but in every case, it would be of a critical nature. For instance, strategic war plans for Europe and, more recently the ambush in Afghanistan. Also, we would consider information on weapons development, high-tech equipment, aircraft designs, and so on to be indicative of a trail that might lead to Casper.

We know from The Otter that all those types of intelligence have been passed by Casper, and we know a few specifics. As an example, which people on our list had access to knowledge of our new air-to-air missile technology three years ago? We know it fell into Soviet hands. So, who could have delivered it?"

Admiral Hollifield leaned back in his chair, took a puff on his cigar, and made a humming sound.

"Well, where do we go from here? John, it is quite commendable that you have narrowed the field to twenty-five. Good job. It's a little mind-boggling that all these individuals, both militarily and politically, are some of the scariest people on the planet in terms of power. I mean, really, your list consists of half of the Joint Chiefs of Staff and their personnel, the Director of National Security Agency, the Secretary of State, and some of the other most powerful members of Congress and military."

"And that's not all, Admiral," Hanraty said. "It is also possible that Casper is merely someone that has access to one of these individuals, socially or otherwise. That would mean, of course, that people are talking critical intelligence out of school."

"You have your work cut out for you, Jake," the Admiral said, pointing the lit end of his cigar at him. "You will have to start interviewing these people. It will have to be subtle so as they have no idea what you are doing. How you are going to do that is beyond me, but General Osborne can be of some help."

Jake smiled, "Admiral, is it too late for me to join the U.S. Navy to swab decks and chip paint?"

1400 Hours
5 January 1982
Major General Seth Osborne (Ret) Residence
Fredericksburg, Virginia

COLONEL JOAN WHITEHEAD (USA Ret) passed blue, letter-sized folders down the table to each member of the Benedict Arnold Tribunal.

"As you know, I have been tasked with the gathering of information on Senator Samuel Zendt. His name has surfaced before, but we are taking a closer look at him since he has been appointed to the Select Committee on Intelligence."

"Yes," Vice Admiral Stanley Monroe (Ret) said. "It is my understanding that after his predecessor was murdered, he finessed his way onto the committee by campaigning throughout the capitol building, promising political favors to both parties. He is more feared than liked."

"What you've heard is correct, Stanley," Whitehead said. "Zendt has strong backing from elements of the left. Zendt is being groomed for greater things. He was a political organizer in Cook County, Illinois. Chicago. Essentially, Senator Zendt is a far-left-wing socialist because that is what some other members of the Senate want him to be. He covers that up well, but make no mistake about it, he is a socialist. If this were back in the days of Joe McCarthy and J. Edgar Hoover, he would be labeled an outright communist. Zendt is smart. He is not going to make any statements that he is pro-Soviet Union, and I'm not saying that he is, but he would certainly like to see a strong, socialist central government and a welfare state. We have no direct evidence that he is financially corrupted, but he is treasonous. When we look at Samuel Zendt, we may well be looking at the future of the United States."

Marine Major General Lefevre sat forward, indicating that he had something to say.

"I know Zendt. I worked with him on a couple of issues when he was on the Armed Services Committee. I believe he has enough support on Capitol Hill to eventually be elected President of the United States, and that is without question his ambition. He is no friend of the military. He has no respect for the military whatsoever, and that is disturbing with him sitting on the Intelligence Committee. He is dangerous, and I don't like him."

"Ok," Osborne said. "I think that we all agree that Senator Zendt is undesirable as far as the Tribunal is concerned. However, there is no indication that the man is corrupt. We simply don't like his political beliefs. His family is one of the wealthiest in the country. He has no need to be corrupt in a monetary sense. We need to stay focused on our objectives. It has never been our intent to control long-term politics other than to deal with corrupt politicians. Hopefully, the voting public will see through Zendt's true character, but from our point of view, we have not identified him as corrupt. I suggest we keep him in view, but, for now, let him pass."

"Agreed," Air Force Brigadier General Robert Perribone said. "The biggest danger with Senator Zendt is the top-secret information he will be carrying around from the Intelligence Committee. If we later find that he is misusing that information, we may want to redefine our use of the word 'corruption'. In the meantime, I agree that we let it pass."

All members of the Benedict Arnold Tribunal nodded their agreement.

CHAPTER 21

1600 Hours
7 June 1982
Lieutenant General Nathan Hawk's Office
The Pentagon
Washington, D.C.

"SIR," Jake asked after glancing at his notes, "to what extent would you say you have had intimate knowledge, or access to the knowledge, of up-to-date strategic war plans for the 8th Army in Europe over the past five years?"

Jake knew the correct answer, but a valid counterintelligence interview technique was to gauge the subject's veracity and his degree of nervousness at being asked the question. Body language and being agitated could indicate that the subject was hiding something.

General Hawk paused and leaned back in his chair. The coffee cup he was holding began to shudder a bit, splashing droplets of coffee over the cup's edge and dropping onto the General's lap.

Jake met the general's eyes, awaiting an answer. The pause was long as the General gathered his thoughts, but Jake continued his stare with an air of expectancy.

General Hawk coughed, not because of anything physical, but to deflect the anxiety that permeated the atmosphere in the room. His coloration had changed. His face was flushed, and it was apparent to Jake that the General was doing his best to avoid outright rage. Still, Jake looked to the General for an answer.

Finally, the General stated, "Well, Colonel, I'll not answer that question. Not only do I find you insubordinate and audacious, but your question is, frankly, out of your pay grade. I am not only a general officer, but I am also your superior officer in Military Intelligence. I'll have to ask you to leave my office. In fact, I am ordering you to leave. I will be reporting your behavior to General Brodrick."

Jake rose from his chair, expressionless. He was neither disappointed in the General's response nor was he intimidated. He had accomplished what he had come for.

One floor down, Jake found an empty office and dialed the number to Admiral Hollifield's residence. The Admiral answered according to military protocol, as he always did.

"Sir, this is Lieutenant Colonel Jacobs. I'm calling to report on my interview with Lieutenant General Hawks."

"Good afternoon, Jake," the Admiral said cheerfully. "Well, you are on the phone, so I guess you didn't get skinned alive."

Jake chuckled at the Admiral's sense of humor, akin to, 'You are on the phone, so you must have survived a grenade thrown at you—in an elevator.'

"Yes, sir. I still have all my body parts, but I suspect my next Army Officer Evaluation Report (OER) will be a disaster.

General Hawk did not specifically mention north Greenland, but I think it would be prudent for me to start buying sub-zero temperature gear."

Admiral Hollifield laughed aloud. "That bad, huh?"

"That's my third interview on the military side, and two of them have had similar results. I think the word will spread quickly to avoid a meeting with me. Other than disregard for me, I'm not sure I gained much information of value. All on the list had the information and opportunity to be our mole. Major General Otis McAvoy, the current commander of the 10th Mountain Division, is not a likely candidate, in my opinion. The man was straightforward, answered all my questions without taking offense, and gave me all the time I needed to do the interview. He struck me as a flag officer that is truly a warrior and a strict Constitutionalist."

"I know General McAvoy," Hollifield said. "He is a warrior. Post-Vietnam, we are seeing fewer of these warrior officers make flag rank. It is becoming more common now to see bureaucrat-flag officers that operate by snuggling up to political benefactors. What about generals Bloomfield and Hawk?"

"Nothing specific on either, Admiral, but I would leave them on the list."

"Why?" Hollifield asked.

"Well, sir, if I'm allowed to use personal instinct, which I know is subjective, I felt that both were defensive to the point that they were hiding something. The nature of what they are hiding doesn't necessarily have anything to do with Casper, but I feel that both have something going on that is a secret. It is like they have done something wrong, and they don't want anyone to find out about it. You know what I mean, Admiral?"

Hollifield laughed. "Sure. I know what you mean. It's like

when Suzanne goes shopping and spends too much money. It's a little game we play. She keeps it a secret, and I know but say nothing. So, Brownfield and Hawk stay on the list. What they are hiding may be insignificant as far as we are concerned, but then one of them might be Casper."

Jake chuckled at Admiral Hollifield's reference to Suzanne. It reminded him of his dad's gun collection. Frequently, a new gun would show up in the gun safe. His dad would always act as though it were a supernatural appearance.

"We need something more tangible. Our line of questioning is leading us nowhere."

"I think you're right," the Admiral said. "Let's go back to The Otter, Yanovski, and see if we can't find a more tangible lead. You never know what he might say that would make our search more productive."

"I'll set it up, sir. See you back at Lejeune next week."

1030 Hours
9 June 1982
Capitol Hill
Washington, D.C.

"HAVE A SEAT, COLONEL JACOBS," Congressman Jess Elliott said as his secretary set a tray of cookies and a carafe of coffee on a small conference table. "I must tell you upfront that I've been warned about you. You have made quite a reputation for yourself in a short period of time."

Jake did his best to make light of the comment.

"Yes, sir, that's what I understand. Rest assured, sir, I mean no disrespect. There is no reason for our meeting to be anything less than pleasant," and Jake had some reason to believe that the meeting would be pleasant.

The Congressman from Arizona had held his seat in the House of Representatives for thirty years. He was a gregarious man, respected and powerful in the realm of American politics. There was no reason to suspect Congressman Elliott of any malfeasance unless one were to question how a congressman became an eight-digit, multi-millionaire from a twenty-thousand-dollar salary at the start of his congressional career. Even now, he only had a salary of seventy thousand dollars. Obviously, the Congressman was an investment genius.

"We'll see," the Congressman said as he poured coffee into both cups. "I agreed to meet with you as a courtesy to Major General Osborne. We go back a ways. He's a good man."

"Yes, sir," Jake said. "I'll not waste your time. As you know, I am with Military Intelligence. My job is insignificant in the grand scheme of things. I've been tasked to simply update the branch on how it might better facilitate congressional members on the use of intelligence matters. With your tenure in Congress, your input would be helpful."

"Really?" Elliott asked, more as a statement than a question. "The grapevine says that you are trying to track down some mystical Russian mole. Is that true or not?"

"Well, sir, it is that grapevine I would be interested in knowing about. If anyone knows how things work around here, it would be you."

"That's the advantage of being an old timer, Colonel," Elliott said. "What do you want to know?"

Jake sipped his warm coffee and then leaned back in his chair. "It's a given that those directly involved in intelligence matters are well informed, but to what extent are other members aware of specific intelligence? Does that grapevine, in your opinion, carry information that is intended to be restricted?"

Congressman Elliott laughed aloud. "Colonel, given a little time, every member of Congress knows everything of importance. The more important the information, the faster it travels, and it travels by seniority. 'Top Secret' doesn't mean squat in these halls. Information is traded like a kid's baseball cards. If another congressman needs my vote, he will trade valuable information for it. If I don't need it, I will hold out until something of value comes along. Colonel, if you are looking for intelligence leaks, you just found an entire building full of them."

Jake remained expressionless. He knew the Congressman expected a reaction, but Jake did not give it to him. Illegitimate, or perhaps illegal, collaboration is well known in Congress for having a life of its own. Admitting that high-level intelligence was used as currency was not a surprise.

"You brought up the subject of a Russian mole, Congressman. If a mole did exist in Congress, would the intelligence passed through the grapevine be of high value to a foreign power?"

"Absolutely," Elliott said. "Now, it might take some finesse for a mole to come up with detailed documents, but a well-connected mole could be a significant threat to the country. I've been concerned about that for years."

"Any prospects as to who might be a traitor, Congressman?" Jake asked halfheartedly.

"Sure," Elliott responded. "Everyone that is not in my political party."

CHAPTER 22

1500 Hours
22 December 1982
GRU Headquarters
Moscow, Soviet Union

COLONEL VLADIMIR ZHUKOV marched sharply into General Alexey Dmitrievich's office, came to a halt precisely three feet from the general's desk, and snapped a perfect salute.

"Colonel Zhukov reporting to General Dmitrievich as ordered, sir."

The General removed his glasses and set them on the papers in front of him.

"At ease, Colonel. How was your trip?"

"Fine, sir, and it is good to be home and in uniform again."

"Enjoy. You won't be home long," the General said. "I know you are anxious for a more suitable assignment, but this one in America is important. You will be rewarded for your loyalty. We have had several communications from

Wellspring. The situation regarding Major General Osborne, and the now Lieutenant Colonel Jacobs, remains passive. Wellspring's take on things is that Osborne is a minor threat, and if elimination of Jacobs became necessary, that would eliminate all threats entirely. Apparently, Jacobs is causing quite a disturbance with his incessant questioning of both military and political leaders."

"What action do you wish for us to take against Jacobs?" asked Zhukov.

Dmitrievich lit a cigarette and deeply inhaled the smoke.

"No terminal action for the moment, but it is necessary for you and your team to increase surveillance. Wellspring is satisfied, for the time being, that Jacob's actions are more of a benefit than a detriment. Jacob's alienation of high-level individuals tends to discredit the very existence of Wellspring. And when Jacobs comes up empty-handed, that will put America to sleep with respect to a mole."

Zhukov remained in the position of 'at-ease' but did so in strict, military fashion. "How detailed are you expecting our surveillance to be, General?"

"You will need to reassemble your full team of six men. I expect you to know where he is and who he is meeting with. Other than that, there is no immediate need to monitor conversations or documents. We will wait for instructions from Wellspring to escalate our actions, should the need arise."

"Anything else, sir?"

Dmitrievich paused, inhaled deeply, and exhaled a cloud of cigarette smoke.

"It would be an interesting maneuver if you could develop a personal relationship with this Lieutenant Colonel Jacobs. Challenging."

1300 Hours
24 December 1982
Camp Lejeune, North Carolina

PATRICK STEPPED through the door of Jake's residence without knocking, with Rebecca and little Sara close behind. Jake came out of the kitchen wearing an apron over his Bermuda shorts and t-shirt to identify who was breaking into his house.

As their eyes met, Patrick came to attention and vigorously saluted.

"The pride of Tennessee reporting to the almighty Lieutenant Colonel Scumbag, as ordered, sir."

Jake's smile was from ear to ear, and Stephen Patrick ran to greet Uncle Patrick and Aunt Rebecca. Always a happy reunion.

"About time you got here," Jake said. "I figured that since you don't know how to use a compass, you were lost like some second lieutenant."

Jake stepped over to shake Patrick's hand, gave Rebecca a hug and a kiss on the cheek, then took Sara out of her arms for the pure pleasure of holding the beautiful child.

"Rebecca, you are as beautiful as ever, and this one, well, she is the prettiest thing I have ever seen. I wish Sara were here to hold Lil' Sara. She would be beside herself."

"We all wish that," Rebecca said. "Not a day goes by we don't think of her. You know that."

Jake smiled, "I do."

Patrick grinned. "So, let's get down to the important stuff. Let's eat."

"Turkey and dressing tomorrow," Jake said. "Today is C-Rations. Just kidding. We are having meatloaf."

Patrick had a look of surprise on his face. "Well, if you cooked that meatloaf, I'll have a bologna sandwich."

"No bologna."

"Ok," Patrick said. "I'll risk the lives of my family if that's the way it is. So, Lieutenant Colonel, how's the spy hunt going?"

"About as well as my career. I've managed to alienate the most powerful people in D.C., and I have nothing to show for it. You will be glad to know that all that abuse and humiliation of our plebe year at West Point was pretty good training. These big wigs can't rattle me. I was a plebe. I was proud of you, by the way, for graduating first in our class at the Command and General Staff College. You are going to be a big shot. I hope so because I may need a little pull to not get kicked out of the Army."

"This assignment may be a high price to pay if you don't find this traitor. Are you prepared for that?"

Jake put his hands on his hips, a familiar indication from Jake that his resolve was solid.

"Patrick, as far as I'm concerned, Casper is responsible for Sara's death. He may not have pulled the trigger, but make no mistake about it; he is responsible. I would walk to the ends of the earth to bring him to justice. There is no price too large for getting that done."

"Understood, Jake," Patrick said. "You know you can call on me anytime for anything if I can be of help. I'm with you, buddy."

"How is Stephen Patrick adjusting to being on a Marine Corps base?" Rebecca asked.

"Now, for that, we are in big trouble," Jake said, waving his arms in the air. "What have I done? I've gone and ruined the boy."

Patrick and Rebecca laughed.

"Don't tell me the Marine Corps has gone and fried his brain with all that 'oorah' business," Patrick said.

Jake shook his head in counterfeit disgust. "I'm afraid so. The boy says he wants to be a Marine Corps aviator, and the Marines around here don't help. For the pleasure of annoying me, they love to dig that hole deeper every chance they get. An Army officer on a Marine Corps base makes life harder than it ought to be. It makes me think of those poor tactical officers at West Point that were not Army. Remember that Navy officer that had his car smashed by an M-60 tank? The look on his face was priceless."

Patrick laughed aloud. "I think about that often. That's the funniest thing I've ever seen. As far as Stephen Patrick goes, maybe you can have him hypnotized to overcome all the brainwashing."

"I'll keep that in mind. Desperate circumstances call for desperate measures."

CHAPTER 23

1400 Hours
7 February 1983
Camp Lejeune, North Carolina

MAJOR GENERAL SETH OSBORNE and Jake sat in plain metal chairs across from Jake's desk. The office was small and reflected military budget constraints, not the opulent furnishings of a general officer in Washington. In his younger days, Osborne had desk duty in offices identical to this one. He admired Jake's sense of decorating his office. The walls were blank. There was no adornment of career to date. There was no West Point diploma hanging on the wall, no display of the two Silver Stars and Purple Heart awards he had received, and no pictures and citations from units in which he had served. His office told a visitor nothing about him. Somehow, he preferred Jake's spartan surroundings to those he had as a flag officer.

"I know not to put you on the spot and ask specific questions about Casper," Osborne said. "I understand the plan, and it is a good one. I'm here, basically, as a goodwill call and to visit briefly with Admiral Hollifield. I hope you don't mind my intrusion."

"Not at all, General. It is good to see you. I hope all is well with you and your family."

"My guess is that your excursions through the Pentagon and Congress are an eye-opener," Osborne said. "Political games and corruption can change one's view of how our republic has evolved."

Jake smiled, "There is some truth to that, sir. I suppose it has always been that way to a degree, but it appears to me that that kind of behavior is becoming more acceptable. One gets what one allows sort of thing."

"Progressive, negative change, I'd say, in the military as well as the public sector," Osborne said. "Our national culture is in transition. Corruption in government is occurring right out in the open, and no one seems to have the courage to hold those people accountable to the law."

"I can't argue with that, sir, but I have a narrow focus. That is, I mostly see the changes in the military. For instance, I have seen some significant changes in West Point between the time I was there as a cadet and when I was there as an instructor. At first, I was very critical of those changes, and to some extent, I still am, but I've come to realize that the Academy and the military are only a reflection of our changing society. Good or bad. Some call these changes modernization or progressive growth. I don't, but some do. I think our Nation is currently declining in its sense of legitimate attitudes toward precepts that founded this Nation and made it great. The academies are simply floating along, conforming to whatever society thinks is now right and normal. That is not the fault of those assigned to command at the academies because they are following the orders passed down by civilian government. Based on our Constitution, the actions of that civilian government are determined by the people. If our culture is changing, or 'what is allowed' is changing, the buck stops with the American people. They are corporately responsible."

"Interesting viewpoint," Osborne said reflectively. "Don't you think that we have a responsibility to defend the Nation against, for instance, corruption in government? I mean, obviously, corruption in Congress is representative of domestic enemies. You took an oath to defend the Nation against enemies, foreign and domestic. How can one uphold that oath and not pursue a domestic enemy as passionately as pursuing a foreign enemy?"

Jake paused and made eye contact with the General. "Well, perhaps you are referring to the several assassinations of members of Congress and a sitting federal judge over the past few years. It is my understanding that corruption and breach of public trust was the likely motive. I do not support that sort of action. It is illegal. One cannot conduct illegal vigilantism and then use the Constitution, the foundation of law and order, as a justification for that criminality. Assassinating politicians, regardless of their corruption, is not defending the Nation against domestic enemies. It is a crime. Granted, corruption should be eliminated in Congress. That would be a right thing. However, to be a right thing, an action must be a right thing done in a right way. Otherwise, it is a wrong."

Major General Osborne smiled. Obviously, Jake was not a candidate to become a member of the Benedict Arnold Tribunal. He was disappointed.

"I couldn't agree more," Osborne said to cover his secretive beliefs.

The Benedict Arnold Tribunal still met regularly to

discuss individuals that appeared to be deeply involved in corruption. Most of those being discussed were members of Congress, but two were federal judges that lined their pockets from rulings favorable to those who could pay. No sanctions for assassination had been approved by the Tribunal for months. As they had hoped, the President was addressing corruption in the legislative branch as well as he could, giving the Benedict Arnold Tribunal reason to pause extreme measures. But if the President was to fail in his efforts, the Tribunal stood ready to proceed in its quest to alter the path of corruption in American government.

"So," Osborne said. "I take it that when you catch Casper, you are looking for due process of law, even though it is flawed, rather than immediate, fatal justice."

"That's correct, sir," Jake said emphatically.

"And what if due process does not convict him?"

"I would be horrified by that," Jake said, "but I would have upheld my oath toward Constitutional integrity."

A film of tears covered his eyes.

"My wife, Sara, would expect that of me. Doing the right thing would honor her."

1400 Hours
1 April 1983
Pan Am Flight 287 out of Dulles
Washington, D.C.

JAKE TOOK his aisle seat in coach on the Boeing 727 and waited as the other passengers found their assigned seats. He was wearing charcoal slacks with a white shirt and a maroon foulard tie under a navy sports coat. Other than a closely cropped haircut, there was nothing about his appearance to indicate that he was anything but a business traveler. He was to spend a few days at the Presidio of Monterey, the California Army base, which was the home of the 229th Military Intelligence Battalion. His objective was to interview The Otter, Colonel Vladimir Yanovski, again. For Yanovski's security, they were to meet on the base to prevent unintended identification of The Otter. A public meeting could have disastrous implications.

Only moments after adjusting his seat, Jake was interrupted by a gentleman indicating that he had been assigned the seat adjacent to his. The man was of formidable stature, middle-aged with salt and pepper hair, horn-rimmed glasses, and business-casual attire. Jake smiled, then rose and stepped into the aisle to allow the man to take the window seat.

"These seats are either getting smaller, or I am getting fatter," Colonel Zhukov said. "I'm looking forward to the time I can retire and don't have to travel at all."

"I understand," Jake said. "A four-hour flight is long when your knees are tucked up under your chin."

"I'm Leonard Petrov," Zhukov said as he extended his hand to Jake. Petrov was a common Russian name, and Zhukov used it on the off-chance that his near-perfect English failed him. An American with a Russian heritage was not by itself a reason for suspicion, but the use of language could be."

"John Jacobs," Jake said as his hand met Petrov's.

"What do you do, John?" Petrov asked.

"Army," Jake responded. "Paper-pusher. Nothing interesting, I'm afraid, but it's a job."

"Well, I'm sure it is more interesting than you let on, especially to a heavy equipment salesman like myself. Talk about boring. I take it you are an officer. Where did you go to college? I went to Arizona State."

Jake was not enthused to have a twenty-questions conversation with a stranger all the way to California. He had to think about his upcoming interview with Yanovski, but primarily, in his line of business, strangers asking a lot of questions was always suspect to some degree.

"A small college in New York." Jake pulled a book out of his briefcase, a subtle hint that he was not interested in a four-hour conversation."

"Family man?" Yanovski pressed.

"Yes," Jake said as he opened the book to a marked page. "One son. I think I will close my eyes for a few minutes, then catch up on some reading."

Liar, Yanovski thought. *You don't have a wife—because I gave the order that got her killed.*

"Sure. We can visit some more later."

Jake was successful at avoiding continuous conversation until a half-hour out from the San Jose International Airport. But Zhukov did make his final bid to get together for lunch sometime back in the D.C. area.

"Do you have a business card so I can call you?"

"No," Jake said. "But I will take one of yours. I'll give you a call, and we can set up a time."

Zhukov fumbled for words as he fictitiously searched for a nonexistent business card.

"I must have left them in my luggage, but I will write down my number."

Jake slipped the scrap of paper with Leonard Petrov's name and number into his shirt pocket.

"I'll give you a call."

1400 Hours
2 April 1983
229th Military Intelligence Battalion
Presidio of Monterey, California

"COLONEL JACOBS, it is good to see you again," Colonel Vladimir Yanovski said with a genuine smile on his face.

Jake returned the smile.

"And you as well, Colonel. I trust you have been treated well."

Though once considered enemies by national politics, under different circumstances, they might have been friends all along. However, those circumstances had dictated that their relationship be one of friendly respect, not one that would lend itself to Sunday barbeques in the backyard. While Yanovski was still called to the battalion occasionally for information as new intelligence developed, he was essentially living the life of an ordinary citizen of the United States. He was known as Simon Solokov, worked as a warehouse foreman, and lived a modest life. His new background cover was that he was originally from the Hill Country of Texas, where his family had immigrated to in 1894 to farm. He loved America. He loved his freedom, far away from the stress of being an officer in the Soviet Army, where he could receive a death sentence at the whim of a superior officer. His business with U.S. Military Intelligence was infrequent, but so long as General Alexey Dmitrievich was the head of the GRU, Yanovski would be an asset of value.

"Things couldn't be better," Yanovski said. "I know I have said it numerous times, but thank you for allowing me to defect to America. Not only did it save my life, but it gave me a life I never would have had in the Soviet Union. Freedom is wonderful."

Jake smiled at the transformation that had occurred in the Colonel's life.

"I'm glad you are happy. I apologize for interrupting your day, but I have some questions. I'm here for more information on Wellspring. Maybe there is something you haven't thought of before."

"Yes, sir. How can I be of help?"

Jake glanced at his notes and the list of questions he had prepared. "You previously indicated that Wellspring was either military or political, but either way, you thought him to be socially well-connected enough to gather intelligence indirectly from others. The purpose of my visit is to narrow the search. That is, military or public figure. Is there any recollection of your conversations with Dmitrievich that would favor one classification over the other?"

Yanovski sat back in his seat in deep thought, sipped his tea, and slowly lit a cigarette. "Well, I suppose there is, but it is no better than speculation. General Dmitrievich did once say that Wellspring had a fairly long period of time that he did not produce much in the way of intelligence of value. A lull, so to speak. Dmitrievich was concerned that Wellspring was less enthusiastic about sending information, but at the time, it occurred to me that Wellspring temporarily did not have access to intelligence. Perhaps a different assignment would be the cause, which might indicate that he is military. However, my personal feeling is that Wellspring is well connected with the United States Congress."

"Why would you think that?" Jake asked. "Theoretically,

the passing of high-level intelligence could come from either source."

Yanovski took another draw on his cigarette before putting it out in the ashtray. "I think it is because Dmitrievich always talked about Wellspring as though he were born royalty. You know what I mean. Born wealthy and raised to be a socialite. It appeared to me that Wellspring must have had social connections with powerful people even when he was a young man before he had a position of consequence himself. I guess what I am saying is that Wellspring was groomed. It is not always the case, but military people tend to come from the middle class in America. That's not so in the Soviet Union. The upper class gets the promotions."

"So, you think Wellspring is a man rather than a woman?" Jake asked.

Yanovski shrugged. "I think a man, but it could be a woman. I don't really have a concrete opinion one way or the other."

"Education?" Jake asked, feeling that he was indeed gaining insight into Casper's identity.

Yanovski paused. "I'm not that familiar with universities in America, but I would think that Wellspring has a very liberal education. Obviously, he is a Marxist. If I'm correct about his upbringing, he was likely of Marxist persuasion long before he went to a university. So, perhaps his university education is not a factor in identifying him."

"What else can you tell me about Wellspring?"

"Not much," Yanovski said, "other than his information was superabundant and detailed. For instance, if he sent information on an advance in military technology, he sent detailed schematics. Almost unbelievable that someone could have that kind of access to intelligence. I mean, who in your government could do that?"

Jake frowned. "Unfortunately, a lot of people. In the Senate and the House of Representatives, information and favors are traded like baseball cards."

"What are these baseball cards?"

Jake laughed. "I'll bring you some the next time I come to visit." Jake flipped through a couple of pages of his notes. "You mentioned a Colonel Zhukov at one time. What can you tell me about him?"

Yanovski pursed his lips to emphasize a quality of gravity to the question.

"He is a Spetsnaz GRU colonel, extremely loyal to General Dmitrievich, and one of the most dangerous men I have ever met. At the time of my defection, he was in the United States in support of Wellspring with a team of six others. If you are looking for him, you are not likely to find him. Zhukov speaks perfect English and can blend into the American environment. He is one of the main reasons I must never be discovered by the Soviets."

"I see," Jake said. "What does this Spetsnaz colonel look like?"

Yanovski paused a moment to dredge up an image of him. "Over six-feet tall, muscular, maybe two hundred pounds of pure muscle, handsome, salt and pepper hair, and eyes that warn you that he is evil."

Jake leaned back in his chair and thumped his West Point Monte Blanc on the open page of his notes. "I think I met Colonel Zhukov yesterday on the airplane. Sat right next to him for four hours."

CHAPTER 24

0900 Hours
11 April 1983
Camp Lejeune, North Carolina

ADMIRAL HOLLIFIELD SAT in an overstuffed leather chair, well-worn as though it had been in use since the days of World War II, while Jake and Hanraty sat on a matching sofa. Conforming to Hollifield's dislike of formality, the three sipped coffee from Styrofoam cups.

"John, why don't you bring Jake up to date on that telephone number he gave you."

Hanraty flipped through his notes until he found the page he wanted. "There is not a lot to tell, but this fact alone is interesting. It is a Pennsylvania number. Philadelphia, to be exact. It goes to an answering service for a Mr. Petrov. When I contacted the answering service, they said that Petrov seldom has a message, but when he does, they mail the message to a postal box in Washington. So, I tracked down the postal box. From the Washington box, the mail is then forwarded to general delivery at the U.S. Senate. That's as far as it can be traced. The message disappears into the massive void of Senate mail."

"Well," Hollifield said. "It's obvious that no one legitimate would go to such lengths to disguise a telephone call. Your thoughts, Jake?"

Jake set his cup on the coffee table. "I'm convinced that this is about Colonel Vladimir Zhukov. We have talked about him before but without any serious conclusions. I don't think we'll get more evidence. I'm convinced that the man that sat next to me on my flight was Zhukov. That means that he is still in the U.S., and he is still here in support of Casper's operation. The outstanding question is why he went to the trouble to approach me. What is to be gained by him doing that?"

"Don't know," Hollifield said, then lit a cigar. "I'm sure he and Casper know you are working to catch this traitor. Perhaps he thought you would be a Chatty Cathy doll and schmooze you into telling him exactly where you are in the investigation and why you were going to Presidio of Monterey. Or maybe Zhukov is just that arrogant, and the encounter was a game to him. Either way, the stakes have been raised. Your investigation, Jake, has become more dangerous."

"I don't think it is more dangerous, Admiral," Jake said. "I think we have simply become more aware or reminded of the danger that has been present all along. Zhukov and his team are here to protect Casper. There is no doubt in my mind that the attempt on General Osborne's life and the death of Sara was ordered by Casper and executed by Zhukov. We are dealing with the same threat. That said, why don't Zhukov and his team kill me now and put an end to the investigation?"

"Good point, Jake," the Admiral said. "Good question."

"It's because they aren't worried about you, Jake, or the investigation," Hanraty stated. "If looking for Casper is a war, we are losing, and they know it. Without a significant lead in some direction other than what we are pursuing, we will never come up with anything but weak circumstantial evidence, a guess as to who Casper is. Casper wins with us flopping around, and if we don't find him, what rumor there is will die."

All three were quiet for a long two minutes. Finally, Admiral Hollifield tapped the ash off his cigar, inhaled deeply, and exhaled his thoughts. "We must keep the pressure on. Casper will make a fatal mistake. I don't know what it will be, but if we keep disturbing the people on our list, he will take some action that will give us another parameter to narrow our search. That parameter might put a big X right on his forehead."

"I think that is exactly right, Admiral," Jake said. "Just thinking out loud, but with enough pressure, anyone on our list that makes a serious effort to stop our search would raise a red flag on himself. I'm not saying that that is the parameter we hope for, but it might be."

"Ok," the Admiral said. "What's your agenda?"

Jake checked his notes. "I have six more flag officers to interview and eleven in Congress. Based on his profile, I'm anxious to interview Senator Zendt, but he keeps canceling our appointments. He is dodging me. I'm sure he is aware of what I am doing. The more he dodges me, the more curious I am about him, especially about his appointment to the Senate Select Committee on Intelligence. Somehow, that appointment doesn't fit his background and experience in the Senate. Anyway, an interview with him should be interesting. I'll keep pestering him until he gives me some time."

"Onward, Gentlemen," Admiral Hollifield said as he rose

from his chair, a sure indication, in Navy-speak, that the meeting was over. "Good job. We will get there. If you need me this afternoon, I will be on the golf course with three Marines. By the end of the day, I'm likely to think that the Navy is nothing but a bunch of guys in a rowboat."

1430 Hours
10 September 1983
Senator Samuel Zendt's Office
The Capitol Building
Washington, D.C.

"THANK YOU FOR SEEING ME, SENATOR," Jake said as Zendt motioned him to sit in one of the two chairs before his desk. Senator Zendt stepped behind his massive walnut desk and sat in an overstuffed leather chair. The undercurrent of Zendt's demeanor hinted at confrontation. He was not pleased to have Jake in his office.

"General Brodrick pretty much insisted," Zendt coldly said. "What can I do for you? I haven't much time."

Jake was expressionless. "I understand, Senator. You are a very important and busy man."

The comment was intentionally made to irritate Zendt slightly and put him on the defensive. One might presume to be important and too busy to deal with a subordinate, but to be openly called on it makes the statement a metaphor for arrogance. Zendt understood the weight of the comment and frowned.

"Yes. Well. Ah, ask whatever you want, Colonel Jacobs. What can I do to help you?"

Jake wasted no time getting to the point of his interview.

"It's a curiosity, Senator, that you ended up as a member of the Senate Select Committee on Intelligence when Senator Prather was assassinated. You were on the Armed Services Committee at the time, which doesn't have much to do with intelligence matters. You are a young Senator in terms of seniority, and for all practical purposes, you had no first-hand experience with intelligence. How do you explain your appointment?"

Jake sat back in his chair and let the pot boil.

Senator Zendt turned red-faced with frustration and anger. "Senator Prather was not assassinated. He was killed by a mugger. It could happen to anyone. It had nothing to do with my appointment to the Intelligence Committee. If I had not been appointed, someone else would have been, and it's a good thing, too. Senator Prather had been in the Senate much too long. His days of contributing anything of value were gone. He lived in the past without any thought about the modern world we live in."

Jake showed no reaction to his thoughts that Zendt had come perilously close to admitting that he was involved in Prather's assassination, which in his mind, moved Senator Zendt up on his list of those that might be Casper. There was the motive of positioning to a better source of intelligence, and there was the supposition that if Zendt was capable of murder, he was capable of espionage.

"Perhaps so, Senator. I mean, it might have been a mugging as opposed to an assassination. Either way, it was fortuitous for you."

"You're impertinent, Colonel," Zendt said in a raised voice. "I know for a fact that you are fighting windmills in your quest to uncover some fictitious spy in Congress. It is ridiculous, and your line of questioning is ridiculous. This interview is over. You can find your way out the door."

Jake did not move a muscle. The interview was not over, and he knew it.

"That's fine, sir. What shall I tell General Osborne, and thereby General Brodrick, and maybe the President? Shall I tell them that you refuse to answer questions concerning the most treacherous traitor in American history? If that's the case, thank you for your time, and I will be on my way."

Zendt froze, and Jake forced the Senator to be the first to speak. A full minute passed. Then two.

"Very well, I do want to be cooperative. I know you are simply doing your job. It can't be easy being the contemptibly obnoxious person you appear to be. What other questions do you have for me?"

An hour passed with Jake asking questions that had Senator Zendt flustered and squirming in his chair. Zendt did his best to be evasive, but when he was, Jake pressed for a direct answer. Finally, Jake announced that he had only one question remaining.

"Senator, you have implied that you had no reason to maneuver yourself to an appointment to the Intelligence Committee because you regularly knew from others in Congress all there was to know on intelligence matters. Apparently, you felt the need-to-know, top-secret intelligence long before you were required to know by your appointment. Why is that? Why did you gather top-secret intelligence when, frankly, it was none of your business? Are you a spy, Senator?"

Zendt was horrified by the question. He was no longer focused on the impertinence of Jake's questions; he was mentally engulfed in survival. His previous answers had unveiled the fact that he gained even the most sensitive intelligence over the years by leveraging whatever power he had and selling favors. He had gone so far in his answers to admit that lobbyists were a source of information of which he regularly took advantage. Zendt recognized that Jake had walked him into a corner for this last question.

"Shall I repeat the question, Senator?" Jake asked.

Zendt did not know how to answer the question, only that he had to answer. Careful with his words, Zendt said, "I most certainly am not a spy. I admit I've known things that I probably shouldn't have known, but that is just how Congress works. It's a game based on who knows what, and one can buy or sell information, top secret or not, to get what one wants. I'm not a communist. I'm a loyal American."

Jake knew that he had spooked Senator Zendt. He could let the Senator off the hook, to an extent, by agreeing with him. But he did not. His intent was to rattle the cage and encourage Casper to make a mistake.

CHAPTER 25

1430 Hours
23 October 1983
Camp Lejeune, North Carolina

JAKE ASCENDED the stairs and walked down the hallway to the office of Admiral Hollifield. His heart rate was slightly elevated from the call he had received, and he was anxious to inform the Admiral of his circumstances.

"The Admiral will see you now," the secretary said, and Jake entered the office. Hanraty sat in front of the Admiral's desk.

Before Jake could say a word, Admiral Hollifield was talking with gravity.

"I don't know if you have heard, but there was a bombing of the Marine barracks in Beirut. I don't know any specifics yet, but it is bad."

"I had not heard that, Admiral," Jake said with surprise, but I did notice a lot of commotion down on the first floor. Marines are running around like World War III just started."

"It may have," the Admiral responded. "There were several hundred Marines housed there."

Jake sat in the worn chair next to Hanraty.

"That explains why I came up here, sir. I just received orders to deploy without any details. I am being airlifted to Hunter Army Airfield, Georgia, in an hour."

Admiral Hollifield and Hanraty looked at Jake in surprise. Though word of the Beirut bombing was still closely held, it was now apparent that a military response was underway.

"I don't know yet which unit I will be attached to," Jake said. "Bragg is home for the 82nd Airborne Division and Hunter Army Airfield for the 1st Ranger Battalion of the 75th Ranger Regiment. Based on my orders, I presume I'll be attached to the Rangers."

Admiral Hollifield lit a fresh cigar with a frown on his face. "Something wrong about that, Jake. Why would they deploy you to Beirut? You're not on anyone's staff. Why would they want a Lieutenant Colonel in Military Intelligence, not currently assigned to a MI unit or to either the 75th Ranger Regiment or the 82nd? Those units have their own MI personnel already."

"Yes, sir. Jake said. "I'm baffled, too, but my main concern right now is Stephen Patrick.

"Don't worry about him, Jake," the Admiral immediately responded. "I'll pick him up and take him home with me. Suzanne will spoil him rotten until you get back."

"Thank you, sir. I know he will be in good hands. Well, I better get over to the airfield. I don't even have so much as a toothbrush, but I will be issued whatever I need."

"Be safe, Jake," the Admiral said. "No telling how long you will be over there. I'll do some poking around to get a few questions answered about your deployment. Somebody had a reason for it."

0530 Hours
24 October 1983
75th Ranger Regiment/1st Battalion
Hunter Army Airfield, Georgia

JAKE WAITED PATIENTLY as the quartermaster sergeant set gear on the counter and checked each item on his list. The first on the counter were two sets of outdated OG-107 Cotton Sateen Utility Uniforms. He preferred these old-style olive drab fatigues from the Vietnam Era over the new Battledress Uniform (BDU), which is not well suited for hot weather.

Over the next half-hour, gear was issued that he knew from experience from his days in the Green Berets he would never need and that he certainly did not want to carry. When the sergeant finally requested his signature, it was apparent that he had been issued gear for a combat mission in the field, not a staff position. His final issue was an M16, 5.56mm rifle, a Colt 1911 caliber .45 pistol, one hundred rounds of ammunition for the rifle, and fifty for the 1911. A quartermaster major stood close by, indicating to each soldier that entered the building that there was a communications blackout. There would be no calls to family. Still, Jake had no idea what was to be his mission and was confused that he had a mission at all.

The 1st Ranger Battalion had been reactivated in 1974, having had a spectacular reputation in World War II and lineage to Vietnam Long Range Reconnaissance Patrols

(LRRP) that patrolled in small teams deep into enemy-held territory. In the Normandy invasion, the Rangers attacked the cliffs at Pointe du Hoc to defeat the German gun emplacements with over a sixty percent casualty rate. The Rangers are a proud light infantry, and Jake was enthused to serve with them, even if he did not understand the assignment.

A young sergeant picked Jake up at the quartermaster building in a jeep, then drove him to a hangar at the airfield, dropped him off with all his gear, and sped away. After Jake changed his uniform and assembled the gear he wanted, which was light compared to what he had been given, he stuffed the remainder in a standard canvas duffle bag and walked to the hangar.

"Lieutenant Colonel Jacobs," a tall, handsome captain said. "I am Captain Mark Fredricks. Welcome to the 1st of the 75th. I'm to escort you to Colonel O'Keefe. He will brief you on your mission."

Jake fell in step as the Captain said, "You probably don't remember me, sir, but I was in one of your classes at West Point. Russian political history."

"I thought you looked familiar. Shall I give you a verbal writ (test) on the way to Colonel O'Keefe's office?"

"We've already been down that road, Colonel," Fredricks said with a grin on his face. "I'm afraid you would be disappointed. Here we are, sir. Colonel O'Keefe is waiting for you."

Jake walked into the makeshift office and immediately recognized the Colonel. O'Keefe had been a Green Beret major when Jake was a butter bar lieutenant with the teams. Jake snapped a salute. "Lieutenant Colonel Jacobs reporting as ordered, sir."

O'Keefe grinned. "Good to see you again, Jake," and

extended his hand. "Looks like we are at it again. Are you ready for a little action?"

"Absolutely, sir."

"I'll give you a brief rundown," O'Keefe said as he stepped to a map hanging on the wall. "Grenada. Any familiarity?"

"Island in the Caribbean," Jake replied, somewhat stunned that Grenada was the mission and not Beirut. "That's about all I know about it though."

O'Keefe continued the briefing, not surprised that Jake knew little of the country. Most people had never heard of it.

"The Soviet Union has been quite busy, using the local Peoples Revolutionary Armed Forces and Cuba to build military facilities on the island. The local military is not much in the way of trained personnel, but the Cuban Army is a different story. Obviously, such facilities are a threat to the United States in that they could launch an offensive and have a base of operations. The Soviet Union is trying to keep their hands clean by fronting their Cuban surrogate. The United States and six Caribbean nations are now involved in Operation Urgent Fury. Our mission is to put a stop to that nonsense. The President is not about to allow a Soviet base in our backyard.

"Yes, sir," Jake said. "I can see why."

Pointing to the map, Colonel O'Keefe continued his briefing. "The short version of the invasion strategy is this. Units of the 1st of the 75th Ranger Regiment will parachute onto the airfield from five hundred feet at Point Salines under cover of darkness. Heavy Cuban resistance is expected. Once the airfield is taken, the 82nd Airborne will drop in to secure the airfield and rescue a group of students on the island. Colonel Jacobs, you are attached as a Military Intelligence officer to 3rd Platoon, Company C, 1st Battalion Rangers under the command of Second Lieutenant Christopher Timmers. You, and the platoon, will parachute into the designated mountain region two miles northwest of Saint David, which is approximately ten miles northeast of Point Salines. The terrain consists of hills to an elevation of three hundred fifty feet with dense vegetation. The platoon's mission is to operate as a scout platoon, reconnaissance in force, to discover and identify any enemy strength, dispositions, and any other information. Any questions at this point, Colonel?"

"No, sir," Jake said.

"Well, I have one or two," O'Keefe stated. "Your assignment to this mission is an anomaly. There is nothing standard about a MI Lieutenant Colonel assigned to this kind of a mission. I've read your file. West Point graduate, Green Beret, highly decorated, and obviously on the fast track since you made Lieutenant Colonel so early in your career. This mission is directly contradictory to that. What's up? Who did you piss off?"

"Just about everyone, Colonel," Jake said stoically, "but I'm not at liberty to talk about it. I have my orders. I'm a soldier. I'm good to go."

"I know you are," Colonel O'Keefe said. "So long as you don't break a leg or get impaled by a tree from a five-hundred-foot jump, the mission is a cakewalk. We have no reason to think there is any enemy activity in that area.

PART THREE

CHAPTER 26

0500 Hours
25 October 1983
Point Salines, Grenada

OPERATION URGENT FURY was initiated for an at-dawn invasion. Immediately, Prussian Field Marshal Helmuth von Moltke's wisdom sprang into reality: "Every plan is a good one —until the first shot is fired."

Captain Richard Merrill, company commander in the 1st Battalion, 75th Rangers was in the lead C-130, prepared for making a surprise attack on the airfield at Point Salines when word came that the inertial navigation system onboard was malfunctioning. The element of surprise would be lost. The flow of C-130s would have to be adjusted in the air by manual means, and that would delay the parachute assault at least a half-hour, hanging the Rangers in daylight exposed to enemy gunfire. The delay put them behind schedule for the Marine assault at Pearls Island, guaranteeing that word would come to the Cubans at the airfield that an assault by the Rangers was imminent. Worse yet, the change in the airflow of the C-130s meant that the Rangers would land in mixed units, thereby losing organizational and tactical unity.

The shuffle of the C-130s and the delay of the assault on the airfield was an immediate miscarriage of the operation's general strategy. The strategy called for a Coup de Main, requiring Rangers/Marines/Air Force/Seals/Army Delta operators to conduct simultaneous rescue and combat operations. The 75th Rangers, with units of the 82nd Airborne coming behind them, were to secure the airfield at Point Salines. The taking of the airfield would eliminate anti-U.S. Marxists' capability to interdict U.S. air and sea routes to Europe and the Middle East. Their secondary mission was to rescue an estimated one thousand American citizens, six hundred of which were medical students. The 2nd Brigade of the 82nd Airborne was to provide reinforcements to the Rangers for completion of the missions. The 8th Marine Regiment was to assault the Pearls Airport at the northeastern corner of the island, nineteen miles from the capitol, St. Georges, and to gain control over the eastern side of the island. The Air Force was multitasked with AC-130 gunships to provide support to troops on the ground, C-141s and C-130s were to land at the airfield to unload troops and supplies, airlift operations, E-3 AWACS communication, and F-15 air cover to forestall any intervention from Cuba. SEAL Teams 4 and 6 were given two objectives. The first was to rescue the Governor-General of Grenada, Sir Paul Scoon, at the governor's mansion in St. Georges, four and one-half miles up the coast, northwest of Point Salines. The second SEAL mission was to secure Grenada's only radio tower and station.

Rotary wing aircraft launched and coordinated from the ships of the USS *Guam* amphibious ready group, and Rangers launched aboard C-130s from Hunter Army Airfield in Georgia. The invasion force approached Grenada. At the planned 0500 hours attack, four hundred Marines made a helicopter assault upon Pearls Airport ahead of the delayed Rangers at Point Salines. The element of surprise was lost for the Rangers.

0500 Hours
25 October 1983
Pearls Airport, Grenada

PEARLS AIRPORT SITS on the coast with its inland perimeter characterized by low-lying mountains and jungle. Special operation forces set four hundred men of the 8th Marines on and around the tarmac of the Pearls Airport. First Lieutenant Mark Volger and his platoon were in the third helicopter to touch ground, and they hustled into a tactical "V" formation, the tip of which led the way to the likely point of contact with the enemy while the sides retained firepower to the front and also protected the platoon's flanks. Gunnery Sergeant Nick Garcia took the point with Volger and his radio operator five yards behind.

Garcia held a steady but cautious pace forward. Lieutenant Volger came to only a few steps behind him.

"Pretty light fire," Volger said as he scanned the terrain. "I was expecting a lot more tracers than this in the air."

Sergeant Garcia kept his gaze to the front. "Me, too, but that may change in a heartbeat. Those tracers are high. I hope those boys over there keep it that way."

Volger did not reply but glanced right and left. Their

platoons in the invasion force were advancing at the same pace. Enemy fire was light, but not all of it was high. In the dim light, he could see tracers hit the tarmac.

No sooner had Volger processed that thought when Lance Corporal Benjamin Alvarado took a through-and-through hit to his left hip and sat down on the tarmac. The platoon Navy corpsman ran to his side. The corpsman, Petty Officer 3rd Class Willard Sorensen, pushed Alvarado down flat on the tarmac and began questioning him as to where he was hit. All Sorensen got from Alvarado was a string of curse words about being taken out of the action.

"I didn't come all this way to get back on that damn helicopter," Alvarado angrily said. "Patch me up, Doc. I'm a Marine. I came here to fight."

Sorensen cut Alvarado's utility uniform away from the wound and began to work his magic.

"Not too bad, Corporal. You are going to live and have a story to tell, but you are going to be in some pain when this morphine wears off. The gals back home will slobber all over you for being a genuine hero."

"Screw that," Alvarado said. "Get me back in action."

Sorensen laughed. "Not a chance, Marine. You're done."

Helos continued to land on the tarmac. Marines disembarked quickly with precision, advanced to their designated sectors, then tactically advanced to meet presumed stiff resistance that never came. As Volger's platoon neared the terminal, he gave the signal to shift into a line position, one squad advancing under covering fire from the other two. Another quick glance left and right told him that other units were doing likewise. As the Marines closed on the terminal, enemy gunfire diminished to a dead stop. The Grenadian soldiers of the People's Revolutionary Armed Forces and a small contingent of Cubans had abandoned their post, slipped into the civilian population, and changed out of their uniforms to disguise their identity. Four hundred Marines advancing on their position was more than they could bear.

0500 Hours
25 October 1983
St. Georges, Grenada

NAVY SEAL TEAMS 4 and 6 were tasked to parachute to the Governor-General's mansion, rescue the governor from enemy forces by assault, and, as a secondary mission, disable Grenada's only radio station and tower. Immediately, Murphy's Law initiated the action with tragedy. One of the C-130s veered slightly off course and dropped four of the SEALS short of the beach and into the water. A miscalculation of the weight of ammunition they carried pulled the four to a deadly depth, and they drowned.

CHIEF PETTY OFFICER Peter Schramp led his team to the veranda doors of the mansion facing the beach by advancing in pairs and utilizing covering fire. Resistance was heavy. The Cuban soldiers defending the mansion were seasoned, many of which had served under Soviet advisors in Ethiopia and Angola, but the SEALS were superbly trained to capitalize on the element of surprise they had achieved. Shramp and two other SEALs kicked the front door open and entered the mansion. Shramp fired two, three-round bursts, killing two Grenadian soldiers that were determined to hold their position. The three SEALs went room to room clearing them and found Governor Scoon, his wife, and eleven civilians huddled in the library.

"Thank God," Scoon said in his heavy British accent.

Shortly, the opposition was dispatched. Several of the Grenadians made it out the back of the residence to escape the SEALs, and within a few minutes, the governor and the mansion were under U.S. control.

0500 Hours
25 October 1983
Rugged Terrain
Northeast of St. David, Grenada

JAKE PRIVATELY QUESTIONED the need for the Ranger platoon to parachute from an altitude of five hundred feet if there was little expectation of contact with the enemy. A seven-hundred or eight-hundred-foot jump would be less risky, considering the terrain and tropical forest. A jump from a higher altitude would make for a softer landing in the treacherous canopy of jungle. At five hundred feet, a paratrooper would only hang in the air about twenty-three seconds. Hardly enough time to make a soft landing. His horizontal speed would be impacted by the speed of the C-130, which would be eighty to ninety knots, or one hundred miles per hour, and his vertical descent would be twenty-two feet per second, or fifteen miles per hour. The speed and the terrain, made for a significant pucker factor.

"Well, it can't be any worse than my jump into

Afghanistan," Jake said aloud to himself as he stepped to the door and jumped.

Dawn was starting to break. There was enough light to dimly make out the dense canopy of trees below but dark enough to hide the dangers that were only seconds away. Ten seconds from impact, heavy automatic weapons fire rose upward from the jungle, tracers lighting up an otherwise lusterless sky as the enemy fired at the descending parachutes. Jake was startled, hair rising on the back of his neck as he drifted the final two hundred feet, helpless to do anything but hang under the canopy of his parachute and gaze in amazement at the flurry of tracers that were hunting him. He glanced to his left and saw a paratrooper limp, hanging from his suspension lines, lifeless, drifting toward the ground. Ten seconds were felt to have entered an alternative reality, slowed to a teeth-grinding deferment of the natural laws of time. Then, another sense of reality struck. His feet punched through the upper branches of a Giant Silk Cotton Tree, twenty-five feet off the ground. As he helplessly fell, he was thrown into one large branch, then another, slapped and gouged by lesser limbs until he came to an abrupt stop when the suspension lines were thoroughly entangled in the tree. He was four feet from touching the floor of the jungle. With one of the quick releases failing on his harness, Jake wasted no time pulling his M-7 bayonet strapped to his leg, slashed the parachute riser, and dropped to the ground.

Jake unslung his M16 and went to one knee to orient himself to the situation. Someone, presumably Second Lieutenant Timmers or the platoon sergeant, Sergeant First Class Alvin Dross, had dropped a blue smoke grenade to rally the platoon to a central point. Under less dire circumstances, identifying a location with smoke would be avoided, but under fire it was necessary to quickly gather a cohesive force. Jake moved in that direction with deafening small arms fire ringing in his ears.

Finding the Lieutenant and the platoon sergeant, Jake gladly joined them to share a barely adequate boulder for cover. Timmers had his 1:50,000 scale topographical map on the ground to identify exactly where they were and to consider a better defensive position if there was one. Timmers pointed to the map. "What do you think, Colonel? Fifty meters behind us is that plateau. Looks to be high enough to give us a defensive position and a slight escarpment which would give us an advantage of a field of fire should the enemy press an assault."

Jake looked at the map. "Looks good to me, Lieutenant. Bound to be some rock up there for cover. We might want to see if we can get an M-60 placed to cut off a surprise from the top of that plateau. I might suggest, if it is acceptable to you, that you put the platoon in a line formation and set up flankers."

"Exactly," Timmers said. "Master Sergeant, pass the word to the squad leaders. Five minutes, then we beat feet to that plateau."

Dross moved to locate the squad leaders and crouched to avoid undo exposure to the small arms fire.

Timmers folded his map and put it away. "Damn poor luck for us to land right on top of those hostiles, sir, especially since there weren't supposed to be any. About half-peculiar, wouldn't you say?"

Jake raised his eyebrows. "I was just thinking the same thing, Lieutenant."

He didn't say it, but the situation was more than peculiar. It smacked of the ambush in Afghanistan that killed that

Green Beret team. That team had walked into an oversized Soviet unit lying in wait to ambush them. So far, this little stroll through the jungle was turning out to look the same. If his intuition was serving him correctly, it was possible that this was a bogus mission set up for the specific purpose of ambushing this platoon, and if that were true, then he was the target. Massacre the platoon. Kill him. Casper evades detection.

Master Sergeant Dross returned, out of breath from scrambling to connect with squad leaders, and slid to cover next to Timmers and Jake. The small arms fire had ceased. "What I'm being told by the men is that we have a least a full-sized company of Cuban infantry stirred up. At least a company. Maybe more."

"Did you locate Sergeant Pentuk?" Timmers asked. "I need that radio."

"Bad news, LT," Dross replied. "Pentuk was KIA on the drop. The radio has a hole through it as big as your fist."

Timmers frowned and glanced at Jake. "Well, I reckon those Cubans have picked a fight with the wrong bunch of badass Rangers."

Again, Jake said nothing, but thought, *Yeah, that's probably what General Custer might have said about the badass 7th Cavalry, too.*

Timmers checked his watch. "Move 'em out. Let's grab some higher ground.

CHAPTER 27

0536 Hours
25 October 1983
Point Salines, Grenada

DAYLIGHT. Thirty-six minutes behind the planned assault, transport C-130s dropped a company unit of the 75th Ranger Regiment on the Point Salines airport. Immediately the Rangers were engaged by Cuban soldiers. Initial intelligence claimed that the opposing force would be construction workers, but it was readily apparent that it was primarily Cuban soldiers. The Cubans were, in fact, a well-trained fighting force. It was only an After Action Report that unveiled that over a thousand rifles and the equipment for a full-strength Cuban battalion were located at Point Salines. 23 mm anti-aircraft guns hammered rounds toward the aircraft but were ineffective. The Cubans could not depress their guns low enough to hit the low-flying C-130s. The Rangers had jumped from five hundred feet, enduring AK-47 fire from the Cubans, and landed hard on the runway in scattered fashion and made haste to disconnect from their parachutes. Mixed units, caused by the shuffling of the aircraft, was a disadvantage, but the Rangers had continuity in their training. They could overcome.

Captain Richard Merrill hit the ground with bent knees, rolled on the ground to absorb the shock, quickly disconnected his parachute, and brought his M16 to a ready position. As he rose from the tarmac, two Soviet-made BTR-60 armored personnel carriers within four hundred yards rushed to meet the Rangers, 14.5 mm heavy machine gun rounds blazing toward his men and splattering off the runway. The Rangers, sensing they were outgunned, took whatever cover they could find, which was mostly nothing at all, as they slammed their bellies to the ground and prayed. Moments passed in desperation as the BTR-60s closed in.

Under fire, Sergeant Francis Danhof prepped his 90 mm recoilless rifle and, within seconds, scored hits on the two armored personnel carriers. He turned the situation from near disaster to a return of momentum in the assault. Moments later, an Air Force AC-130U Spooky II gunship entered the scene from seven thousand feet to bring destruction to the Cuban anti-aircraft emplacements and provide ground support for the Rangers. The Spooky II's 25 mm five-barreled rotary cannon and M102, 105mm howitzer put Merrill's men back on their feet for the assault, and the sky filled with the next wave of descending parachutes.

"Hotwire those dozers and clear those personnel carriers out of the way," Captain Merrill shouted above the roar of battle to the company's First Sergeant. "Have the men fall in behind the dozers for cover. Follow me. Continue the advance."

Heavy small arms fire from the Cubans continued from

the roof of the terminal and from surrounding buildings, with Rangers returning overwhelming firepower to their positions.

After initial reports at the Pentagon of action on the ground, the next phase of the plan was executed. Two battalions of the 82nd Airborne Division at Fort Bragg were airlifted to Point Salines. Wave after wave of landing parachutes increased the firepower delivered to the Cubans. By 1000 hours, fifteen hundred paratroopers were on hand to terrify any remaining Cuban defenders.

As the battle continued on the tarmac, First Sergeant Philip Tully led two platoons to the True Blue Campus, where a number of American students and other Americans were being held captive. An exchange of small arms fire was briefly intense. Ignoring his own safety Sergeant Delbert Winsel ran through a hail of bullets, crashed through a door on the south side of a building, took a forward roll, and came up firing his M16 in three-round bursts into two shocked Cuban soldiers while a third, unleashed wild shots toward the sergeant from a Soviet pistol at close range. When his weapon jammed, Winsel instinctively threw his M16 at his attacker, like he was passing a basketball back in Alabama, and rushed the man who was trying to kill him. They both went to ground, and Winsel pulled his combat knife from his leg sheath. The struggle was short. Winsel punctured the Cuban under the sternum, then shoved the tip of the knife into his heart. As his Ranger brothers entered the room to assist, Winsel sat on the floor, shaking uncontrollably from the rush of adrenalin that ran through his body. On his feet again, he and his squad searched the buildings from room to room. Contact with the enemy was soon non-existent. The Cuban soldiers that were dedicated enough not to throw down their weapons and run, died.

Within hours the Point Salines Airport was secured, a

THUNDERING WHITE CROSSES

perimeter was established, two hundred fifty Cuban prisoners were taken, and one hundred thirty-eight medical students were rescued at the True Blue Campus adjacent to the airfield.

1000 Hours
25 October
Governor's Mansion
St. Georges, Grenada

HAVING FOUGHT their way from the beach to the Governor-General's mansion, rescued the governor, and secured the building, the battle had just begun for SEAL Teams 4 and 6. A helicopter extraction had been planned for the SEALs and Governor Scoon. The extraction was to be executed within forty-five minutes of taking the mansion. But that did not happen. Enemy resistance was heavier than expected, and the SEALs were forced to seek other options. The mansion came under heavy fire from Cuban armored personnel carriers and infantry. The SEALs did not have anti-tank weapons to deal with the firepower of the armored vehicles. Using their automatic weapons and grenades, they held off the attacking Cubans from defensive positions in and around the mansion. The SEALs were armed with 5.56 x 45 mm M-16s and one Stoner 63 Light Machine Gun of the same caliber. Continuous small-arms fire and the deadly effectiveness of rifle-fired grenades from the Cubans increased, forcing the SEALs to consolidate civilians to an upstairs room for their safety.

Under heavy attack from Grenadian infantry and turreted armored personnel carriers, the SEALs needed air support.

Senior Chief Petty Officer Foster Chadwick recognized that they were outgunned.

"Find that SAT phone and get it to me right now!"

After Hull Technician 1st Walter Yamashita had moved to each SEAL location on the perimeter to find the satellite phone, he returned to Chadwick in minutes.

"Ok, so, you aren't going to like this Senior Chief. Somehow, the SAT phone got left behind on the insertion aircraft. We don't have a SAT phone."

Senior Chief Petty Officer Chadwick closed his eyes and bit his lip.

"Well, Yamashita, that's sure-fired disappointing. That puts us in a pickle. We can't call in air support."

Yamashita said nothing.

They had radios, but they could not communicate with the Air Force gunships that were above St. Georges. The Army radios could communicate with the Air Force, but the Navy could not. An Army Delta Force operator was in the vicinity, doing what Delta's do, and heard the SEALs' calls for support. He relayed the need for support to the Air Force. Within fifteen minutes, an Air Force AC-130 Spectre laid down fire on the advancing enemy with its 20 mm and 40 mm cannons while another Spectre was dispatched to join the fray. The gunships turned back the enemy assault, but after two hours, they flew off to refuel. The SEALs made a plea for reinforcements at the mansion.

Since the mansion was located in an area where St. Georges civilians resided, the use of Navy gunfire from ships or jet aircraft was not a viable option. Command chose a lesser option. Two Marine AH-1T Super Cobra attack helicopters from the USS *Guam* were ordered to attack the nearby Grenadian-held Fort Frederick, which was directing the attacks on the mansion. At 1300 hours, Chief Warrant Officer Carlton Weeks and his co-pilot, Warrant Officer Randall Warhime, flew their Cobra overhead with the support of a second Cobra. They were met by Soviet ZU-23 anti-aircraft guns. A half-hour later, the Cobras made their fifth attack, and the Weeks-Warhime Cobra was hit by three antiaircraft rounds. Both engines were disabled, and the pilot and co-pilot were both injured. Though wounded, Weeks managed to crash-land the Cobra on a sports field in St. Georges, and the wounded Warhime pulled the pilot from the burning wreckage.

Above the sports field, the second Cobra laid down rocket fire to keep Grenadian soldiers away from the pilots and called for a rescue. A Marine CH-47 made a heroic landing under fire and rescued the pilot, but the co-pilot, Warhime, was killed by Grenadian small arms fire. The Cobra above continued to provide cover for the evacuation, but it was also hit by antiaircraft fire, killing both pilots. At 1340 hours, it crashed at sea.

Orders were issued to bomb Fort Frederick, and central command consulted with the Army advisor, Major General Norman Schwarzkopf, Jr., to achieve an envelopment maneuver. Two rifle companies of the 22nd Marine Amphibious Landing Unit off the USS *Manitowoc* were ordered to make an amphibious landing north of St. Georges.

At 1530 hours, thirty Grenadians and Cubans, supported by armored personnel carriers, advanced toward the mansion. Senior Chief Petty Officer Chadwick, bypassing his weakening radio, used a long-distance calling card to call Fort Bragg in the United States for help. An AC-130 received the patch by radio from Chadwick's telephone call and could hear the firing instructions given to a fire control officer at Fort

Bragg. With that information, the C-130 laid down fire on the advancing Grenadians and turned them back.

MEANWHILE, as the SEALs battled Grenadian and Cuban forces at the Governor's mansion, the SEALs that had been tasked with securing the radio station and radio tower in St. Georges found themselves in a precarious situation. They were outnumbered, outgunned, and close to being overwhelmed by the attacking opposition. Like their brothers at the mansion, they had radio problems and could not raise command to request support. They beat back wave after wave of attacks, but when they ran low on ammunition, a joint decision was made that their position was unsustainable.

"Rig our C4 explosives on the tower and in the radio station," Hull Technician 1st Jett Ritter said to Machinist Mate 1st Lee Rooney. "We don't have a choice. We barely have enough ammo to make it to the beach. If we're lucky, we might be spotted and get some air support."

"And if we are not so lucky?" Rooney asked.

Ritter laughed out loud. "How far can you swim, Sailor?"

A half-hour later, the team left the radio station. The explosions destroying the tower and radio station lit up the sky and provided a diversion for their escape. Resistance to the beach was light, but the Cubans soon became aware of the SEAL's retreat and were in immediate pursuit.

Arriving at the water's edge, Ritter said, "Wouldn't you know it? There's not an aircraft in sight." He glanced over his shoulder and saw a dozen Cuban soldiers running toward them, firing wild shots in their direction. "Well, ok then. It's the water. Let's go."

Without hesitation, the team entered the water and started swimming toward the open sea. Cuban bullets peppered the water around them.

As they swam further out to sea, Quartermaster 1st Marvin Wartner said, "Join the Navy, the recruiter said. Make your life an adventure, the recruiter said."

They all laughed.

"Keep swimming," Ritter said. "We should make it to Florida in about two months."

1300 Hours
25 October 1983
75th Ranger Platoon
Northeast of St. David, Grenada

THE CUBAN INFANTRY company had made two assaults on the platoon. Had the Cubans a choice, they would have preferred to have had the high ground rather than yielding it to the Rangers. While the Rangers had a slight advantage of cover, the Cuban infantry had mass, an overwhelming force in numbers. It was an offensive siege of sorts. It was only a matter of time before the Rangers ran out of ammunition and were crushed by attrition. Captain Alonzo Mondragon had his orders. Annihilate the Ranger platoon down to the last man, and he had nearly two hundred trained soldiers to complete his mission.

Captain Mondragon ordered mortar rounds to precede the second assault. The mortars sent metal and rocks in every direction. During the assault, three Rangers were wounded, including Lieutenant Timmers, whose left femur was shattered by shrapnel. The medic saved his life with a tourniquet to stop a profuse bleed. He was conscious, but for all practical purposes, he was out of the fight. "Dadgummit," he said to Jake. "This is downright inconvenient. I reckon you are in command, Colonel."

"No," Jake replied. "You are still in command of your platoon. I'll follow your orders and help all I can. We'll get through this together."

Timmers looked at Jake, his eyes expressing gratitude.

"Well, alrighty then. I know your background, Sir. I have every confidence that you will keep these yahoos alive."

"Any orders, Lieutenant?"

"Well, Sir, we are going to run short of ammo and water pretty quick. The men need to gather those AKs in front of us tonight and all the ammo and water those dead Cubans were carrying. A radio would be nice."

"Done, Lieutenant," Jake replied. "Smart move. We are expected in St. Georges day after tomorrow. When we don't show, it's likely command will send an aircraft to search for us."

"Where's that goofy Tennessee hillbilly when you need him," Jake mumbled.

"What's that, sir?"

Jake smiled, "Oh, my roommate from West Point, Patrick McSwain, is a Cobra pilot. It would sure be nice to see him overhead about now. Where are you from, Lieutenant?"

"College Station, Texas, sir," Timmers replied. "Commissioned from Texas A&M."

"Ha, just up the road from my hometown. Ever heard of Comanche, Texas?"

Timmers smiled. "You betcha, Colonel. I've driven through there. Nice little town. You married?"

Jake paused. "Married my childhood sweetheart. She is the only woman for me, ever," he said, not wanting to share that she was dead.

"Children?"

"A son," Jake said. "Stephen Patrick. He's my everything."

Jake motioned for Master Sergeant Dross to rally the squad leaders to his location. Three minutes later, he was passing the Lieutenant's orders down the platoon's chain of command.

"The Cubans have numerical superiority. Make every round a hit. One round, one dead Cuban. Every Ranger in the platoon is a sniper today."

CHAPTER 28

1900 Hours
25 October 1983
Governor's Mansion
St. Georges, Grenada

DIRE CIRCUMSTANCES GIRDLED the SEAL team at the mansion. They were in danger of being overrun by a force that was numerically superior to theirs. Fortunately, the Marine amphibious force soon made an uneventful landing on the beach north of St. Georges and prepared for the landing by helicopters of Fox Company from Pearls Airport. For the SEALs at the mansion and the Marines en route for their rescue, the atmosphere was one of high anxiety that the units would not be in time to save the SEALS.

Twenty Grenadian soldiers had made another assault a couple of hours before midnight and managed to place themselves close to the mansion. The SEALs found outside cover the best they could, but they were perilously close to running out of ammunition while the attackers were gaining ground. As the Cubans made their attack, an AC-130 used its cannons to beat them back, forestalling the overrunning of the mansion and the recapture of Governor Scoon. Until fuel was an issue, the AC-130 remained attack-ready until 0400 hours on the 26th. By dawn, two Marine infantry companies, thirteen amtracs, and five tanks inched toward St. Georges. As light peeked over the horizon, Golf Company, Force Recon Marines, arrived at the mansion and joined the twenty-two SEALs. Within three hours, Governor Scoon and his wife were airlifted to the USS *Guam*. Miraculously, none of the SEALs were seriously wounded, and the mission to rescue the governor was successful.

Senior Chief Petty Officer Foster Chadwick and First Lieutenant Arthur Pettigrew (USMC) leaned against the retaining wall on the seaward side of the mansion. Chadwick pulled a Meal Ready to Eat, or MRE, out of his pack and began to search through it for something edible.

"You got here barely in the nick of time, Lieutenant," Chadwick said. "I don't know if we could have survived another attack. We would have had to throw paperclips from the governor's office in another half-hour."

Pettigrew laughed. "Admirable stuff you and your team did here. Glad we could help out."

1530 Hours
26 October 1983
Open Caribbean Sea
West of Grenada

"HOW MUCH FURTHER?" Machinist Mate 1st Rooney asked as he continued to swim.

Jet Ritter smirked. "You sound like my kids on a road trip."

"Yeah," Marvin Wartner said. "How much further? How much longer, Daddy? Can we stop for a hamburger?"

"Zip it," Ritter said. "You are all a bunch of babies."

The laughter was drowned out by the sound of a Navy reconnaissance aircraft approaching at two hundred feet for a better look. They would not have to swim the fifteen hundred miles to Florida after all.

"How's that for service, Wartner?" Ritter said. "A hamburger coming right up."

Half an hour later, the SEALs were picked up and delivered to the USS *Independence*.

2300 Hours
26 October 1983
75th Ranger Platoon
Northeast of St. David, Grenada

THE PLATOON medic tended to Lieutenant Timmers's leg wound. It was swelling and discolored, and he was in and out of consciousness. "We need to evac the Lieutenant. If we can get him to a hospital, that might save his life, but I wouldn't take any bets on saving his leg."

Jake frowned. The possibility of an extraction did not appear to be something that was going to happen anytime soon. Command did not suspect they were in a jam yet.

"Do all you can. The Lieutenant is a fine officer. He needs to survive all of this."

Jake turned to Master Sergeant Dross. "I need six volunteers. Two from each squad. We are going out to get weapons, ammo, and water."

"I'll get the six men and take them out, Sir," Dross said.

Jake started refreshing his face paint. "No. I'm taking them out."

Dross reluctantly shook his head in the affirmative and moved toward the squads. Seven minutes passed, and six Rangers appeared.

"Five minutes, gentlemen. Take your pack, empty of course. We are going to gather some AKs from their dead, as much ammo as we can gather up, and any canteens we can find. Take your sidearm and knife. We will low crawl out and back. Be as quiet as you can be, and maybe they won't start throwing lead at us. When you have all you can reasonably haul back here, get back to these rocks."

The six men emptied their packs, refreshed their face paint, shed any gear that could make a noise, and made sure a round was chambered in their Colt 1911. Five minutes quickly passed—quicker than they might have imagined.

Jake smiled, an expression to encourage confidence. "Ok, men. Follow me."

Jake slid out from the boulder in a low crawl and started making his way downslope, looking for a dead Cuban from which he could snatch his equipment. The six men followed one at a time from behind the boulder to do the same. A crescent moon was all the light they had to do the unpleasant job. Jake had only crawled twenty feet before coming upon a face-down Cuban soldier. Though he already knew the Cubans had come close to overrunning their position, it still surprised him that he found a dead one so quickly after leaving the boulder. As he approached, Jake drew his knife on the off chance that the man was only wounded and not dead. Finishing him was not a pleasant thought, but he would do what he had to do to maintain silence. Jake rolled him over and was thankful that the soldier was dead. He slung the AK-47 around his neck, slipped a half-dozen magazines and a canteen of water into his pack, and crawled further downslope in search of more supplies.

Coming upon the fourth soldier, Jake was startled when the Cuban opened his eyes wide, clenched Jake's shirt, and started to loudly moan. Jake could see in the moonlight that the man was not really a man but rather a boy, maybe sixteen or seventeen years old. The fragments from a Ranger's grenade had torn a large hole in his abdomen, releasing his entrails onto the dirt and rocks. Jake put his left hand over the young soldier's mouth to silence him, then slashed the boy's carotid artery.

The Cuban infantry was over-confident in their numerical superiority. They did not expect the Rangers to crawl out from the rocks into the open. Not a shot was fired. Jake and the Rangers returned to the boulders with two dozen AKs, several hundred rounds of ammunition, and enough water to last for days.

CHAPTER 29

0700 Hours
27 October 1983
Point Salines, Grenada

COLONEL O'KEEFE, regimental commander of the 75th Ranger Regiment, cornered Brigadier General Oliver Wotell at the command post inside the terminal building. Wotell was on Major General Schwarzkopf's staff, and was as gruff and demanding as his boss.

"Sir, if I may have a moment," O'Keefe said.

Wotell set his papers down on the table and met O'Keefe's eyes. It was his personal policy to give a subordinate his undivided attention if he agreed to talk to him at all.

"What is it, Colonel?"

"Sir, one of my platoons was tasked to parachute into the jungle northeast of St. David on the 25th. That unit has not been heard from since. Frankly, sir, the mission is a mystery to me. I can't see that the Grenadians or Cubans had much strategic incentive to have any troops in the jungle between St.

David and St. Georges. Yet, I have a platoon of thirty Rangers that appear to be missing. There's not been any radio communication whatsoever, and they were due in St. Georges late yesterday."

Wotell looked at his map on the table.

"Looks like less than twenty kilometers. Not much of a hike if they didn't encounter some resistance. No radio contact, you say?"

"That's correct, sir."

Wotell looked up from the map and paused for a moment.

"I tend to agree with you, Colonel, about there not being a strategic reason for the Cubans to have troops in that area. But you never know. I tell you what, Colonel, if that platoon doesn't show up in St. Georges by 1800 hours today, we'll send out a reconnaissance aircraft to locate those men. Report back to me then."

COMBAT OPERATIONS CONTINUED throughout the day. The Grenadians and Cubans had ditched their uniforms and gear to hide among the civilians or jungle. Once the Marines fully arrived in St. Georges, they occupied the surrounding forts and other objectives while meeting little resistance. While the Marines secured St. Georges, the Rangers and 82nd Airborne advanced across southern Grenada. Having met heavy resistance at Salines and Grand Anse, the general consensus was that the enemy might have sufficient troops to counterattack. Based on that, the Rangers and paratroopers moved to clear all phase lines, leaving zero pockets of resistance. The situation had become a strictly infantry operation. The condition of the airfield at Point

Salines had put them in a position where helicopter gunships were not readily available for ground support, leaving them with dependence on naval gunfire and air support. Again, communication became a problem. The Army radios could not directly communicate with the USS *Independence*. The paratroopers on the ground had to connect with Fort Bragg for a fire mission and wait until that message was sent to the Navy.

The military barracks at Calivigny were still an unachieved objective. Major General Schwarzkopf was planning to take the barracks on the 28th, reasoning that there was little expectation of resistance. However, higher command insisted on Schwarzkopf's Rangers taking the barracks during daylight hours of the 27th. The paratroopers were close, but the orders required the use of the Rangers to be inserted by helicopters. Minutes before dark, naval gunfire pounded the barracks and Corsairs dropped ordinance to add to the effect. UH-60 Black Hawk helicopters inserted the Ranger battalions, and by 2100 hours, Calivigny Barracks was secured.

Throughout the 27th, communication issues and other problems continued to plague the operation. Cuban snipers opened fire on an airborne battalion. A Navy liaison team called the USS *Independence* for an air strike, and Corsairs attacked without clearance by the 82nd Airborne 2nd Brigade fire support personnel. As a result, the Corsairs strafed the brigade command post. Several troops were injured, some seriously.

1730 Hours
27 October 1983
75th Ranger Platoon
Northeast of St. David, Grenada

THROUGHOUT THE DAYLIGHT hours of the 27th, the Cuban infantry continued to press the attack on the Ranger platoon. When the first wave found a wall of fire from AK-47s, the sound being distinctive, they knew the error they had made during the night. The Ranger's resupply of weapons and ammunition proved deadly. Jake estimated that at least a third of the Cuban force lay dead on the escarpment to the front of the plateau.

The second and third attacks proved equally deadly to the Cubans, but once again, the Rangers were perilously close to running out of ammunition. "Ten to twenty rounds of ammo left per man, Colonel," Master Sergeant Dross said as he squeezed behind the boulder with Jake and Lieutenant Timmers. "That's not enough to hold off another attack."

Jake frowned. "I was afraid of that."

"What are your orders, sir?" Dross remained silent as Jake thought of options.

"Well, Master Sergeant," Jake said, looking Dross in the eyes. "We are going to do what Rangers do. We are going to go kick some ass and drive those Cubans off this hill."

Dross smiled.

"K-so, we are not going to let the enemy walk up here and kill us just because we're out of ammo. As the Cubans launch their next attack, we are going to take the offensive. We'll charge them with the ammo we have left and use the bayonet after that. We will put them into a disorderly retreat for one hundred yards with us hot on their tail, pick up ammo on the way back to these boulders, and continue the fight."

"Hooah, Sir," Dross said.

"Inform the men. Pull the men in tighter," Jake said calmly.

Minutes later, the Rangers had closed the gaps between them, and Jake could see the Cubans forming forty yards downslope for another attack. From the previous attacks, he knew it would take less than ten minutes until providence would determine the fate of himself and each of the Rangers. Jake stepped out from the boulder that provided him cover.

A bullet splattered the loose rocks two feet behind him. Jake did not flinch at the near miss.

"Gentlemen," Jake said. "This is the day you have trained for. This is a day made for you, a Ranger in the 75th Ranger Regiment. I don't know if each of you is a believer in Jesus Christ. If not, this is an excellent time to find Him. If you fall today, believer or not, you are soon to know the glory of God. If you survive this charge, know that you are a part of the finest light infantry in the world, the 75th Ranger Regiment, and know that God still has a plan for you. Lock and load. Fix bayonets!"

Jake glanced over his shoulder and saw a line of Cubans advancing.

"Yell at the top of your lungs. Let them know you are coming to kill them. Ready? Follow me."

Jake headed downslope, yelling as loud as he could, and twenty-one Rangers followed, doing the same. Their charge was redolent of Colonel Chamberlain's charge at Little Round Top at Gettysburg against Alabama Confederate forces. The Rangers used their remaining ammo effectively, and Cubans fell where they stood. With ammo spent, the charge continued.

Jake crashed his body weight into a soldier, executed a parry right to deflect the enemy's rifle, swung the butt of his M16 into the Cuban's chin, then downwardly slashed his bayonet diagonally, left to right, opening the man's chest, before thrusting the bayonet into his throat.

It was mayhem, but short lived. The Cubans were terrified. They did not expect such fierceness from the Americans. They dropped their weapons and ran into the jungle as fast as they could. Jake paused and surveyed the situation. Dozens of Cubans had fallen, and the action had come to a stop.

"Give the order to withdraw," Jake said to Dross, who was by his side.

Expecting a counterattack, the Rangers made their way up the escarpment, gathering ammunition along the way. No sooner had Jake arrived back at the boulder than he heard the distinctive sound of a reconnaissance aircraft.

CHAPTER 30

1800 Hours
27 October 1983
Point Salines, Grenada

AS FAR AS combat is concerned, Operation Urgent Fury was quickly turning to clean-up details and administration. The airfields were being cleared of debris, combat patrols were clearing pockets of resistance, and prisoners were being interrogated to add depth to intelligence matters. Aircraft sorties arrived and departed, taking wounded and civilians out of Grenada while the new government was being established, and world governments were being notified, much of which was media play and propaganda.

A Navy reconnaissance aircraft reported the sighting of the missing Ranger platoon northeast of St. David. A part of that report was that the platoon was backed up against a plateau, fighting off a much larger force. Once reported, central command was determined to react in support of the platoon, but oncoming darkness complicated the situation considerably, and the lack of radio communications made naval gunfire or supporting air support perilous.

2000 Hours
27 October 1983
75th Ranger Platoon
Northeast of St. David, Grenada

"THE PILOT SAW US," Master Sergeant Dross said. "We'll be getting some air support soon."

Jake took a long drink of his warm canteen water. His appearance told the story of their circumstances, his face blackened but for pink around his eyes showing the stress and exhaustion of their battle, and his uniform was torn to shreds with small flesh wounds oozing blood.

"No doubt about that. Our problem is that the Cubans are reforming for a counterattack. Our aircraft are not going to know where to lay down fire. The last thing we need is to get strafed by friendly fire."

"Ideas, sir?" Dross asked. "We'll do whatever we need to do."

"Yeah," Jake said. "Round me up a haversack field bag, a dozen angle-head flashlights, and a half-dozen yellow and red smoke grenades."

Understanding immediately what Jake was thinking, Dross said, "I'll go, Colonel."

"I'll go, Sergeant. I could use the exercise," Jake said. "Go get me what I need. We are running out of time."

Returning five minutes later, Dross handed the field bag to Jake. "Orders, sir?"

Jake opened the bag and surveyed its contents. "They are going to send Cobras. Maybe some A-7 Corsairs. As soon as you hear them, drop green smoke in several places inside our perimeter. Light it up with as many flashlights as we have left. Those Cobras have searchlights. They'll pick up the green and know where we are located. I'm going to mark the Cuban positions with red and yellow. The pilots will know what to do. Don't let Lieutenant Timmers and these boys die today, Master Sergeant."

"I won't let you down, sir."

Jake moved to low crawl down the escarpment. Sergeant Dross pulled on Jake's arm. "This is a dumb idea, Colonel."

Jake gave the master sergeant a half-hearted smile. "Yeah. A really, dumb idea."

Jake slowly inched his way downslope, the sharp rocks of the escarpment cutting and scraping his already bleeding legs and arms. He had to work at controlling his breathing. Adrenaline pumped through his veins, and he could feel his heart pounding. Twenty minutes passed, and he knew he was within feet of the Cuban line. He could hear muffled conversations in Spanish. For no rational reason, he recalled being a floater as a plebe to a 1st Regiment table at West Point. He had the same feeling of being in enemy territory as he did then. It was frightening.

No sooner had the thought passed through his mind than he heard the distinctive sound of two incoming Marine Cobras. Jake reached into the satchel he was dragging and pulled out a red smoke grenade. He pulled the pin, came to a kneeling position, and lobbed the grenade in the direction of the Cubans. Following that, he lobbed two angle-head flashlights before continuing his low crawl down the Cuban line another twenty yards. He repeated the action with red smoke and flashlights. As the Cobras came in low and close, he doubled the number thrown. The Cubans were confused, engulfed in red and yellow smoke.

Jake came to a dead tree lying on the ground. At two feet in diameter, it was the best cover he was going to find. After scraping out a few inches of dirt with his hands, he wedged his body under the tree. Another five seconds and he would have been too late. The lead Cobra opened fire along the line, generously applying a wall of lead and killing Cubans in its first pass. The top of the dead tree, too, took the fierce power of the AH-1 Cobra, and if Jake had not been under it, the bullets would have found their mark in his body.

The second Cobra followed the first. Fifty yards from the Ranger's defensive line, two Navy A-7E Corsairs dropped ordinance to engulf the retreating Cubans in shrapnel and flames. The Corsairs were armed with M61A1 Vulcan 20mm Cannons, loaded with a thousand rounds each, AGM-65 air-to-ground missiles, and Mark 82 unguided bombs. They dropped it all on the area marked with yellow and red smoke. The battle was over. Captain Mondragon was dead, and his men that were still alive were in complete rout.

As the Cobras continued to circle overhead, Jake crawled out from under the tree. He stood and attempted to dust himself off but immediately realized that his good intention to be neat was ridiculous. Slapping his cuts and scrapes was a painful reminder that a neat appearance was not a requirement.

Jake made it upslope a half-dozen steps before Master Sergeant Dross and three other Rangers found him. Dross stopped, put his hands on his hips, and said, "Well, Colonel, I reckon the Army needs to come up with a commendation or two for you."

"Good to see you, Master Sergeant," Jake said. "Real good to see you. The men ok?"

"The men are fine. Those Cobras and Corsairs put the Cubans on the run. What's left of them."

"No medals," Jake said, "but I could use a drink of water."

1500 Hours
28 October 1983
Hunter Army Airfield, Georgia

EXFILTRATED FROM THE JUNGLE, Jake and the unwounded Rangers stepped off the C-130 that had carried them from Point Salines Airfield. The wounded had first been airlifted to the USS *Guam* then, if seriously wounded, like Lieutenant Timmers, they were immediately flown to the field hospital in Jamaica. Jake's gratitude for stepping onto American soil again brought a rush of adrenaline.

Jake walked forty yards toward the main building with his gear. A crowd had gathered to greet the soldiers, almost exclusively wives and family members. As he approached the crowd, two people stood out that made him smile. Admiral Hollifield and Patrick stood side-by-side, somewhat stunned by Jake's appearance. They had not expected to see him looking so exhausted and war-torn. His fatigues were in shreds, his face was still darkened with camouflage grease paint, and his cuts and scrapes oozed light red serous drainage.

"Damn, son," Admiral Hollifield said. "You look like hell."

Jake laughed while shaking the admiral's hand and replied, "I tried to keep up a snappy appearance, Admiral, but it just didn't work out."

Patrick gave Jake a hug and a brotherly slap on the back. "You do look pitiful. But I've seen you look worse. Boxing took its toll on you a couple of times."

"Well," the admiral said. "We have your uniform. Let's get you to a shower and shave, and then we'll visit."

"Looks like we need to get you about a hundred Band-Aids, too," Patrick said.

"Always the exaggerations," Jake replied. "By the way, Patrick, where were you with that Cobra of yours when I needed you?"

Patrick smiled. "I wish I had been there for you. I would have had your back for sure."

AN HOUR LATER, Jake walked into the Officer's Club and found the Admiral and Patrick sitting in a secluded area reserved for flag officers. A shower, shave, and his fresh uniform had transformed him. Except for his superficial wounds, Jake looked like he had sat behind a desk through Operation Urgent Fury.

"Stephen Patrick?" Jake asked immediately.

Hollifield grinned. "He is fine. Suzanne is spoiling the tarnation out of him. He'll be anxious to see you."

"And Rebecca and Baby Sara?" Jake asked Patrick.

"Ha," Patrick said. "I don't know why, but she has been driving me nuts, worrying about you. Sara is the life of the party, as always. Otherwise, there isn't any news other than Rebecca is pregnant again."

"Oh, wow," Jake said. "That's fantastic. Do we have any idea who the father is?"

Patrick looked over at the Admiral with a mock smirk on his face. "I'm going to tell her what you said, Jake. She'll put cyanide in your beer."

Jake laughed. "You did better than alright when you married Rebecca. She is awesome. Congratulations on the baby. That's wonderful."

"You two give me a headache," the Admiral said. "On a more serious matter, what's your take on this crazy deployment you got to Grenada, Jake. In all my years in the service, I've never heard of such a thing. No warning. Sending a Lieutenant Colonel to do the job of a 2nd Lieutenant, and the bizarre circumstances of throwing that platoon into a hostile environment with absolutely no strategic value whatsoever."

"That just about sums it up, Admiral," Jake said. "I can't prove it. Yet. But I can't think of any valid reason for that mission, except that it was intended that the platoon be massacred and me dead. Admiral, I think I stepped on some toes in my investigation of Casper. In fact, I think I stepped directly on Casper's toes. He wants me stopped."

Admiral Hollifield paused and lit a cigar. "I think you are right. You know, we have been looking for another parameter to narrow our search for Casper. I think he may have handed that parameter to us on a silver platter. You didn't get killed. I'm sure that frustrates him to no end. We have our list of suspects. Now we need to find out who initiated the orders to send that platoon, with you attached, into the jungle for no reason. That was an ambush. Pure and simple. Those Cubans knew the platoon was coming and exactly where it was going to touch ground. The Soviets and the Cubans are not dumb. Landing in the middle of an oversized company was planned."

"Those are my thoughts, also, Admiral."

"Do you like anyone in particular for being Casper at this point?" Hollifield asked.

Jake thought for a moment. "Well, Sir, without any real

support for my opinion, just about anyone in the chain of command, from the chairman's staff down, could have influenced those orders. However, I think Senator Samuel Zendt looks awfully suspicious. He dislikes me and finds me dangerous to his ambitions. He is a well-camouflaged Marxist, and his appointment to the Senate Intelligence Committee is dirty. I'm of the opinion, Sir, that he had something to do with the assassination of Senator Prather. It was Prather's death that created the opportunity to better his knowledge of intelligence matters. He came unglued when I asked questions about Prather.

"He's not my favorite criminal on Capitol Hill either," Hollifield said. "Ok, Jake. Take a few days to quit bleeding, and let's up the pressure on Casper."

CHAPTER 31

0900 Hours
1 November 1983
The Pentagon
Washington, D.C.

VICE ADMIRAL BROWNFIELD, General Brodrick's, Director of Intelligence, met Jake at the door to his office. While dreading Lieutenant Colonel Jake Jacobs' second visit, resembling more of an interrogation, he put a smile on his face and acted as though they were the best of friends. In terms of his capacity to ingratiate himself to accommodate any given situation, he was impeccably qualified to achieve his ambition of becoming a U.S. Senator.

"Welcome, Colonel," Brownfield said as he steered Jake toward a coffee service. "I'm glad you safely made it back from Grenada. I understand that things got a little dicey for you."

"It's nice to see you, also, Admiral Brownfield," Jake replied. "There was a moment or two of excitement, but things went well."

"Good. Good." The Admiral poured Jake's coffee and then moved toward his office sitting area. "What can I do for you today, Colonel?"

Jake smiled, "As you may or may not know, Admiral, I was attached to a Ranger platoon for military intelligence purposes. The main conversations in the Pentagon these days are after-action analysis of Operation Urgent Fury. So, I needed to meet with you regarding that Ranger platoon's mission in Grenada."

Brownfield averted his eyes, indicating to Jake that he had hit a nerve. "I don't follow, Colonel. Just what is it you are needing to know?"

Jake sipped his coffee and leaned back in his chair. His long pause was causing a disturbance in Brownfield's body language. Brownfield crossed his legs, set his coffee on the table, crossed his arms at his chest, and frowned. Brownfield felt threatened. It was a game of who would speak next. Jake held his silence.

Admiral Brownfield lost the game after a seemingly long minute. "Why would I know about a unit's assignment, especially a unit as small as an Army platoon? Now, if you were to ask me about the strategy for the fleet, or the 82nd Airborne, in Grenada, then I might have some information for you. But a platoon, no."

Again, there was a long pause and Jake's silence. For the second time, Bloomfield lost the game. "Why are you asking me about that Ranger platoon? What is it you want to know, Colonel? I've already said that I don't know anything about it."

"Who ordered that mission, Admiral?" Jake asked without facial expression."

Brownfield's face reddened, not from anger but rather

from the perceived threat that he was about to be intertwined in a damaging scandal.

"I don't know, Colonel. I think you will have to ask that question at the command structure below me."

Ten minutes later, Jake walked out of Vice Admiral Brownfield's office. He did not know, with any conviction, if the Admiral was involved in the orders that intended to massacre the Ranger platoon, but he was certain that he had lit a fire that would send a wall of flames throughout the chain of command.

1800 Hours
5 November 1983
Capitol Beltway
Washington, D.C.

THE WORKWEEK WAS FINISHED. Jake had changed into civilian clothes and was happily anticipating a long weekend with Stephen Patrick. It was a six-hour drive down I-95 to Camp Lejeune. His plan was to walk into the house before midnight, catch a few hours of sleep, and make a colossal breakfast when Stephen Patrick crawled out of bed. After that, the plan was to do whatever Stephen Patrick wanted to do. Something, or nothing.

Jake cruised the Bronco in the far right lane at seventy miles per hour while vehicles sped past him from the inner lanes. He was anxious to get to Lejeune, but not at breakneck speed. He turned on the radio, and 50's Rock and Roll set him to tapping his thumb on the steering wheel. Bobby Freeman's

Do You Want To Dance blared through the speakers. Jake turned up the volume.

A white van slowly inched its way up to pass him on the left side of the Bronco. As the cab of the van pulled even with the Bronco, Jake glanced at the vehicle. There were two men, a driver and a passenger. Both were looking at him. It struck Jake mildly odd, then the van accelerated. As it pulled forward, the sliding door of the van opened. Immediately Jake saw a third man in a kneeling position with an automatic weapon. As Jake reacted by hitting the accelerator, bullets ripped into the side of the Bronco and shattered glass. Jake reacted—not by conscious decision but by instinct. He made a hard turn of the steering wheel to the right, crossed the shoulder of the road, and dashed down the long, grassy drainage ditch between the interstate and the frontage road running parallel to the interstate. The Bronco bucked and fishtailed from one side to the other down the steep slope. At one point, the vehicle went to two wheels on the ground. Jake counter steered, as one would on ice, and the action set all four wheels back on the ground. The Bronco bounced over the curb of the frontage road and slid to a stop on pavement.

Jake glanced over his shoulder, looking for the van. It had pulled to a stop on the side of the interstate. A minute later, the van eased into traffic and disappeared. Heart pounding, Jake pulled forward, made a right turn at the first street, and found a strip mall with a full parking lot. After pulling his Colt 1911 from under the driver's seat, he pulled a roadmap from the glove compartment. He needed an alternative route to Camp Lejeune. Technically, reporting the attack to the police was required, but Jake knew what the attack was about. Casper wanted him dead. Jake's priority was to get to Camp

Lejeune as quickly as possible and to make sure Stephen Patrick would be safe.

0600 Hours
6 November 1983
Camp Lejeune, North Carolina

JAKE HAD PLACED a call to Admiral Hollifield minutes prior to midnight from his residence. The admiral was not upset with the late-night call that awakened him. He was accustomed to such calls when they were at an emergency level, and he was aware that no one in their right mind would call at midnight about some trivial matter. Stephen Patrick was at the admiral's residence. After listening to Jake's report on the I-95 incident, Hollifield placed a call to the Officer of the Day, and within minutes a dozen Marines were posted around his residence and Jake's.

The following day, Admiral Hollifield walked into his office promptly at 0600. Jake and John Hanraty were already there and rose when the admiral entered.

"Good morning, gentlemen," the Admiral said as he hung his coat and hat. "I didn't sleep a wink after your call last night, Jake. I reckon you stirred up a hornet's nest in Washington this week."

"No doubt, sir," Jake replied. "I got out of that jam without a scratch, but my Bronco is shot to pieces."

"Thank God you made it out unscathed," Hollifield said. "Now we need to figure out what to do next. We can't have you running around Washington with Casper, or someone else, trying to kill you. Any ideas?"

Jake scooted to the edge of his chair and leaned forward.

"Yes, sir. Colorado. I think I will take thirty days leave and go to my cabin outside Durango. If they are going to keep coming after me, I would prefer to have them do it on my ground. I would have the advantage."

Admiral Hollifield had a look of surprise on his face. "No way, Jake. You have no idea how many might be coming your way."

"Well, I sort of do, Admiral. According to The Otter, there are six Spetsnaz in the U.S. at Casper's beck and call. If I go to Colorado, it will draw them out. There is a chance that we might find out who gave them their orders. Taking offensive action beats sitting around waiting for them to shoot me in the men's room. That would be an embarrassing way to go down."

Admiral Hollifield leaned back in his chair, sipped his coffee, then lit his first cigar of the day.

"I see your point, Jake, but I don't like it," he said. "You against six. Those are really bad odds, and they are Spetsnaz. Those guys are well-trained killers."

"Do you have a better idea, Admiral?"

"What if we could improve those odds?" Hanraty asked. "I mean, what if we could put some men with Jake in Colorado?"

"Might work," Jake said. "But they would have to be out of sight. Otherwise, the Spetsnaz might wait for a better opportunity. They would know that I can't stay in Colorado indefinitely."

Hollifield tapped his cigar on the edge of his ashtray. "I think we could make that happen. I could quietly arrange through the Joint Special Operations Command (JSOC) a team to help set a trap. It would be SEAL Team Six or Delta Force. Those guys are always excited to sit in the woods and eat MREs."

"What are the legalities of an operation like that inside the United States, sir?" Jake asked.

"I'll take care of that," Hollifield responded. "Their mission is counterterrorism. If this situation doesn't fit their purpose, I don't know what does."

CHAPTER 32

2000 Hours
9 November 1983
Chesapeake General Hospital
Chesapeake, Virginia

COLONEL VLADIMIR ZHUKOV parked on the first floor of the parking garage at the Chesapeake General Hospital and took the stairs to the third floor. He was a half-hour early but taking the chance of tardiness was out of the question. No one, as far as he knew, had ever met with Wellspring. General Alexey Dmitrievich had sent him orders for the meeting. That was all he knew. A reason for it was not given. Not much made Zhukov nervous, but a meeting with Wellspring set him on edge. He could not shake the thought that when Wellspring had used him, for whatever he wanted done, Dmitrievich would give orders to terminate the only man that had met the mole the Americans called Casper.

Zhukov walked to the south end of the garage and leaned against the retaining wall overlooking the hospital. There did not appear to be a lot of foot traffic at this hour, but a few people exited the elevator and walked to their parked cars. Zhukov thought it smart for Casper to set the meeting in a place that had some human traffic. Hiding in plain sight would be more secure than attempting to be isolated. People pop-up unexpectedly no matter how secretive one plans.

Standing against the retaining wall, Colonel Zhukov could see anyone approaching. He felt underdressed to be meeting with someone like Casper. The man was a legend. A full-dress uniform seemed appropriate, but for the fact that it was not. Baggy, black sweatpants and a gray hoodie gave him the appearance of any number of Americans at eight o'clock in Chesapeake, Virginia. He looked like he belonged.

Punctually, a gray sedan pulled into a parking space twenty yards from where Zhukov was standing. A tall-statured man emerged from the car and walked slowly toward him. An observer might take him for a dapper gentleman in his charcoal slacks, crimson sweater, navy short trench coat, and topped with a made-in-Spain fedora. Coupled with horn-rimmed glasses, it would be difficult for anyone to accurately describe him.

At five feet from where he was standing, Zhukov was stunned. He had seen the man many times, both in photographs and in person. But to now realize that this man was Casper was shocking.

"Good evening, Colonel Zhukov," Casper said. "Thank you for meeting with me."

"Yes, sir," Zhukov stumbled. "My pleasure, sir."

"I'll get straight to the point, Colonel. Lieutenant Colonel John Paul Jacobs represents a significant risk to our mission. His interrogations are 'stirring the pot,' so to speak. The more people think there is not a Casper, the better. He is having the opposite effect. You and your team have made three attempts to eliminate this threat, and you have failed three times. Wouldn't you agree, Colonel?"

"Yes, sir," Zhukov said, embarrassed that he was being scolded by a man he held in high regard.

"Your sharpshooter missed him in Colorado and killed his wife. That did nothing but make him determined to get revenge by finding me. The failure in Grenada was the biggest fiasco I've seen. Your advisor to the Cubans had all the assets he needed to take out that Ranger platoon and terminate Jacobs. That was a colossal failure, and it sent Jacobs on the hunt for who issued the orders to put him with that platoon. It's only a matter of time before he runs that down. Unbelievable. Colonel you failed to get Jacobs on I-95. How hard could that be? You are Spetsnaz. A street gang could have done better."

Casper paused. Zhukov remained silent.

"What I hear is that Jacobs has gone to his place in Colorado. Here is what I want you to do. No, this is what I expect from you. Get your team to Colorado and take care of business. No long sniper shots. No bombs. I want him terminated, and I want your hands on his cold, dead body. No failure this time, Colonel. Do I make myself clear?"

"Yes, sir," Zhukov responded. "I will take care of it."

"Personally," Casper said. "I am holding you personally responsible. Get this done, and General Dmitrievich will get you and your team back to Moscow for reassignment."

Without another word, Casper turned and walked back to his car.

Colonel Zhukov watched Casper drive down the ramp to exit the garage. He was shaken by the ordeal. Not only was he shocked by Casper's identity, but he was visibly shaking from being reprimanded. The one thing he held in certainty was that his life depended on killing Lieutenant Colonel Jake Jacobs.

2000 Hours
9 November 1983
The Ore House
Durango, Colorado

MASTER SERGEANT BRENDON ZAPKA met Jake at the door of the Ore House. Jake did not know his name, and he did not ask. Both were casually dressed in jeans, boots, and medium-weight western-style jackets, but Zapka looked like a local blue-collar tradesman or rancher. His medium-sized beard and below-the-ear haircut underneath a well-worn, pecan-colored Stetson presented little curiosity to the other guests in the restaurant. Jake thought the Master Sergeant to be five years his senior, and he was taken by the man's stature, which belied his military occupation. Zapka was five foot nine inches tall and weighed, maybe, all of one hundred fifty pounds.

"Let's eat," Zapka said.

Jake smiled, thinking that this soldier needs to eat.

"The steaks here are outstanding. They are large, and they'll cook it just the way you like it."

A pretty, young waitress led them to a table, took their drink orders, and stepped lively toward the kitchen.

"Let's eat first, then down to business, if that is alright with you," Jake said.

"Absolutely. No sense ruining a good meal. Where are you from, sir? I think I hear a little bit of Texas or Tennessee."

"Guilty," Jake said. "Originally from Comanche, Texas. Having a roommate from Tennessee for four years didn't help matters. How about you?"

"The West," Zapka said. "I grew up on a small ranch."

"How did you end up in the Army?" Jake asked.

Zapka laughed. "I ask myself that same question a lot. Poor judgment, I suppose, but not really. I graduated from a state university with a degree in agriculture and had no idea what I wanted to do. So, I joined the Army."

"You didn't want to be an officer?" Jake asked.

Zapka grinned. "I didn't take ROTC. I wanted to be in for a couple of years as an enlisted man. As it turns out, I'm pretty good at it."

Jake nodded that he understood. He did not want to press the questions. Master Sergeant Zapka was a quiet professional. Soldiers in the 1st Special Forces Operational Detachment-Delta (1st SFOD-D), better known as Delta Force, did not talk about themselves or their operations, exercising their Code of Silence. If an operator did talk, he would be blacklisted. Under the command of the Joint Special Operations Command (JSOC), Delta was used for various clandestine classified missions, primarily counterinsurgency. The units specialize in close-quarter combat, hostage rescue, and high-value target extraction. Jake knew little about Delta Force, and only a handful of people knew more.

Most of what he knew bordered on the mystical. They rarely wear a uniform, which conceals their identity, and generally, they shun the traditional philosophies of military life. Regarding capability, some might argue which is better: SEAL, Green Beret, or Delta. The argument is unavailing. All three units are the best combat marksmen in the world, and woe be it to someone on the butt end of their business. Having been a Green Beret, Jake had a first-hand appreciation for the training and skills of Delta Force. They primarily recruit from units in the Army, like the Green Berets or the Rangers, or other airborne units. But unlike the SEALs, Delta also recruits exceptional candidates from other branches of the service. It is not unusual to find SEALS or Recon Marines in the Delta teams. Delta finds well-trained and qualified individuals and sends them to badass graduate schools. One is not likely to ever know who they are or what they do.

"Excellent meal," Master Sergeant Zapka said as he pushed his plate forward. "That ought to last me for a few days. Ok, sir, here is where we are. We have a team of four, plus our troop commander. I am the team leader. The troop commander is holed up in a local motel room, and he will coordinate communications and deal with civilian authorities as need be. Two operators are outside the restaurant as we speak, and two operators are already on-site at your cabin. We have your back."

"I don't know if the Spetsnaz will show up, but I'm pretty sure they will," Jake said.

"We have a topographical of the terrain. Could you sketch out the specifics?" Zapka said as he handed Jake a napkin.

Jake pulled his academy Monte Blanc from his pants pocket and sketched the cabin and the significant physical details of the situation. "Are your men visible?"

Zapka smiled. "They are at the woodline behind the cabin. The Almighty Himself would have difficulty spotting them. They have covered the flanks, and they have a visual on every access. A mouse couldn't get to that cabin without us knowing about it."

Jake nodded, indicating that he had every confidence in the Delta team.

"We need you inside the cabin unless it is breached. Do you have an exit plan?"

"I do," Jake responded. "I can surface twenty-five yards behind the cabin from a well."

"Weapons?" Zapka asked.

"Ithaca 37 12-gauge, Colt 1911 .45 ACP, six-inch stiletto, and a tactical tomahawk," Jake replied. "I have plenty of ammo and magazines."

"No offense, sir, but are you skilled with that tomahawk?"

"Escrima," Jake said.

Zapka smiled. "That's good enough for me. Now, we'll keep the operation as silent as possible, but rounds fired will draw the local authorities. For legal reasons, it is preferable that the Spetsnaz engage first, but circumstances will dictate that. Our actions will be in response to a hostile threat. The county sheriff will likely be on the scene within an hour. Once action is initiated, liaison support will be inbound to deal with the sheriff, and you will be exfiltrated when the mission is completed. The FBI will be madder than a box of rattlesnakes poked with a stick. Technically, something like this is their jurisdiction. The bigwigs at JSOC will have to handle that. My team will not be available to answer questions. We will be gone, and so will you."

"I can't help but be a little curious as to why the FBI has not been involved," Jake said.

"You're lucky, I guess. If this were an FBI operation, some guy in Washington wearing a suit would be out to make a name for himself, and there would be fifty agents stomping around with flashlights and noisemakers. They would look good, but the Spetsnaz would be on the other side of the highway laughing their ass off."

"I see," Jake said. "What is my job in all of this?"

Master Sergeant Zapka laughed. "You are the bait, sir."

2300 Hours
9 November 1983
The Cabin
22 Miles from Durango, Colorado

THE THICK, rough-cut wood shutters were closed and padlocked. Light from within the cabin was obvious enough, but from the outside, one would not be able to define a target. Jake changed into his tiger stripe fatigues and boots, camouflaged his face and hands, readied his weapons, and climbed into the cabin's attic. He was ready for an assault when it came—if it came at all.

Gunnery Sergeant Kenneth Shanahan, a Delta Force operator recruited from Marine Corps Recon, positioned himself three feet inside the woodline, one hundred meters west of the cabin. Wedged under a fallen tree and covered with a five-by-nine Ghillie banket, one would have to step on him to find him. His position gave him a clear visual of the access road leading to the cabin, the grassy valley to the west, and the rear of the cabin. Protruding from under the fallen tree, Shanahan's camouflaged XM21 Sniper Rifle was primed for a target. The rifle was a national match grade M14, built for accuracy, and it was, at present, geared with a Starlight scope for night vision and a direct connect sound suppressor to a Vortex Flash Hider.

Army Staff Sergeant Michael Neel lay prone, covered by a Ghillie blanket, halfway between the highway and the cabin and fifteen yards from the access road. If the Spetsnaz came down the access road, he was close enough to hear their heartbeat. Like the other three members of the team, Neel carried a Colt XM177 Commando, a variant of the M16, commonly called the CAR-15 (Colt Automatic Rifle-15). All armed government personnel have their favorite sidearm. Delta Force is not an exception. They religiously carry the Colt M1911A1 in .45 ACP for its knock-down power and sheer deadliness. Popped center mass with a .45 caliber round, and it is game over.

Army Master Sergeant Zapka and Petty Officer 3rd Class Joseph Rooney joined the tactical situation by midnight, low crawling at a snail's pace to positions twenty yards, right and left, of the cabin door and blending into the tall grass. Rooney was a SEAL. He loved the Navy, but he loved Delta more. He often joked that being an operator was like being a Texas Ranger. One war, one Delta.

By 0200, the temperature was down to thirty-five degrees. It is cold if one is lying motionless on the damp ground for hours. Not to disappoint, a dark-colored van approached from the east. The van slowed, almost to a stop, as it approached the access road to the cabin, then crept forward two hundred yards down the highway. It stopped for less than a minute, turned off its lights, and made a U-turn. At the access road, it stopped.

CHAPTER 33

0300 Hours
10 November 1983
The Cabin
22 Miles from Durango, Colorado

CHIEF PETTY OFFICER Rooney was not called 'Lunchbox' for nothing. He was always hungry. As he lay in the tall grass with the temperature dropping, he could not decide whether he wanted a cheeseburger and fries or a pulled pork sandwich and onion rings. The sound of three rapid squelches through his headset diverted his attention. It was time to go to work. Hostiles were incoming.

Marine Gunnery Sergeant Kenneth Shanahan reported into the microphone that touched his lips. "I have a visual on two, I say again, two individuals nearing the woodline at two hundred yards, approaching from the west."

"Can you identify?" Master Sergeant Zapka responded.

"KLMK camo (Kamuflirovannyi Letnyi Maskirovochnyi Kombinezon), black watch caps, and it appears they are carrying the AK74 carbines. They are tactical," Shanahan said. "Not your typical Colorado turkey hunters."

The van continued to be motionless at the access road. "Wait, one," Zapka said. He was waiting to see what activity evolved from the van. If it turned onto the access road, or if personnel from it moved toward the cabin, he would then make the call that an aggressive, hostile action had been initiated.

From the attic gable vent on the north side of the cabin, Jake had a view of the access road. But for a utility light nearby, the road was dark. Two minutes passed, then there was a loud pop, sparks flying at the top of the utility pole, and shards of glass hitting the ground. The cabin was engulfed in darkness. Jake made his way through the attic and dropped himself to the hallway floor.

"Well, ok then," Zapka calmly said into his microphone. "I reckon we have our hostile situation. I saw the muzzle flash at the highway. It seems that they have at least one Dragunov Sniper Rifle."

Three single squelches from the team signified an acknowledgment.

Master Sergeant Zapka wanted to eliminate the threat of the two Spetsnaz soldiers coming toward the cabin from the west, but he thought it favorable that the remainder of the assault group think they were still a tactical asset. "Two hostiles coming from the west on your left flank. Quietly terminate. I say again. Quietly terminate."

Zapka immediately received a one-squelch in acknowledgment.

Gunnery Sergeant Shanahan scanned the area with his Starlight scope. One Spetsnaz was in the woods. One was in the clear, walking slowly several yards behind the first. At a smidgen over one hundred yards, Shanahan had an easy shot with the M21 Sniper Rifle. He pulled the crosshairs to the tip of the Spetsnaz's nose, adjusted with movement, took a deep breath to hold, and pulled the trigger. The 7.62 x 51mm NATO round removed most of the Spetsnaz's face from the nose up and dropped him like a stone.

Colonel Zhukov gave the order. Four Spetsnaz' exited the van, spread themselves ten yards apart in a squad line formation, right and left of the access road, and moved forward. The van inched onto the access road, lights off, having maximum firepower to the front from the four walking Spetsnaz. Zhukov saw no need for extraordinary precaution. He had overwhelming odds in his favor against one American Lieutenant Colonel.

"Well," Master Sergeant Zapka said into his microphone. "That's interesting. We have four Russkies on the ground and moving forward. Unless that van is driven by a robot, we have more than the expected six Spetsnaz."

Three single squelches followed.

Jake set himself prone on the floor of the master bedroom with the 12-gauge in the dark. The front door was a lighted, clear target. The trap door to the tunnel he and Patrick had constructed for the auxiliary water pump was open for a quick exit if needed. His mind kept returning to the fact that he needed at least one of the Spetsnaz alive to interrogate. Otherwise, the attempt on his life would yield no clues.

On his left flank, Gunnery Sergeant Shanahan caught a glimpse of the Spetsnaz a skosh within the woodline and making good time moving toward the cabin. Shanahan drew two quick conclusions. First, the Spetsnaz was not aware that his buddy that had crossed the field with him was dead, and second, he had no idea that he was in a perilous situation. As his target neared, Shanahan picked his spot behind a large tree, squatted before covering his head and shoulders with the Ghillie blanket, and pulled his Randall seven-inch stiletto from its sheath.

The Spetsnaz kept his AK-74 carbine in a ready position, but he did not concern himself with snapping twigs underfoot, making noise. He was focused on preventing the American target from escaping from the back of the cabin.

As the Spetsnaz stepped two paces past the gunny's tree, Shanahan quietly dropped the Ghillie blanket, clutched the man's face between his forearm and bicep, inserted the stiletto to the hilt in the back of the neck, then shoved the handle left then right. With the brainstem severed, the Spetsnaz was dead before Shanahan could release him to the ground.

"The west is clear," Shanahan reported.

Three single squelches replied.

The van sped up. It covered the distance to the cabin quickly, wheeled through the front yard, and came to a stop inches away from the first step of the porch. The sliding side door of the van opened, and two Spetsnaz stepped onto the porch. The first rushed to the door with a thirty-pound forcible entry battering ram. With two swings, the door cracked. A third hit broke two hinges, and the door flew open. The second Spetsnaz rushed through the door.

Master Sergeant Zapka and Chief Petty Officer Rooney opened fire on the four Spetsnaz moving forward on foot with their CAR-15s. Now realizing that they were not dealing with only Jake, the Spetsnaz returned fire. The firefight was fully engaged. Zapka turned momentarily toward the van and fired a three three-round burst through the windshield of the van to kill the driver and disable the van. He then refocused on the four Spetsnaz returning fire. With the driver dead and the van disabled, the odds of a Spetsnaz escape were dwindling. Zapka's primary concern now was the presumption that the Spetsnaz were now inside the cabin and his hope that Jake had dropped into the tunnel for an exit.

The first Spetsnaz crossed the threshold of the front door and was met full-force with triple-ought buckshot from Jake's Ithaca-37. He went airborne, landing back on the porch.

The other Spetsnaz immediately entered the room, firing wildly with his AK-74 carbine. Jake attempted to pump another round into his shotgun. It jammed. With no time to clear the Ithaca, Jake rushed the attacker, knocking the Spetsnaz off balance enough to frustrate a killing shot. Instinctively, Jake pulled his tomahawk connected to his load-bearing tactical harness, planted his feet, and initiated a downward right-to-left figure-eight attack. The downward sweep slashed the Spetsnaz's right leg an inch above the knee. Without hesitating the momentum of the figure eight, Jake stepped forward and to his left, bringing the downward left-to-right stroke of the tomahawk in contact with the back of the Spetsnaz's neck, driving the bit deep.

As the Spetsnaz fell to the floor dead, the butt of a rifle stock slammed into the side of Jake's head. He went to the floor on his back, dazed. Colonel Zhukov jumped on Jake, straddled him, and held a six-inch Soviet Army NR-40 Combat Knife to his throat.

"We meet again, Lieutenant Colonel Jacobs," Zhukov said. "You have been quite a pest."

Still dazed, Jake tried to move against Zhukov's weight but could not.

Zhukov smiled. "From the sound of things outside, I think neither of us will live to see another day. No matter. Even after performing my duty of terminating you as ordered, my country will not allow me to live. I know too much. It is unfortunate for both of us.

Jake struggled again to no avail, feeling the sting of the blade on his neck.

"I do admire you, though, Colonel," Zhukov continued. "You have come very close to finding Wellspring. Very close. However, it is too late. Even if you knew, it would not do you any good because you are about to die."

Jake blinked. "Well. If you are going to kill me, tell me who Wellspring is. I deserve at least that much. It won't make any difference to you or Wellspring."

Zhukov paused, then conveyed a beastly look in his eyes as though he were toying with a captured prey. He leaned over, his knife still on Jake's throat, and whispered in his ear.

As Zhukov moved to sit up again, Jake freed and swung his right arm with his academy ballpoint pen clutched in his fist. The barrel of the pen punctured Zhukov's left eye. Jake pulled his hand back, opened his palm, and smacked the end of the pen with force. The pen penetrated Zhukov's brain, and he convulsed with involuntary muscle contractions.

Jake rolled Zhukov to the side, recovered his tomahawk, and stood over the twitching, convulsing body of the Spetsnaz colonel. He was prepared to attack, but in less than a minute, Zhukov ceased to move. He was dead from a massive brain bleed. Jake stared at the Monte Blanc logo, a white six-pointed star that had replaced Zhukov's eyeball.

The four Spetsnaz in front of the cabin lay dead, and Master Sergeant Zapka cautiously entered the front door of the cabin. He surveyed the situation. Jake stood next to Zhukov's body.

"Well," Zapka said, "you've been busy. You alright?"

"Yeah," Jake replied. "It was touch and go for a few

minutes." Blood dripped down the side of Jake's head from a gash, his head hurt from the blow he had taken from the butt of Zhukov's rifle, and blood oozed from the shallow slits on his throat.

As they debriefed each other, they heard the distinctive sound of a Blackhawk landing in the meadow close to the cabin. "The military police out of Fort Carson are here," Zapka said. "They'll mop up this mess." Zapka turned and walked out the door.

Minutes later, Lieutenant Colonel Michael Holland walked through the door wearing a Class A uniform and introduced himself as though this were a social gathering.

"Two dead here, one on the porch, and seven scattered about. You had quite a night. Let's get you on that Blackhawk and out of here. I'll handle the local authorities that are on their way as we speak."

Holland stared at Zhukov. "That's an oddity. What's with his eye?"

Jake shook his head. "That's my ballpoint pen, Colonel, and I will be wanting that back. The Delta operators. Are they ok?"

Holland smiled. "No problem about the pen. I'll make sure you get it back. Delta operators? What Delta operators."

CHAPTER 34

1000 Hours
10 November 1983
Fort Carson, Colorado

SHORTLY AFTER LANDING at Fort Carson by Blackhawk helicopter, Jake was taken to the post hospital to have his injuries checked out. Although his injuries were minor, the doctors wanted to ensure that he did not have a concussion from the blow to his head. Jake was frustrated with the loss of time. His head was spinning, not from having a rifle butt slammed against his head but rather from the words Colonel Zhukov had whispered in his ear. Questions looped through his mind. Should he call Admiral Hollifield? Should he wait until he could see him face-to-face? What proof was there other than the word of a Soviet Spetsnaz colonel? Would the Department of Justice take action based on the accusation, or would they demand the unreasonable and require a chain of unattainable physical proof before they would act? Would this revelation cause embarrassment to the highest levels of government to the extent that the result would be a massive cover-up?

Doctor Marlow, a major, finally entered the examination room with a medic. Jake had sat in the cold room in his underwear for about as long as his patience would bear.

"You're a lucky man, Colonel Jacobs. As far as the tests show, there are no skull fractures, and there is no indication of a concussion."

Jake smirked. "That's good. All I have to worry about is catching pneumonia."

"Sorry about that," Marlow said. The medic pulled a blanket out of a closet and handed it to Jake.

"You can shower down the hall, and we will have a clean set of fatigues for you within the hour. The medic will change your dressing after your shower. You should change it a couple of times a day or until you are tired of messing with it."

1900 Hours
10 November 1983
Marine Corps Air Station
Cherry Point, North Carolina

THE ARMY BEECHCRAFT C-12 Huron came to a stop, the airstair for passenger deplaning was lowered, and Jake set foot on the tarmac of the air station at Camp Lejeune. The door of the terminal opened, and Admiral Hollifield stepped out. Jake saluted, and the admiral returned it.

"I swear, Jake," the Admiral said. "Seems like every time I see you lately, you're wearing a new set of cuts and bruises."

Jake smiled, "It does seem that way. Could easily have been worse. Much worse."

"Hanraty is at the office," Hollifield said. "Let's have a chit-chat, and then we'll get you home."

A twenty-minute drive put them in Admiral Hollifield's office. Hanraty stood to greet Jake. He was surprised to see Jake with a bandaged head and a fatigue uniform that had no indication of unit or rank. A private would be more identifiable.

"Ok," the Admiral said as he sat in one of the leather armchairs. "Thanks for the call on a secure line. That's not exactly the kind of information that should be shared on an open telephone call. There's no telling who might tap into the conversation."

Jake spent the next fifteen minutes giving the Admiral the details of the events that had taken place in Colorado, including Zhukov's last words whispered in his ear. Since the time of the phone call from Ft. Carson, Hollifield had thought of nothing else.

"You can thank Major General Carpenter at JSOC for the helpers you had at your cabin. That help was at no small risk to his career. It was a bold move, but obviously, a necessary one."

"Yes, sir," Jake said. "Those helpers, as you call them, were spectacular."

"We must proceed with caution," the Admiral continued. "Without some strong substantiation, we really have no place to go with this information. We must view it as another lead, albeit a strong one, but only a lead at best. It is not a sufficient reason to take legal action. Revelation by a KGB Spetsnaz colonel is not exactly a reliable source. Do you agree?"

"I do," Jake said, "but under the circumstances, I personally think the information is accurate. Zhukov thought he was about to kill me. He would have no reason to give me a false name. If he thought he was going to leave me alive, I could understand how it might have been a smoke screen to throw us off the track of discovering Casper's identity."

Hollifield lit a cigar and blew a cloud of smoke into the air.

"I agree with that, but we don't know for sure. There is a possibility of either scenario. The Department of Justice would laugh us out of their office without facts to verify the accusation. What are your thoughts, Hanraty?"

"No doubt that is right, sir," Hanraty said as he sat forward in his chair. "Our problem is that everyone will want proof, and the Department of Justice is broken as far as I'm concerned. They won't pursue a case unless it is a slam-dunk win, easy, and politically correct. One possible solution would be to turn it over to the FBI. This is their job."

Hollifield smirked. "The upper echelons of the FBI are as politically motivated as the Department of Justice. Congress certainly wouldn't deal with it. Most flag officers in the military are outstanding, honorable men and women, but there are those that are where they are because they are political sycophants. They would bury the accusation. No. For now, neither the FBI nor the Department of Justice is a viable solution. It is up to us to continue the investigation and come up with irrefutable proof. Suggestions? How are we going to do that?"

A full minute passed in silence as Hollifield continued to puff on his cigar. It was frustrating for all three that they were close enough to Casper to reach out and touch him, but they were trapped in the machinations of bureaucracy. Finding enough proof to encourage legal action appeared to be impossible.

Jake broke the silence. "Since we have a specific suspect,

what if we go directly to those that planned and executed Operation Urgent Fury? We might get a senior officer that remembers how that Ranger platoon was injected into the battle plan. It's not as good as having the Soviet Union cough up the specific transfer of intelligence, but maybe if we keep pushing, one small lead will lead to another until we have something that cannot be ignored."

Hollifield continued to puff on his cigar and tapped the long ash into his ashtray. "I don't know that we have an option. I have a relationship with most of those officers. Perhaps I can get some specifics. Major General Carpenter at JSOC and Major General Osborne may open some doors. I'll let General Osborne know where we are on this and contact General Carpenter. Jake, while I am doing that, you get some rest and spend some time with Stephen Patrick."

1030 Hours
12 November 1983
Major General Seth Osborne Residence
Fredericksburg, Virginia

A LIGHT DUSTING of snow covered the ground, and General Osborne had a fire blazing to knock the chill in the air. He took Admiral Hollifield's coat and hung it on the coat rack in the foyer.

"Another winter has arrived, and my joints are in rebellion," Osborne said.

"I need to move to Arizona," Hollifield replied. "Who would have ever thought that age would become our greatest enemy."

Osborne laughed. "Getting old never crossed my mind until a couple of years ago. Ignorance of youth."

A quick visit to the kitchen to pour a mug of coffee preceded their sitting by the fire in Osborne's den.

"What do I owe the pleasure, Admiral? Fredericksburg is a little out of your way on a cold morning."

"I just needed to update you on this Casper business, and I thought it best to do so away from Washington."

"I appreciate that," Osborne said. "I've heard rumors that there was some calamity in Colorado with Lieutenant Colonel Jacobs. A few in Congress are all up in arms about it. They've stormed General Brodrick's office, and as you might imagine, the FBI is screaming their head off about a military operation taking place on American soil. I've been dodging Brodrick because I don't have anything to tell him. So, thanks for coming by to bring me up to speed."

"Well, Seth," Hollifield replied, "Concerning Colorado, I'll just say that the action there was necessary. Casper made an attempt on your life, and he has made three attempts on Colonel Jacobs' life. One of which resulted in the death of Jacobs' wife."

"I'm aware of all that."

"Apparently," Hollifield continued, "Casper sent ten Spetsnaz to Colorado to kill him. There was action taken to interdict that plan. Granted, local law enforcement and the FBI have reason to take issue with the action, but in the long run, that will sort itself out."

Osborne sat back in his chair and sipped his coffee as he absorbed what Hollifield was telling him.

"Why were the locals and the FBI not used?"

"Well, I'll answer that question with a question," Hollifield said. "How would you envision that situation turning out if local law enforcement and the FBI were charged with protecting Colonel Jacobs from an assault by ten Soviet Spetsnaz Special Forces soldiers?"

General Osborne paused, then smiled. "I see your point. Total chaos, I suspect."

"Exactly."

"So, did anything positive come out of this, other than Jacobs not being killed?"

"That's why I'm here, Seth."

CHAPTER 35

1400 Hours
13 November 1983
Headquarters, 75th Ranger Regiment
Fort Benning, Georgia

COLONEL BRIAN REESER met Jake at the door of his office, cordially greeted him, and offered a beverage. Jake poured himself a glass of cold water and sat with the Colonel at his small, round conference table. Reeser was a West Point graduate and a decorated Vietnam veteran.

"Welcome back to Benning, Jake," Reeser said. "Best I remember, the last time we visited was at the Army birthday ball here at Benning. Have you been back to West Point lately?"

"Not lately, sir," Jake replied. "I had a three-year tour as an instructor but have not been back since. And you, sir?"

"Yes. I was there last week. There have been a few changes since we were cadets. Some of them I like, and some I don't."

Jake smiled, "That sums up how I feel, too. Most of the

changes are positive with respect to the academic curriculum and technology. I hope to get another assignment there someday."

"I would like to do that someday as well," Reeser said. "For now, I'm very happy commanding the 75th. What can I do for you, Jake?"

Jake sipped his water before jumping into the reason for his visit. "I'm sure you are aware of all the details of what is now known as the lost Ranger platoon in Grenada."

"I am," Reeser said with a frown. "I'm none too happy about that situation. In fact, I am still spitting mad. You performed magnificently, by the way. I have put you in for commendation. That platoon should never have been given that assignment."

"How did that assignment come about, sir?" Jake asked. "That is the purpose of my visit today."

Colonel Reeser moved to a set of flip-over maps, fumbled through a half-dozen, and stopped when he came to the map of Grenada. He pointed to the area west of St. David where the platoon had been.

"As you know, Operation Urgent Fury was essentially under naval command. That is not unusual, and it is not a point of criticism. As far as the 75th is concerned, our job is to execute our part of an overall plan. We had some tactical input, but the big picture came from a higher level of command."

Reeser moved his pointer to St. Georges.

"If, and I say again, if, the planners intended a hammer and anvil tactic, that is, to use the invasion forces at St. Georges to act as the hammer, and the platoon moving west to be the anvil, then tactically, this all makes sense. The two movements would have smashed the opposition. However, a legitimate hammer and anvil maneuver would have required a much larger force than a single platoon. A battalion could have done it, but not a platoon. Poor planning, in my estimation."

"Who gave the orders to place the platoon in that position?" Jake asked.

"Well, indirectly, I did. So, I take responsibility for executing the orders I was given."

"I appreciate that, Colonel," Jake said. "Spoken as a true leader. Honorable."

Reeser nodded, indicating that he appreciated the comment. "Not being a hammer and anvil tactic, the platoon operation was slated for military intelligence. That's where you entered the picture. It was to be a reconnaissance in force to gather intelligence between St. David and St. Georges, which in my estimation, was not necessary. Air reconnaissance would have accomplished that. We are talking about, what, six to twelve miles? Even if a reconnaissance mission were legitimate, putting a lieutenant colonel with that platoon as the military intelligence officer was ludicrous."

Jake sat forward in his chair. "Based on your assessment, sir, would you find it conceivable that the mission for that Ranger platoon was a planned ambush?"

Reeser sat down in his chair, drank from his water glass, and crossed his legs.

"Actually, Jake, I think that is exactly what it was. An ambush, and you were the target. I have made noise about it up the chain of command, but I've been ignored."

"I don't mean to sound like a broken record, sir, but how or who could have put that platoon in that situation?"

"Well, it was a military intelligence operation," Reeser said. "The order had to come from someone powerfully connected to Military Intelligence."

"Could it have come from someone on the Senate Intelligence Committee?" Jake asked.

Colonel Reeser paused in thought. "Interesting. Sure, but there would have to be cooperation on the military side for such an order to be issued in the plan of battle."

"How about the office of the Chairman of the Joint Chiefs of Staff or one of the chiefs?"

Reeser blinked at the level of authority Jake was considering.

"I hesitate to say, but sure. Any one of the chiefs of staff or their individual staff directors could have slipped in the order. And any one of them could have been influenced by a member of the Senate Intelligence Committee. Still, it would likely be someone at the intelligence level. In the chairman's office, Admiral Brownfield controls the Directorate of Intelligence, and each of the chiefs also has an intelligence component. The Director of Defense Intelligence and his staff could influence a battle plan. That would be Lieutenant General Nathan Hawk. Are you seriously thinking that someone at that level of military authority set up an ambush in Grenada?"

Jake sat back in his chair and put on his face of nondisclosure.

1400 Hours
14 November 1983
Camp Lejeune, North Carolina

THE CONFERENCE ROOM adjacent to Admiral Hollifield's office had been prepared for a meeting of four. An array of refreshments was made available, courtesy of the

Marine Corps, and notepads were set at each chair. To downplay any assertion of authority by rank, Admiral Hollifield had instructed there be two chairs on both sides of the table. The pecking order was a bit confusing. Major General Osborne led the Casper investigation, but Admiral Hollifield was the ranking officer. Hollifield's seating arrangement eliminated any awkwardness.

Osborne's five-hour drive from Fredericksburg seemed like less to him. He had been mentally consumed with thoughts about Casper, legal ramifications, and, more importantly, proof. Driving through the gate at Camp Lejeune, he concluded that damning circumstantial evidence would be all that could be mustered. There would be no indisputable evidence. There would be no solid proof that there was an exchange of intelligence documents between Casper and the Soviet GRU. To make matters worse, he knew that the legal system, the FBI, and the Department of Justice would do nothing. It made him angry that the most treasonous spy in the history of the United States would remain free from prosecution.

Following pleasantries, they took seats at the table. Admiral Hollifield opened the conversation.

"Gentlemen, our purpose this afternoon is to discuss what we know, what we think we might know, and how we should proceed with the investigation. General Osborne, this is your investigation. We are here to assist you."

"Thank you, Admiral," Osborne said. "I have purposely been outside the details to avoid having to report your findings to others. That was appropriate. What I would like is for each of you to elaborate on your findings."

Jake opened a folder that contained his notes and began an hour-long briefing. He deferred research findings to John

Hanraty, but he did cover his interviews, specifically identifying subjective and objective conclusions, details about the lost platoon in Grenada that might implicate Casper, and the Spetsnaz assault on his cabin in Colorado.

John Hanraty nervously ran through his methodology of creating a list of possible suspects based on long-term, consistent access to top-secret military intelligence. He then discussed a list of individuals that had the capability to insert orders, directly or indirectly, to the battle plan of Operation Urgent Fury. To summarize his presentation, Hanraty unveiled a colorful Venn diagram, showing the overlap of individuals meeting both criteria. Four names fell into the common area of the diagram. One of those names was the name that Colonel Zhukov had whispered into Jake's ear.

"So, there you have it, General Osborne," Admiral Hollifield said. "Am I convinced of Casper's identity? Yes. I am. Is this information objectively conclusive? No. Not in my opinion. Is there sufficient evidence to force the FBI and the Department of Justice into action? I don't think so. I don't believe they would even initiate their own investigation. Even if they did have hard proof, I think this would still be too politically explosive for a lot of people."

Osborne was silent, as were the others.

CHAPTER 36

0930 Hours
15 November 1983
The Jefferson Hotel
Washington, D.C.

MAJOR GENERAL SETH OSBORNE was pleased with The Jefferson, a recently renovated hotel near the White House. It was a luxury hotel with spacious rooms and opulent surroundings. Compared to the hotels he usually stayed when in Washington, it was like the Taj Mahal. The room service breakfast had been perfect. He showered and meticulously prepped his dress blue uniform with his two stars and five rows of service ribbons he had been awarded, including the Combat Infantry Badge, Purple Heart, and three ribbons for valor in combat. Tending to his uniform was a commonplace task requiring little thought. He had placed the ribbons and badges on the blue coat countless times.

General Brodrick's recruitment of him to verify the

existence of a spy had not been too demanding on the freedom of his retirement. However, on this day, the assignment was frustrating and disappointing. Contrary to Brodrick's expressed opinion that there was no spy, Osborne now knew that Casper existed and who he was. In less than four hours, he would meet with General Brodrick and report his findings.

1000 Hours
15 November 1983
The Pentagon
Washington, D. C.

GENERAL BRODRICK'S secretary announced the arrival of Senator Samuel Zendt. The general slid the report he was reading to the lower right-hand corner of his desk, then tapped the edges of it so that it was perfectly aligned.

"Send him in, Mrs. Turnicky."

Senator Zendt brushed past the secretary and approached Brodrick's desk in a confrontational manner.

"General Brodrick, what's this nonsense about that Lieutenant Colonel Jacobs not being investigated by the FBI over all that commotion in Colorado? It was a violation of federal law. The military must be held accountable."

Brodrick sat back in his chair, surprised by Senator Zendt's demeanor.

"Have a seat, Senator."

Zendt sat in front of the general's desk and waited for the response he demanded. Brodrick paused to collect his thoughts.

Firmly, Brodrick said, "As you and I have previously

discussed, Lieutenant Colonel Jacobs has been on assignment to investigate the possibility of a spy. Well, there isn't one. Major General Osborne will be here this afternoon, and his orders will be rescinded. Jacobs will be reduced in rank back down to major, and he will be reassigned elsewhere. As far as that commotion in Colorado is concerned, you are mistaken that the military and civilian authorities will not be looking into it. These things take time, and it is complicated. You will have to be patient."

Senator Zendt was calmed by a portion of what Brodrick had said. "Ok. I'll be patient, but I fully expect that situation to be disclosed and appropriate action taken against those responsible. I'll rely on you to see to it."

Brodrick was expressionless. He would humor Zendt, but the Senator was not his superior. He owed Zendt, neither personally nor officially, any explanation whatsoever. To calm the raging waters, he would play along with the senator for the time being.

"As far as this spy business is concerned," Zendt said, "I'm glad to see that good judgment has prevailed. Having one of your officers running around insulting members of Congress and insinuating that they are anything but honorable is misguided. I've never believed that there is a mole. There is no spy."

1300 Hours
15 November 1983
The Pentagon
Washington, D.C.

MRS. TURNICKY ESCORTED Major General Seth Osborne into General Brodrick's office, poured iced tea into glasses, and set them on the coffee table in front of the General's overstuffed leather chairs. Without a word, she exited the room and closed the door behind her.

Osborne sat in one of the chairs, knowing which of the four was General Brodrick's. Brodrick made an entry on his calendar at his desk, then crossed the room to sit with Osborne.

"Good afternoon, General," Osborne said. "Two weeks until Thanksgiving. Do you have plans?"

Brodrick sipped his tea, then responded.

"Yes. My wife and I are traveling to California to visit our daughter and her husband. It won't be a long trip, but an enjoyable one. How about you?"

"No plans this year, General."

"So, what can you tell me about that fiasco in Colorado with Lieutenant Colonel Jacobs?" Brodrick asked.

Osborne set his glass of tea on the coffee table and leaned back in his chair. "The short version, sir, is that ten Soviet Spetsnaz Special Forces soldiers assaulted Colonel Jacobs' cabin intending to kill him. Their plan failed. Jacobs is very much alive, and the ten Spetsnaz are dead."

Brodrick clearly indicated that he was agitated. "I've seen a vaguely written report on the incident, but I'm unclear about how one of our Special Forces teams was involved. Who ordered that team to Colorado? Let me rephrase that. I know the orders came from Major General Carpenter at JSOC, but I want to know who was behind Carpenter's order."

Osborne remained expressionless. "I wouldn't know anything about that, sir. You know how these Special Forces types are. They march to the sound of their own drummer.

However, it's a good thing they happened to be in the neighborhood."

Brodrick frowned, his anger apparent. He knew that Osborne had to be lying, and his flippant answer was infuriating.

"It was illegal for them to be there. It was illegal for a military action to take place on American soil. If Jacobs needed protection, then the FBI should have provided it. Why was that not the case, General?"

Osborne leaned forward, sipped his tea, then set his glass back on the table.

"Because we are talking about insurrection, General. Because we are talking about a treacherous, traitorous Soviet spy. It was a military operation in direct response to an attack on the United States by a foreign power."

"It was not," Brodrick vehemently said. His face turned red with anger and his hand was shaking as he did all that he could to contain his rage. "Your assignment on this matter is terminated. There is no spy. Your orders are hereby rescinded. Your position on this is nonsense, and I will have no more of it. Jacobs will be reassigned, and you can go back to being retired. I have already given the order to reduce Jacobs' rank to major."

"It is not quite over, General," Osborne said calmly. "You see, General, the commander of that Spetsnaz force was a Soviet colonel. His name was Colonel Vladimir Zhukov. He may have been an excellent soldier, but Lieutenant Colonel Jacobs was better. Before he died, Zhukov told Jacobs who Casper is, or should I call him Wellspring, General?"

Shocked, Brodrick gripped the arms of his chair, his face turned ashen.

"You are Wellspring, General," Osborne stated. "You are the traitor to this country."

Brodrick stammered. "Th—that's ab—absurd," as he bolted upright in his chair. His controlled anger was now uncontrolled rage. "How dare you make such an accusation. I'm the Chairman of the Joint Chiefs of Staff."

Osborne had a revolted look on his face. "You are the chairman, General. But not for much longer."

Brodrick needed a rational and overpowering disclaimer to discredit Osborne's accusation, but instead, in his state of hysteria, his words had a confirming effect.

"You have no proof of such a thing."

"But I do. I had a nice, long visit with Vice Admiral Brownfield. It was you who ordered him to slip the Military Intelligence mission into the battle plan in Grenada. It was you who coordinated the ambush of that Ranger platoon. It was you who ordered three attempts to have Jacobs killed. It was you that Colonel Zhukov identified as Casper, the traitor to his country. The closer Jacobs got to tracking you down, the more frantic you became to silence him. All the evidence points to you, General."

Silence prevailed for a full minute. Osborne stared at the general with a look of hatred and disgust as Brodrick probed his mind for an avenue to escape the accusation.

General Brodrick closed his eyes and exhaled heavily, resigned to fact that Osborne knew the truth.

"Ok, Seth," the general said. "It doesn't really mean anything that you know. I am Casper, and I am proud of it. In twenty or thirty years, the United States will be a communist country. The Soviet Union will win this war. Communism will win, and I will have done my duty. You have nothing on me. There is no actionable proof that I am Wellspring. No one will listen to you. No one will believe you. You are a disgruntled, fired general officer, and my military service record will stand on its own. That's why I hired you. Granted, going after Jacobs has been a mistake. If I had not done that, you would not have the slightest clue."

Osborne remained silent, letting Brodrick tighten the noose around his neck.

"I will be in this office for at least a few more years, and after that, I will still be influential in Washington. You have laughable circumstantial evidence. Even if there is an investigation, it will be dropped. Now, get out of my office."

General Osborne smiled, reached behind his back, and withdrew from his waistband the two-inch barreled Colt Cobra .38 he had carried in Vietnam. Brodrick tensed, the threat to him escalated.

"I agree with you, General," Osborne said. "The FBI, the Department of Defense, the Department of Justice, and even Congress will bury the truth. It would be too big of a scandal to admit that you are a traitor. And you are right. Circumstantial evidence will not put you behind bars or dangling at the end of a hangman's rope."

Brodrick was speechless. Beads of sweat rolled down his back. "Look, Seth, this is ridiculous. You won't get me to confess to the authorities at the point of a gun, and I don't believe you are going to shoot me. You won't get away with doing that. If you pull that trigger, there will be Military Police here in a matter of seconds. There's nothing for you to gain."

"No gain for me, General," Osborne said. "Gain for the United States of America. I am a patriot, General."

Brodrick started to speak when Osborne fired three quick rounds into Brodrick's chest and one round to his forehead. Only seconds passed before Mrs. Turnicky reacted to the sound of gunfire and opened the door to Brodrick's office.

J.M. PATTON

Major General Seth Osborne put the barrel of the Colt Cobra in his mouth and pulled the trigger.

CHAPTER 37

1530 Hours
15 November 1983
Camp Lejeune, North Carolina

JAKE AND JOHN HANRATY walked into Admiral Hollifield's office together, chatting about how cold the weather had turned. The Admiral was seated at his desk, cigar in hand, and held a dispirited facial expression. The seriousness of their call to meet was nonverbally conveyed.

"I'm glad that both of you are still on deck this afternoon," Hollifield said. "I've just had a phone call from the Pentagon with some shockingly bad news.

Jake tensed. From his perspective, such an announcement usually involved someone's death.

Hollifield continued. "I don't have much in the way of details, but Major General Osborne shot and killed General Brodrick earlier this afternoon, then shot himself.

Jake was stunned, and his thoughts jumped from one to another in rapid succession. The death of General Osborne.

Casper is dead. What does this do to proving Brodrick's guilt? How will this play out politically and in the media?

Admiral Hollifield paused, shook his head from side to side, and set his cigar in the ashtray.

"I haven't had time to properly consider the ramifications, of course, but I do have some initial thoughts. There will be waves of unintended political consequences and constitutional ones as well. We'll never know for sure, but I think General Osborne did this because he knew that Brodrick would never be properly investigated, tried in a court of law, and convicted. Everyone would be scrambling to cover their ass. He took justice into his own hands. He bypassed the Constitution. I do take exception to that, but on the other hand, I can't help but be somewhat pleased that a traitor, especially one in Brodrick's position, has met his just reward."

Jake and Hanraty both nodded to indicate that they understood the admiral's emotional conflict.

Hollifield retrieved his cigar from the ashtray and filled the air above his desk with smoke before continuing. "It's going to get interesting politically. Unofficially, I am issuing you a gag order. I am restricting all information and findings we have gathered on this assignment. Our findings will be considered hearsay, and legally that would be correct. There would have to be a trial and conviction to be otherwise. I suspect that this will play out as a murder-suicide. The government and the military will call it that, avoid all rumors of Casper, and close the books. Too embarrassing to parade the Chairman of the Joint Chiefs of Staff as a Soviet spy in front of the American people. I'm not suggesting there will be a cover up. I simply think the government will take the line that the incident is murder-suicide and let the truth lie dormant. Our mission is over."

"I have no problem with that, Admiral," Jake said. "I'm not saying that I approve of General Osborne's actions because I don't, but the situation does violate my sense of honor. The villain, in truth, will be portrayed as an innocent victim, and a man seeking righteous justice, though misguided, will historically be remembered as a villain."

"What about Senator Zendt?" Hanraty interjected.

"Well, John, justice for Senator Zendt will have to wait for another day," the Admiral said. "I do suspect that we will see Zendt as President of the United States in a decade or two. And, Jake, I understand what you are saying. Speaking of injustice, I received notification this morning that your rank has been reduced to that of major."

1000 Hours
9 January 1984
The Oval Office, The White House
Washington, D.C.

ADMIRAL HOLLIFIELD NOTIFIED Jake a week earlier that the two of them were invited to meet with the President. The invitation, presented in a genteel manner, was an order. A half-hour after the meeting time, they sat outside the office waiting. Hollifield was relaxed. He had been to the Oval Office many times. Jake? Not so much. He had made many enemies in the pursuit of Casper, and it did not seem out of the realm of possibility that the President was about to reprimand him.

"You are going to drive me to drink if you keep checking your watch," the Admiral said.

"Sorry, sir. I'm a little nervous."

Hollifield laughed. "With all the decorations you have for valor, and you're nervous about a meeting. You have nothing to worry about, Jake."

The door to the Oval Office opened, and an executive secretary asked them to enter. The President walked toward them with a broad smile on his face, dissipating thoughts Jake may have had about a reprimand. After shaking hands, the President motioned for them to sit.

"Thank you for taking the time to visit with me," the President said, as though attendance were voluntary. The President sat, and the Admiral and Jake did as well.

"It's nice to see you, Mr. President," Hollifield responded. "And the First Lady, is she doing well?"

The President smiled. "She is. She sends her warmest regards and told me to invite you and Suzanne to California in April. We are having a good old fashion barbeque on the ranch. You do have a cowboy hat, don't you? I'll provide the horse."

"As a matter of fact, I do. I'm sure Major Jacobs has one. He is a Texas boy."

"Major," the President said, "you are invited, too. Bring that son of yours with you, Stephen Patrick, I believe. We'll put him on a horse. He'll have a great time."

Jake was more relaxed. So far, this did not feel like a butt-chewing kind of meeting.

"Stephen Patrick and I would be delighted to attend, sir."

"Very good. Something to look forward to."

The President crossed his legs as he leaned back in his chair.

"Ok. Let's talk a little business. General Brodrick first. Thank you, Admiral, for filling me in on the situation this past month. My staff looked into it, and there is no doubt in my mind that General Brodrick has been a spy amongst us for years. Shameful. Shameful for his treachery and shameful that we didn't do a better job vetting a man in such a powerful position. The accepted position by all concerned, including the public, is that Major General Osborne murdered Brodrick over some unknown grievance, and he then took his own life. There were some speculations about Casper, but the media was not able to run with it, and neither was anyone else. Don't get me wrong. There is no cover-up, and there will not be one. It is simply a fact that there is no evidence to support an indictment of Brodrick's guilt."

Hollifield and Jake remained silent but nodded that they agreed with the President.

"As for you, two," the President continued. "A superlative job. Your country owes you its deepest gratitude and utmost respect. But, as you know, the work you have done cannot be given the recognition it deserves. Major, your actions in Grenada were amazing. Under normal circumstances, you should be awarded the highest honor our country can give. But again, your service in Grenada would open wounds that are not in the best interest of the country, and with the damage this assignment has done to your career, it's not likely that you would receive a thumbs-up from the military or Congress. You have paid a high price, Major Jacobs, the greatest of which is the loss of your wife. I wish I could have met her."

"Yes, Mr. President," Jake said. "Losing Sara is the most horrible thing that can happen in my life. As far as the rest of it goes, I'm fine with it. If I might suggest, sir, Lieutenant Timmers and Master Sergeant Dross were the heavy lifters in Grenada. Lieutenant Timmers lost a leg. He, and Dross, performed to the highest standards of the 75th Ranger Regiment."

"I'll see to it," the President said. "By the way, here is your pen back. It needs some deep cleaning. You will have to tell me about it sometime. I know most of where it has been, but I'd be interested to hear it from you. So, what are your plans going forward, Major? Assuming you plan to stay in the Army, what would you like to do?"

Jake leaned forward. "I've given that some thought, Mr. President. I think a normal career path for me is an unreasonable expectation. I have, at minimum, another ten years on active duty. I would like to get my doctorate and spend as much time as possible assigned to West Point as an instructor."

The President smiled. "A doctorate from one of the Ivy League universities?"

"Possibly, sir," Jake quickly replied. "But I think I would prefer Baylor, or Rice. Spending some time back in Texas would be appealing."

"How fast can you pack your bags for West Point, Major?"

EPILOGUE

1030 Hours
25 December 1996 (15 Years Later)
The Cabin
Durango, Colorado

FIRST LIEUTENANT STEPHEN PATRICK JACOBS, United States Marine Corps, sat in an overstuffed leather chair, feeling the warmth of the fire blazing in the fireplace. Fragrant steam rose from the cup of apple cider he held with both hands, and he smiled at the noises of family he heard around the cabin. Santa had made his appearance in the night. Colorful wrapping paper was strewn around the room, the children were busy with their new possessions, the Christmas tree twinkled with red and blue and green lights, a foot of snow was on the ground, and comforting voices and laughter from the women could be heard from the kitchen. A feast was in the making.

"Where's the old man?" Brigadier General Patrick

McSwain asked as he swayed into the room wearing baggy khakis and a gawd-awful red Christmas sweater. He plunked himself down in a matching chair opposite Stephen Patrick. "He didn't go back to bed, did he?"

Stephen Patrick chuckled. "Dad? No way. He's gone up to visit Mom."

"In this snow?" Patrick asked, not really surprised.

"Come sunshine, pouring rain, or a freezing blizzard—Dad hikes up that mountainside every day to sit at Mom's grave. He hauled a wrought iron chair up there years ago. He will sit there and talk to her for an hour or so. Who knows, but it wouldn't shock me to find out that she talks back to him."

"Well, their love for each other was one of a kind," Patrick said. "So, when are you going to tie the knot and get married? You're a hot shot, Marine aviator. The women are probably trying to beat your door down."

Stephen Patrick laughed. "When I love someone as much as Dad loved Mom, I'll gladly take the plunge."

Suzanne Hollifield walked over to Patrick and handed him a steaming cup of apple cider. "Sitting by the fire needs a cup of cider to go along with it," she said.

Patrick stood and gave her a hug. As she walked back toward the kitchen, he commented, "That's one of the finest ladies the world will ever know."

"No doubt," Stephen Patrick said. "I'm sure she misses the Admiral a lot."

"They were quite a team. She took his pancreatic cancer and death like the grand military wife that she is. The whole time they were married, he could have been killed many times. His death has been on their doorstep for over fifty years. A military wife is as much a soldier as the man she loves and supports. My Rebecca is the same way. My admiration and love for her is beyond description. Magnificent women."

"I hope to do so well," Stephen Patrick said.

"So, F-18 Hornet driver. I'm proud of you, and I know your dad is over-the-top proud. Now, if we could just get you to transfer to the Army, we could overlook that Naval Academy business."

Stephen Patrick laughed out loud.

"It's Dad's fault, you know. It was those years that we lived at Camp Lejeune that did it. From the moment I first saw a Harrier jump jet making a vertical landing at Cherry Point, I knew I wanted to be an aviator in the Marine Corps. Even all those years back at West Point with Dad teaching, I never changed my mind. I was so nervous about telling Dad that I wanted to go to the Naval Academy instead of West Point."

Patrick smirked. "Well, the Naval Academy does make a pretty good second choice, I guess. Your namesake, Steve Ross, is laughing in heaven. He was a great guy—Steve, your dad, and your mom. For me, they put Comanche, Texas, on the map."

"Second place, huh?" Stephen Patrick was quick to say. "Navy wasn't second place at the Army-Navy game this year."

Patrick frowned. "Navy must have cheated."

"Cheated my foot. We gave Army a thrashing," Stephen Patrick said with a smile on his face."

"Your dad has done some amazing things with this cabin. Three or four times the space. Room for a lot of people."

Stephen Patrick laughed again. "Oh, so now you want to change the subject. Can't say as I blame you. But, yes, Dad has turned this old cabin into quite a house. He wanted to make it a place where our entire family could gather, and he did that.

He has turned into somewhat of a real estate baron. He has bought a lot of property around Durango, and has been developing some of his properties in Telluride. He built two luxury residences in Telluride and sold them within a week of being on the market."

Patrick sipped his hot apple cider. "Well, he will never sell this place. Your mom is here. This is where he will spend the rest of his days."

"No doubt. He still lives in this old part. The original cabin. The rest of the house he built for us."

"Just as well," Patrick said casually. "I spent four years at West Point listening to him snore in the lower bunk. Rebecca accuses me of snoring, but I know she is just making that up."

Stephen Patrick paused, sipped his cider, and leaned over with his forearms on his knees.

"Considering everything that Casper business did to his career, Dad enjoyed his years teaching at West Point. I'll admit, I will always be angry that military politics prevented him from making full colonel. He deserved better. Did you know that at Marine Corps Officer Basic School, they still talk about what he did in Grenada. He is a legend."

"A legend," Patrick said as his eyes misted over and his mind outpoured with memories. Their days at West Point, made all the more bearable by their brotherhood. Their first meeting with Admiral Hollifield and Suzanne in a Philadelphia restaurant. The brigade boxing tournaments, and the victories they had achieved together. Steve's death, and his funeral at Annapolis. The Green Berets, and Jake's decorations for valor. Jake waltzing into a Soviet outpost in Afghanistan to recruit a defector. Sara's death, the devastating cost for doing his duty to find Casper. And Grenada, combat action worthy of the Congressional Medal of Honor.

"He quit caring about rank a long time ago," Patrick forlornly said. "Your dad accomplished more than any soldier I know. Duty-Honor-Country. Your dad has given a full measure."

ABOUT THE AUTHOR

J.M. Patton is a retired Assistant Professor of Mathematics at New Mexico Military Institute (NMMI). His academic major was mathematics: NMMI '69JC, USMA x1973, Baylor University, M Ed Wayland Baptist University. He has a love for Christ and a passion for strict construction of the Constitution. He and his wife Debbie live in rural New Mexico. They are the parents of five sons and have sixteen grandchildren.

You are invited to find more about the author on his website at JMPattonAuthor.com

ACKNOWLEDGMENTS

Special thanks are due to my wife, Debbie, for her support of me in long hours of writing, being lost in thought, and a messy office.

Also, Frank Eastland, Raeghan Rebstock, and Nancy and Bob Lanning of Publish Authority were indispensable in putting the three novels of the *A Full Measure* trilogy into the hands of readers.

THANK YOU FOR READING

If you enjoyed *Thundering White Crosses,* book #3 in the trilogy *A Full Measure,* we invite you to purchase books #1, *West Point,* and #2, *Drums of War,* and share your thoughts and reactions in reviews online and with friends and family.

Publish Authority

Printed in the USA
CPSIA information can be obtained
at www.ICGtesting.com
LVHW060759130823
755069LV00009B/265